John McCabe is a geneticist who lives and works in Birmingham. He is the author of three novels, *Stickleback*, *Paper* and *Snakeskin*.

Acclaim for *SNAKESKIN*

'Coincidence is just another tool of fate. And John McCabe uses this tool like a master craftsman, creating a thoroughly enjoyable comedy of errors . . . Every twist and turn of *Snakeskin* makes you wonder just how many sub-plots McCabe can introduce into one book and it's a pleasure to watch the whole story unfurl'
Punch

'McCabe's madcap third novel is Carl Hiaasen meets John O'Farrell by way of Leslie Neilsen. Hi-octane hi-jinx' *Mirror*

'The absurd situations through which the hapless and avaricious Ian tumbles in his attempts to protect his illicit fortune from the real Millennium Bug unleash countless comic observations. Some of these are convincing and genuinely funny, some puerile or simply off the mark, but the tale of borrowed identities and karmic payback is in the main a success' *The Bookseller*

'A painfully funny thriller . . . part Mike Leigh grimness, part Hollywood action flick, expect to see the film of the book in a multiplex near you soon' *Heat*

'*Snakeskin*'s compelling tale depicts the adventures of Brummie Ian Gillick, a man struggling to save his own neck while simultaneously destroying his own identity . . . While the readers are invited to laugh at the obsessive behaviour of each character, they are also coaxed into reflecting on how real they actually are. Scary stuff'
The List

'A fantastically gripping plot, and exceedingly sharp, original prose' *Arena*

'Thoroughly entertaining, topical novel . . . McCabe's devilish sense of fun wakes up amongst the pocket protectors and low-nutrient junk food – and has the last laugh. Hilariously misanthropic, with all the nasties finding their comeuppance at the end of a tale that's half-bile, half smiles' *I.D.*

'McCabe has woven an intricate but absorbing tale of deception and betrayal. Like his previous two books – *Stickleback* and *Paper* – it's cleverly written with a strong sense of place'
Birmingham Post

www.**booksattransworld**.co.uk

PAPER

'I could say that McCabe writes as Nick Hornby would if Nick Hornby were locked in a laboratory for a year. But that would be glib. The writing is original, entertaining and compelling'
The Times

'A fine and highly original thriller. Hitting you with a series of unexpected outcomes, it provides us with an interesting twist in this well-used genre' *City Life*

'Through the unlikely medium of farce, *Paper* puts real flesh on the truism that science is a cultural enterprise. Not cynical so much as "slightly bruised", McCabe perfectly captures the intellectual and institutional frustrations that oppress the "poor bloody infantry" of science' *New Scientist*

'With its grungy setting, down-beat style and depressed male protagonist, it places itself right at the centre of its genre'
The Times Literary Supplement

STICKLEBACK

'Witty and incisive about the preoccupations of modern life'
Observer

'Not only do you have a compulsive read on your hands, you also have a fascinating profile of the ritualized mediocrity of contemporary living' *Big Issue*

'A witty, fast-paced novel' *Glasgow Herald*

'A rampant roar through the stultifying world of office life. This is a wonderfully funny little thriller with a firm grasp on the frustrations of everyday life. McCabe is a terrific new voice'
Midweek

Also by John McCabe

STICKLEBACK
PAPER

SNAKESKIN

John McCabe

SNAKESKIN

A BLACK SWAN BOOK : 0 552 99873 7

Originally published in Great Britain by Doubleday,
a division of Transworld Publishers

PRINTING HISTORY
Doubleday edition published 2001
Black Swan edition published 2002

1 3 5 7 9 10 8 6 4 2

Set in 11/12pt Melior by
Kestrel Data, Exeter, Devon.

Black Swan Books are published by Transworld Publishers,
61–63 Uxbridge Road, London W5 5SA,
a division of The Random House Group Ltd,
in Australia by Random House Australia (Pty) Ltd,
20 Alfred Street, Milsons Point, Sydney, NSW 2061, Australia,
in New Zealand by Random House New Zealand Ltd,
18 Poland Road, Glenfield, Auckland 10, New Zealand
and in South Africa by Random House (Pty) Ltd,
Endulini, 5a Jubilee Road, Parktown 2193, South Africa.

Printed and bound in Great Britain by
Clays Ltd, St Ives plc.

For Joshua and Alison

Acknowledgements

Stickleback, *Paper* and *Snakeskin* owe a huge debt to Chris Jones.

Supporting cast:
Bill Scott-Kerr at Transworld, Bill Hamilton at A. M. Heath,
Frances Coady and Gail Lynch at Granta Books,
Kate Hurley at Hurley Lowe

Special Guest Appearances:
John, Rose and Tim McCabe

Friends and general hangers-on:
Mark, Reuben, Andrea, Jo, Wendy, Martin,
Neil, Jayne, Jim, Greg, Tony, Dave

Excess Baggage

In Departures, surveying my life as it stood so far – two bags of almost waist height, grey canvas and leather, elephant scrotum in volume – I couldn't help but feel inadequate. Everything I owned except flesh, bones and an expanding beergut sat on a conveyor belt, which had sighed as it received the cases. The large LED digits under the check-in counter blinked in unsteady disbelief, surged to 32, retreated to 25, managed a quick recount, and settled on 28 kilos. Thirty-one years of age and only 28 kilos of possessions. Almost a kilo per year. It didn't seem right somehow. I was gaining weight quicker than this. For all the money I had accrued and spent, everything I owned in the world could fit in the boot of a Fiat Cinquecento. In fact, a push-bike with panniers would probably do in an emergency. But this was no hard luck story of an impoverished traveller. I was wealthy, and was starting to notice a trend. The more money I spent, the emptier my suitcases became.

I handed over my passport and the stewardess squinted at the serial killer photo. As she tapped away at a hidden keyboard I made a mental list of the belongings I had abandoned at various junctures. Their sheer bulk would have filled the aeroplane. Tables, chairs, sofas, beds, drawers, cabinets, wardrobes, cars, televisions, videos, hi-fis, computers, books, magazines, pots, pans, mugs and a single unused ironing board. The last three years of my life had been characterized by the sporadic need to leave a place in a hurry. The stewardess scrutinized my ticket. Cars in particular nagged away at me. They were living objects, almost, standing idle by roadsides, running out of tax and permits, fluids seeping gently from slowly seizing engines, life blood dripping away onto indifferent tarmac. I glanced up. The stewardess had cleared her throat and was looking a little sheepish.

'I'm afraid the maximum allowed luggage is twenty-five kilograms,' she said. 'You are three kilos over.'

'Even for Club?'

'I'm sorry, sir, yes.' She glanced down at my two suitcases. 'Excess baggage will cost you thirty-four dollars.'

'Excess baggage?' I asked.

'Yes.'

'You're telling me I have *too many* possessions?'

The stewardess tilted her head slightly and regarded me for a couple of quiet seconds. 'Sorry, sir,' she said. 'I will have to ask you for the thirty-four dollars.'

I handed over two twenties and headed for the Club lounge, unburdened of my existence, save for a distinctly anorexic carry-on bag, and tried to salvage some hope from the situation. I might have fewer possessions than a Trappist monk who had fallen on bad times, and a similar number of girlfriends, but I had at least managed to find one criterion by which this could be described as excessive. I regarded my hand luggage with new-found enthusiasm. This small bag represented roughly 10 per cent of something which was, in the right circumstances, an embarrassment of belongings.

In the lounge, a pretty hostess brought round some wine. Cars, then, had been abandoned by roadsides, and although I missed them it had often come as a relief to be unburdened. There was always something wrong with them – I seemed to have a knack for buying shoddy machinery. I owned an unreliable Peugeot when I needed dependability, a spectacularly impractical Jeep in urban France, a lacklustre Toyota Four-Runner on the mean streets of Los Angeles. The houses and apartments I had lost, however, were a different matter. These were my spaces, tiny regions on the surface of the planet that I had owned and occupied, safely ensconced within walls, cosseted by beds and supported by floors. I had *feelings* for these places. My house in Birmingham was damp and haunted by memories; my apartment in Nice shady and sedate; my condominium in southern California bright and cool. Just thinking about each property was enough to change my mood; like the memory of a smell, never quite tangible but still there, somewhere, lurking. But also lurking was a fear of ever returning to those places. As I swallowed some more wine, misgivings struggled to the surface. This wasn't so much a fear of flying as a fear of flying home.

Palm Trees for Horse Chestnuts

It had begun as a half-awake thought, which streamed into my consciousness like the Los Angeles light squeezing through the gaps in the apartment's blinds. I screwed my lids tightly shut and turned away from the window, trying to dismiss the idea. But it was too late: I was awake, and I was nervous. I squinted at the clock. 7:43 a.m. I wasn't due to be awake for another seventeen minutes. The dream could be over, I realized, just with a change of date. Catch 21 was about to fuck me roughly from behind.

Clearly, I had to do something, and quickly, though this would mean returning to England. It wasn't that the idea didn't appeal, just that I had already journeyed through homesickness into a perpetual state of acceptance – in the United States of Acceptance – and eventually convinced myself that I never wanted to return. This was, I imagined, the usual safety net of feelings which protects the unhappily exiled from the fall of isolation abroad. In the instant that I appreciated I had no choice in the matter and would have to go back to England, the resignation to a life spent abroad evaporated, and I found myself suddenly homesick.

Looking around my room, I remembered friends and family who had occupied no more than fleeting moments of thought over the last few years, and an unwelcome sensation of betrayal came over me. I rang them sporadically, of course, but it was the refusal to grant them time in my mind or space in my heart that rankled with me now as I turned the shower on and scrubbed myself clean. England, I said to myself, towelling my damp shoulders. England. I dragged my trousers over semi-dry legs. Birmingham. I laced my trainers. Birmingham, I repeated, ruffling my hair. Birmingham, England, I sighed, gazing out into the blurry Los Angeles sunshine. Fall in southern California for autumn in the West Midlands. Palm trees for horse chestnuts. I shook my head slowly and turned away from the window, scanning the room for the telephone. It was lolling on its back on the sofa. I took it with me as I began hunting through under-used cupboards for my suitcases.

Thirty hours later and I was sitting by the ocean. I watched as waves flung themselves onto the beach in lazy, sighing acts of completion, having delivered their single message, before dissolving back into the quiet murmur of the majority. From here I could see clumsy 747s struggle into the sky and bank north or south over the water. Tracing their trajectories back to earth, LAX airport was about ten miles away to the south-east. Time to leave another country. I stood up, brushing the sand off my clothes, climbed into my car and pointed it towards the airport.

With two suitcases in the pressurized hold, my hand luggage safely stowed above, and a few odds and sods in my pockets, I reclined my seat. My lightweight life on an aeroplane. The first leg to Chicago had been fine. At such short notice, no direct flights had been available. Now was the long haul to Heathrow. I sighed and surveyed the furry seats of Club. It was always like this – furry, for some reason, and grubby, almost like naff car seat covers. Most spaces were taken, a few were empty. The usual air of smug executive travel. A scruffy type to my right and across the aisle. British, by the looks. A fat Yank sitting next to him. A forty-something blonde with sunglasses trying to muster an air of discretion in front. Two well-dressed French girls with light sweaters hanging over their shoulders, grips in their hair. The usual rabble. The British guy makes a stab at conversation, but I'm far too caught up in my own troubles to help him out. All I can think about are the questions at Customs. I take a large swig of my drink and try to recall how I ended up in this mess.

Plants

It is the rue de Plaza, Nice, France, 8:30-ish in the morning, a year ago. I am whistling my way back from the boulangerie. The sun has been up for hours, and the streets, which have been scrubbed and washed by an invisible nocturnal workforce, are three-quarters dry. She will be here tomorrow. Finally. I cross the street and head up the hill. The Moped Wars of the city's narrow streets are beginning again in earnest, and one combatant, which looks like a particularly undernourished motorbike and sounds like a very unhappy wasp, zooms down the side of traffic, perilously close to the pavement. I watch as drivers sound their horns, and I wonder whether I should take the Jeep down to pick her up at the airport. I worry suddenly that there won't be enough room for her luggage. If I know Sue, and I think I do, there will be luggage. And not the sort of luggage that might fit in an open-top Jeep. In fact, as I think about it, whistling my way up the rue de Concourse, the plane will need a fucking roof-rack to carry Sue's belongings. No, a taxi will do fine. Could even rent one of those stretch limo things you only see in May when Cannes is in full swing. Christ knows where they hide them the rest of the year. Probably lurking in ridiculously stretched garages somewhere, like slumbering giants. I key in the security number on the iron gates, which sweep gently open, inviting me to step into the shady courtyard at the rear of my apartment.

After breakfast (one croissant, lightly buttered, two pains au chocolat, au naturel, a glass of orange juice, one cup of tea) I pace around for a while, trying to see the apartment with virgin eyes, imagining how it will look to her when she sees it for the first time. The fresh morning light pours in and livens it up, and what strikes me is that there is nothing living in any of the rooms. True, there are a few species of fungi inhabiting the back of the fridge, and some mouldy lines of grout amongst the otherwise spotless bathroom tiles, which the maid steadfastly refuses to scrub, but there isn't even so much as a plant to be seen about the place. It has never really crossed my mind to buy one, and even if it had, I probably would have dismissed the notion on the grounds of the effort involved in watering it. For the purposes of appearance, though, and with the knowledge that when she arrives she will probably take charge of the watering duties, I resolve to get some plants. I check my watch. It is just before ten. Her flight lands at 18:30 the following day. I do a rough calculation on my fingers, and smile. Thirty-four finger-hours, and she will be here. As I have a final wander around the rooms of the apartment, a song comes on the radio and I turn it up. Previously, the song had meant nothing, had been irritating in fact, but recently it has begun to pick me apart, gently, teasingly, almost enjoyably. I listen to the English words, and recognize that it is toying with my feelings, now that I have feelings to toy with. Before, I was immune. Tomorrow afternoon. I take a sharp breath, which seems to bypass my lungs and head straight for my stomach instead, and realize that I'm actually quite nervous about her arrival. I mean, why else would I be thinking of buying pot plants, of all things? After a little more pacing, I have another quick reckon up of items that might make the place look liveable, pick up my wallet and keys and set off into town.

This was the last time I ever saw the apartment in daylight, and the penultimate day I spent in France.

I pull the blind up and stare out of the triple-glazed aeroplane window. A small patch of condensation has gathered between two layers of the perspex. Beyond it lies a silent world of insanely beautiful clouds and endless piercing sunshine. Up here, above the clouds, it is always sunny. I glance around as the passenger seated next to me, who has already introduced himself as Darren, begins to stir in his sleep.

Lumbered

Around the fifth day in Colorado, Dr Darren White realized he had to leave America. Mainly, though, he had to leave Richard. He had thought he could manage, but he was wrong, and was beginning to lose it. The choice was simple – Darren or Richard. One of them was going to die if they shared a room any longer. Of all the roommates at all the conferences in all the world he had to get lumbered with Richard.

After the second day, Darren had stopped attending lectures and just stayed in his room. No-one except Richard noticed. At a conference of 700 delegates, a single truant was hardly going to make headline news. While Darren did his best to cling to some sanity within the cool, sighing hum of the air-conditioned hotel room, Richard greedily consumed as much of the conference as he could. And whereas Richard and the other delegates were spending long hours debating small points, Darren was spending long hours avoiding Richard. He tried ringing his girlfriend Karen when his roommate wasn't around, but never seemed to get the timing quite right. She was either out or asleep. He listened to his own confident voice on the answer machine time and time again, telling him that they weren't there right now, which was obviously true, one of them being in America, and that if you left a message they would get back to you, which was patently untrue, because he left his number several times and nobody ever got back to him. Darren became worried that something had happened to Karen, something bad. And then worse. He started worrying that something good had happened to her, and she had moved out, perhaps to live with someone stable.

While avoiding the conference was fine up to a point, after five days Darren realized he was in trouble. The rest of the attendees were almost ready to pack up their slides and laser pointers and disperse to various corners of the globe, eagerly returning to their laboratories to impart their new-found wisdom. Darren, however, had very little to impart when he got back to Manchester. What was he going to say? Oh yeah, went to a few lectures, got a bit freaked out, stayed in a lot. This was unlikely to justify the expense of sending him abroad. When Darren first planned the trip, he optimistically budgeted to take a week off after the event to explore Colorado. So far he had explored nothing more remote than the back of the TV. Richard had crawled under his skin and attacked him from the inside. He rang the airline and brought his return date forward to the following day. And so, twenty-four hours after picking up the phone in his hotel room he was boarding a plane from Colorado Springs to Chicago, squinting in the sun, to catch a connection back to the relative sanity of his life in Manchester. Mainly, though, he was catching a plane away from the relative insanity that was Richard.

The first leg, five hours on a narrow-bodied jet next to a large man who must surely have been dipped in itching powder at some stage of his life and had never recovered, was a bad start. But the real fun had begun when he landed. On his right for the second leg of the journey was the salad-dodger who had encouraged him to complain. On his left, and hogging the window, was a man of similar age, who had introduced himself as Archie when they sat down.

He was five ten at a stretch, smartly dressed and reasonably good-looking in the right lighting. Conversation hadn't been particularly forthcoming, but later, in between bouts of trying to sleep, Darren made another attempt to talk to him.

The Exchange

Darren turned to face me as I looked away from the window and began to thumb through the in-flight magazine.

'So, Archie,' he began, 'have you been on holiday?'

It took me a second to respond to the name. I really wasn't much good with aliases. 'Sort of,' I replied, shifting in my seat to face him.

'Anywhere interesting?'

'Yes.'

'Where?'

It wasn't that I wanted to be uncommunicative. I was just uncertain of what lay ahead. Talking seemed to make things worse. 'Los Angeles,' I told him. And then, to try to coerce more than two words into my reply, added, 'And Nice.'

'And I suppose you still have all your luggage with you?'

'Yes.' In fact, I had my whole life with me. 'Why?'

'They've managed to lose mine.'

'Really?'

'Yeah. That's why I'm up here with you affluent types, and not back there,' he said, thumbing towards the rear of the plane.

I became more interested. 'What – they left your luggage behind?'

'They didn't so much leave it as send it somewhere else.'

'Pisser. And what, you have to hang around in London?'

'No. I think they'll send it on to me, or I can collect it later.'

'And you've got all your important stuff in the cases?'

'Case,' Darren corrected. 'Yeah, everything. Even my wallet, with all my English money in it, which is a bit of a downer. Not sure what I'm going to do. Might have to ask an airline rep to lend me some cash to get back to Manchester.'

'That's no good.' An idea was forming. 'Listen,' I said after pausing to think for a couple of seconds, 'why don't I lend you the money to get you home? I've got plenty of sterling on me and you look vaguely trustworthy.'

Darren scrutinized me for a second, unsure of why a total stranger should be offering to lend him money. 'No. I couldn't.'

'Come on. Seriously.'

'No, really.'

There was a moment of hesitation this time. He was thinking about it. I tried to make it easier for him. 'Look, I've dealt with airlines before. They're happy to take your cash and accidentally send your entire belongings to a brothel in Botswana, but I've never heard of them being particularly desperate to lend you any of their money.'

He smiled politely. I could see he was coming round to the idea. 'How would I get it back to you?'

'Give me your address and number, I'll get in touch as soon as I know where I'm staying, and you can post it to me.'

'But it doesn't seem fair on you . . .'

'Oh, come on, sod politeness. I hate seeing people stuck in a mess that a few quid could get them out of.'

Darren seemed to wait long enough for it to appear

gracious to accept. 'OK,' he said. 'And thanks. I'll make sure you get it back.'

The ice broken, the money and address exchanged, we continued to chat as the plane ground out the miles between land masses. 'So how come they lost your luggage?' I asked him.

Lost

The counter man looked harassed. Airport staff always do, their skin exuding a distressed sort of greasiness that seems to climb out of their pores to bask in the artificial light. Darren could see before he got to the front of the queue that this wasn't going to be easy. Propping elbows on the counter, he drummed his fingers against his forehead. He wanted the man to know he was angry before he even opened his mouth. Certainly, when Darren did open his mouth, the effect would be diluted in the wide river of his inaptitude for confrontation. So he continued to drum for as long as it felt as if he wasn't milking it too much. How can I help you? the man asked in a weary tone of voice which sounded as if it would have been happier asking How can I chop you into pieces? Darren ceased drumming and told of his predicament. To the airport man, this wasn't a predicament. To him this was a whining Limey complaining about something or other of little interest to him, one more piece of someone else's shit to deal with before lunch, one more thing to moan about to his wife when he got home, one more outpouring of anger to soak up with his greasy skin. Without saying anything the man snatched Darren's ticket and began to tap violently away at a keyboard hidden under his side of the counter. He might have been playing Tomb Raider for all Darren could tell, but, if he was, he didn't look to be doing very well. After a few more seconds he stopped and glanced up.

'Heathrow, right?' he said, his head tilting back on the 'right'.

'Yes. Heathrow, England.'

The man narrowed his eyes. 'Heathrow, England,' he repeated slowly.

'There isn't another Heathrow, is there?'

'Nope, there's only one Heathrow. That's not your problem, son.'

'Well, what *is* my problem?' Darren asked, quickly wishing he hadn't, because the man looked as if he was about to tell him.

'Your problem is that your luggage has missed its connecting flight.'

'What connecting flight?'

'Looks like we couldn't get it on your flight from Colorado – let me see – baggage overbooked, so it was sent via Houston to Chicago.'

'So?'

'Well, it missed the Chicago flight.'

'What do you mean it missed its flight?' Only hours before he had been dragging it around with him like a bad memory. Now his luggage was apparently jet-setting of its own free will.

'I mean it didn't manage to catch the thirteen hundred hours transit for Chicago.'

'What the hell was it doing – last minute shopping?'

'I appreciate your sarcasm, sir,' he said, clearly not appreciating Darren's sarcasm, 'but your luggage won't be able to join you on your flight today.'

Darren felt a little let down. He had been travelling with his suitcase now for several days and they had got quite used to each other. To hear that it didn't have the time to join him on his final flight was a little upsetting. 'So when might it be able to join me?'

'The next connecting flight will be, let me see, sixteen thirty-eight hours, that will get here at twenty hundred hours, next flight to Heathrow . . .' he glanced up at Darren, making sure he was prepared for the worst, 'not until tomorrow.'

This wasn't by any means the worst news in the world. Had he been offered the chance before the journey began of getting home safely but without his luggage, Darren would have been reasonably happy with the arrangement. However, airports take the reasonable out of people. In airports, a minor inconvenience becomes a major betrayal. A slap in the face becomes a kick in the bollocks. Darren resolved to get even. 'I want some compensation,' he said, throttling the instinct to add 'as long as that's OK with you'.

The man picked up a phone and asked for a name Darren didn't catch. He turned round, aware that he was causing a bit of a queue, and caught the eye of an adipose American standing at the adjoining Business Class counter.

'They messin' you abou'?' he asked. Darren nodded sheepishly. 'Tell you what you wanna do. Tell 'em you wanna upgrade. Tell 'em they're messin' you aroun' an' you wanna upgrade.'

'Right,' he said. That was a lot better than his plan. He'd been aiming for a free taxi when he got home or maybe some complimentary drinks on the plane. An upgrade sounded a whole lot better. The check-in man finished his call and sighed. Darren readied himself to be assertive, which, with his distinct lack of skills in this area, was just as likely to get him downgraded to the luggage hold. The man half smiled at him.

'On behalf of Air USA we would be happy to upgrade your Standard seat to Club. If that would be acceptable with you, sir.'

Sir. This was pay-day. Darren wanted to kiss his sweaty pores. For the sake of appearances, though, he tried to look disappointed. After all, this was an airport, where normal rules of etiquette don't apply. In addition, and of importance in the body language of the traveller, he was now a punter who was firmly at home with executive lounges and slightly wider seats. 'I suppose that would be OK . . .' he acknowledged reluctantly.

Darren had found himself with nearly three hours to kill until the connecting flight to Heathrow. Bored and fatigued in equal measure, and still fazed by the previous eternity spent in close proximity to a fidgeting giant, he wandered the endless walkways of O'Hare airport. Every category of tat you could possibly imagine gathering dust on a mantelpiece somewhere was available for purchase, and was being snapped up by similarly weary travellers who had lost either all sense of reality or the will to live, or both. Shopping was, he reasoned, something to do which didn't involve either flying or waiting. Darren decided to try to drink the time away. He managed a couple of beers and began to feel rather good before his flight was called.

And here he was in Club, feeling slightly wider and slightly furrier. With a glass, rather than a beaker, of wine in his hand, he scanned the list of suggested movies. One title jumped out at him. He had read the book, and therefore crossed it off his list, because Darren had a general rule with books and films – never try to do both. For some reason there exists an extravagance of good books which have made bad films and good films which have come from poor books. Rarely is there a good film of a good book. They almost appear to be mutually exclusive. Darren examined the rest of the many films open to the Club Class traveller. Mainly they were movies he hadn't heard of, new releases in America which had yet to slouch their way across the Atlantic to disappoint cinema-goers in England. Darren gambled on one of the selections. It was probably crap, but it was free, and it wasn't as if he could go anywhere. And they were serving copious alcohol and distributing ice creams. And he wouldn't even have to return it to the video shop afterwards. All in all, Darren found it difficult to find a single reason why he shouldn't watch the film. A healthy amount of white wine was decanted into his glass by a stewardess who was obviously too attractive to be wasted on Standard Class. He glanced back at the small screen in front of him and had one more go at dissuading himself from watching the film. Swallowing the wine, he highlighted the relevant option and settled back in his ample seat.

Fact-finding Mission

I was once again gazing out at the perfect stillness we were busy hurtling through. Six hundred and two miles an hour, 37,000 feet above the Atlantic. It doesn't matter how rational you are, it never quite makes sense. Part of me still believes that air travel is an elaborate hoax of some sort. Darren appeared to have given up on whatever he was watching.

'Didn't you fancy any of the films?' he asked, noticing that I wasn't doing anything.

'Not really,' I said, turning to face him. 'You?'

'I tried to watch one but lost interest. Haven't been sleeping since I came away.'

'Jet lag?'

'Something like that. I don't know, it's just my job . . . I don't know if I was ever cut out for . . .' He paused, looking momentarily uncomfortable.

'For what?' I asked, genuinely curious. It was in my interest to learn as much as I could about Darren.

'I'm in trouble when I get back.'

I nodded, not just to encourage him to talk to me, but because I was very much in the same boat. My troubles, however, were likely to occupy a far larger boat than Darren's. In fact, to continue the maritime theme, my boat was a colossal supertanker which was due to run aground at any moment and sink in a big oily mess. 'What have you done?'

'It's what I haven't done. I went to a scientific

conference in Colorado, but didn't go to any of the lectures.'

This didn't seem the most dangerous situation I had ever come across. 'So?'

'I started a new job in Manchester – moved there from Sheffield a few months ago – and they paid for me to go to the conference on a sort of fact-finding mission, you know, report on all the new developments in our area. Trouble is, I can't think of a single thing to tell anyone when I get back. I sort of lost the plot a bit. I was forced to share a room with this lunatic, and I'm either going to have to invent a shedload of stuff or come clean and admit that I fucked up.'

'So make some stuff up.'

'Like what? I mean, easier said than done.'

I sat and thought. I wanted to help him, really. I was about to make his life a whole lot more interesting, so I might as well sort his problems while I still could. 'OK, so they must give you a booklet or programme or something when you arrive at one of these conference things.'

'Yes.'

'And do you still have it?'

'Yeah.'

'In your suitcase, I suppose.'

'No, it's up there.' He nodded at the overhead locker. 'In my briefcase.'

'So get it out. Start reading it. Memorize sections. Surely there's information about each talk in there?'

'Abstracts,' Darren said. 'One for each talk – a sort of summary.'

'Well there you are. Problem solved. Read the abstracts of the lectures you should have gone to, note the important points, elaborate here and there . . . I mean, as long as you don't stray too far from the summary you can't go wrong.'

'Yeah, but you don't get much of an idea from an

abstract about the validity of the data, you know, about how convincing it is. Science is, after all, an inexact science.'

'So apply some technology to your situation. Toss a coin. Pick abstracts that don't interest you and write "unconvincing" in the margin, and ones you do like the look of and write "convincing". I mean, who's going to know?'

Darren reached up and retrieved a volume which looked like a slim phone book, maybe of a sparsely inhabited area, from his case. 'Ah,' he replied, sitting down, 'there's the problem. There were two people from my department there. One, Richard the lunatic, isn't coming back for a while. The other is, though. The esteemed Dr Wilkes.'

'Who's he?'

'She's Sarah, and she's a pain in the arse. Loves her job, lives for it. Does fuck all except sleep and work. Puritanical as hell. She went to the conference. Separate flight and everything, but she's going to know I wasn't in any of the lectures, and that everything I say is going to be bullshit.'

'Come on, surely there were lots of people there. Maybe you just didn't run into her. Lectures often mean different things to different people. I mean, you're talking like you want to get into trouble.' Darren glanced at me, and I thought there was more than a hint of guilt in the look. 'Read the brochure or whatever you call it. It will be OK. Trust me, I'm an expert at bluffing my way through work. I've made a career out of it.' On this rare note of honesty I decided to shut up. Nice once again made its way into my thoughts.

Frenzy

He is standing there, nearly looking at me. Sips a small beer, checks his watch. Looks mean, as mean as I remember him from Birmingham. I stop abruptly, try to get a better view. It is definitely him. He is ten yards from me. My legs are trembling. He glances up and sees me. My lungs shrink. There is a shout. I turn round. Sprint. Don't hear the words. Never look behind. Scream across the road. Round the corner. Down an alley. Through a courtyard. He is chasing, his large Doc Martens slapping the pavement. Flat out. Over a small fence. Another shout. Tear through a park. Out into traffic. More shouts, French this time. Moped skids to a stop. Dash across another road. More tyre noise a couple of seconds back. Into a shopping district. Fewer cars, more people. No voices, just the pain of quick, cold breaths. Bumping into shoppers. Jump a small dog. Glance back. Can't see him. A pram. Swerve to one side, catch a table with my left thigh. The corner stabs me. Dead leg. Keep running, uneven now. Left leg refuses to bend. Swearing. Slowing. Look round. Still can't see him. Losing momentum. Keep running. Pain sapping my stamina. Frenzy subsiding. Can't believe it. Barely running. Enter a shop, hobble to the back. Leg aching. Prop myself against a shelf. Panting, sweating, swearing. Scanning the door. He doesn't come in. Grip my temples. Steady myself. Panic giving way to fear. Stomach muscles gripping tightly to new-found dread. Try to persuade myself I'm mistaken. Shaking, unconvinced. People staring. Clench my arms around my abdomen. Scan round for a rear exit. Emergency fire door. Drag myself towards it. Back out into a yard. He doesn't enter the shop. Stop and think. How could he know where I am? Breathe slower. Friends? Someone has told him. The Expats. Blood-tasting saliva. Bastard Expats. Spit. Saliva dribbles out over my chin. Sharp pain in my leg. Open the gate at the back. Glance up and down. Cobbled alley, few exits. Step back into the courtyard. Try to breathe. Wonder why he is here, instead of terrorizing minor villains in the West Midlands. Inspect the alley once more. Empty and quiet. Overlooked by nice apartments. Recognize one which Marcelo showed me around. Wish I'd taken it. Would have somewhere to hide. Wait one more second, then walk warily towards the end of the alley, one leg refusing to work.

A Ready-made Life

I met Marcelo just as hotel life was beginning to lose its sparkle. Marcelo was Argentinian and worked as an estate agent. He said he might have some properties I could look at and I decided to give it a go. Not that I was seriously thinking about buying a place in Nice – it had never been my intention to stay even this long – but I was acutely aware that after only fourteen weeks of my French odyssey I was becoming more institutionalized than was natural even for me. I craved something more than the four walls of my hotel suite. Five or six and maybe I could breathe again. Marcelo took me on a quick scan of several apartments of variable quality and consistently high price, indicating the good points and glossing over the bad, as was his job. I reminded him of key World Cup outrages perpetrated by his fellow countrymen whenever he seemed to be trying to con me. He brought up the sinking of the *Belgrano* whenever I chided him for being unfair and dishonest. We got on well, and became friends for a few months. I began to come round to the idea of buying a place.

One day I got a call from Marcelo telling me he had to leave the country. Something had gone wrong in Argentina and he had to return. He was never specific, but I guessed from the obvious terror in his voice that a potential loss of money was involved. What about buying a flat? I asked him. You will 'ave to buy eet from someone else, he told me solemnly. We met for a goodbye drink. He was upset, but also annoyed that he was going to have to give up his own rented apartment. Now, if there's one person you want to inherit an apartment from, it's an estate agent. I asked him if it was furnished, and he replied miserably that it was, and he didn't want to ship all his furniture back to Argentina. Again, my eyes lit up. I was in the market to buy. Marcelo needed to sell, and, given the circumstances, cheaply. Here was a ready-made life to step into. An apartment with gas, electric, phone and TV already set up, carpets underfoot, curtains over windows, lampshades over bulbs, pictures on walls, utensils in cupboards, fittings in the kitchen, fixtures in the bathroom, and with all the necessary furniture comfortably installed. This wasn't so much moving into new accommodation as stepping into pre-assembled living. It was a lazy man's dream come true, the Pot Noodle of changing address. We went to the apartment and I offered to buy his possessions and take over the lease. On the way back to the hotel, I offered to buy his car as well, which similarly was already taxed, insured and tested. In a couple of hasty hours I had progressed from the relative immobility of living out of a suitcase in a hotel room to the upward mobility of a smart car and an equally well-bred and much sorted apartment. One of the few aspects of Marcelo's life that I didn't inherit was his soul, which seemed a shame, having come so close to buying an entire life from someone. As he was an estate agent, it had long since been unavailable for purchase, having passed on to Satan for safe-keeping. However, a few weeks later, I was able to add one more piece of his life to my collection.

One More Piece

No-one can quite hear anyone else. I get the sudden impression that she is simply guessing what I'm saying. Certainly, I am doing the same for her. I talk some more and watch her. Every sentence I finish receives the comment of either 'cool' or 'nightmare', or both when she can't make up her mind. From time to time she just nods. She is, I imagine, listening to the tone rather than the content. I try to catch her out by telling her I have a tiny, tiny cock, but in a boastful voice. Cool, she says. Not that it bothers me. Really, I have no interest in Nadia other than having sex with her. I hope she feels the same. It is difficult to tell when I can only half hear her conversation, but I get the steady impression that things aren't going well, and sense that she couldn't be less interested in me if she tried. In fact, as I observe her more closely, I realize she *is* trying, and making an exceptionally good job of it. I continue to monitor her unflagging uninterest and it depresses me. This is a waste of time for both of us. She doesn't have to be so actively indifferent towards me. The message has been received loud and clear and doesn't require any further hammering home. Surely now she is just doing it for her own enjoyment.

Nadia gives out some more unsolicited information about herself. From what I can gather, she is from Washington, and is spending a year 'bumming around

Europe'. I smile at the unintentional innuendo, which is the only bright spark I can salvage from her dreary conversation. She hasn't bothered to keep in touch with Marcelo. I tell her I would be quite interested in hearing from him, particularly in light of the duff car he has sold me. Nightmare, she says. The noise is beginning to tire me out. Aware that this is going nowhere, I suggest that we go somewhere quieter, a place I might be able to get a taxi home from when she isn't looking. Cool, she answers.

We walk past a homeless African girl who is giving out leaflets to people. I decline one, but wonder what they were advertising as we head towards a taxi rank. Nadia continues to talk, telling me her day has been ruined by an unsatisfactory session at the gym. She wore her kick-boxing shoes and found them unsuitable for the running machine. She will now have to do an extra twenty minutes' work-out the next time she goes, which won't be until she has bought some new sneakers, maybe blue to go with the Nik-*e* baseball cap she always, always wears at the gym, but maybe red ones are cool as well, but what do you think, is it, like, a nightmare to wear red with green, or would that be cool, I don't know maybe I'll ring Mom and she will know, she always does, she's cool about some things, you know, so what are your parents like? I stare into her eyes. I have been busy cursing myself over the decision to leave the noisy bar, where I was at least spared the trauma of being able to hear what she has to say. But the p-word interrupted my private melancholy. Parents. A quick stab of guilt, a minor flush across my face. Mum and Dad, whom I haven't seen for nearly two years. I walk on. Nadia has started where she left off, with little interest in anything outside her irrelevant existence. Because my parents are, like, cool, you know, about some things, but I get really pissed at them, like my dad buys me this car, and I'm like, Daddy, if I wanted a status symbol

I would have bought one myself, like he doesn't understand, he says airbags are what you need, and I'm like . . .

I have a good idea what she's like. We approach a tired Mercedes taxi at the front of the queue. The driver is reading a book and waits to finish his sentence before glancing up at us and starting the engine. I give my address and Nadia stares at me. I thought we were going to another bar, she complains. I tell her she is free to, but I am tired and need to go home. She is silent, and looks like she is trying to pout. I desperately try to imagine what Marcelo saw in her. True, she is slim and attractive, but as with most young people who have been born into the satisfaction that money brings, she whines as if the world is against her. I smile as I recall Marcelo's broken understanding of the English language. Maybe to him she was charming company. Then again, maybe she was just fun to have sex with. We approach my street. She has said nothing for several minutes, which is a godsend. The taxi stops and I open the door to get out. Aren't you going to invite me in, she enquires. I tell her that I am very tired. She appears slightly crestfallen. Too tired to fuck me? she asks. I hesitate. She leans over and kisses me. The rules have suddenly changed. Maybe not, I say. We shuffle out of the car and enter my apartment block. Nadia leads the way. She has, after all, been here before.

Iron Lung

Darren reclined his seat and attempted to sleep, which seemed to be the fashionable Club Class executive thing to do. And if it was good enough for them, he reasoned, it was more then adequate for a second-rate scientist from Manchester. As he tried to make himself relax, though, thoughts of the conference began to nag away at him. Transatlantic conferences should be classified as an Olympic event. They are stamina trials, triathlons for the brain, the three endurances being learning, alcohol and jet lag. For one day, the brain is happy, excited by new surroundings, new people, new possibilities. After this, it becomes successively more knackered and craves the apathy of its usual existence. Day Two generally isn't too bad. The first hangover of the campaign and the first yawns, both abated by caffeine. More worryingly, the first doubts. Everybody else is doing better work than you are, everybody else is brighter than you are. Day Three, the second hangover, the second series of doubts. You drink to stay awake at night, and drink to get to sleep before dawn. In short, you drink to fool your body clock into believing you are keeping sensible hours. Day Four sees the first missed lectures, and Day Five the first missed sessions. Most conferences have the good grace to bow out around Day Five, with attendances flagging and delegates sagging. Some will stretch on, though, into a tortuous Day Six, with only the superhuman or the superstitious staying the distance, their tired brains fit to burst. For the truth of the matter, Darren readily accepted, was that the brain is a lazy organ. Darren's brain, in particular, excelled in this department. But in its laziness it stands alone in the body. Lungs, for instance, aren't prone to the sort of lethargy that the brain has spent idle hours developing. Kidneys don't doze off for a few hours now and then; hearts don't run out of enthusiasm and decide to miss out on a few beats. Eyes don't shut themselves down to loll behind tightly closed eyelids. In fact, so unpopular is this selective behaviour that the brain has sectioned itself safely off into its own bone-protected cavity. Smart move. But if other organs could think we'd be in real trouble. Dialysis would be a daily event, iron lungs would be sold by the dozen, pacemakers would be fitted at birth and guide dogs would be available to all. Darren closed his eyes and yawned, and his brain prepared for another partial shut-down. If it hadn't been for sharing a room with Richard, the conference might have been all right.

Sounds of Silence

Suspicious sounds of disguised masturbation thrust their way across the room and into Darren's ears. He peered at the bedside clock-radio. 5:53 in large red digits of misery. 5:53 in the fucking morning. He had managed two and a half hours' sleep. Darren's sticky eyes glued themselves shut again. His ears, on the other hand, remained wide open. The sounds continued with renewed enthusiasm, puffing and panting now readily audible. This was horrible. The beds were a mere forearm's length apart. The proximity of the sleeping arrangement hadn't seemed to faze Richard at all, though. Darren, on the other hand, had spent a vigorous five minutes trying to force the beds further from each other when Richard had been in the bathroom on the first evening of their incarceration. Despite a good deal of pushing, pulling and pleading, the heavy beds had remained more or less rooted to their spots, with Darren achieving little more than a minor hernia and a kingsize mattress that hung a couple of feet off the edge of its frame.

The panting started to increase, with his roommate seemingly counting strokes. This was information Darren could happily live without. Fifty-one, fifty-two, fifty-three . . . Arghhh! The noises abated. Darren pretended to be asleep. The only thing worse than listening to someone masturbate in the bed next to you was that person becoming aware of the fact you had heard. Darren wondered whether he would be able to sleep now without going to the toilet. His bladder was awake and demanding attention. There was a movement between the blind and his eyes: Richard was walking towards the bathroom, and Darren studied his erect form. He was wearing a tracksuit and trainers and appeared a little flushed. Just before the bathroom, Richard stopped, peered closely at the floor, and lay down. Darren sat up in bed, intrigued. What was the pervert doing now? Richard took a deep breath and began again. Fifty-four, fifty-five, fifty-six . . . Darren slumped back to the prone position. The fucker was doing sit-ups! Although mildly reassured that Richard had obviously not been wanking, Darren still experienced a sick feeling of disgust. Masturbation was one thing, but exercise? At six a.m.? Richard conceded defeat at sixty-two. Standing up and noticing his apparent interest, Richard asked whether Darren would care to join him on a quick jog. Darren told him with uncharacteristic restraint that he would rather not, if it was all the same with him.

'But you're going to the first session?' Richard asked.

'What's it on?'

Richard picked up his programme, which was folded at the relevant page. 'The genetics of host–parasite interactions.'

'Maybe not,' Darren muttered. 'Think I'll save myself for the sessions I'm really interested in.' Darren had promised his boss faithfully that he would garner as much knowledge as possible from the trip. To conserve his stamina, therefore, he intended to attend only the most relevant seminars.

'You see, I often find,' Richard said, bending to touch his toes and straightening again, 'that you can learn a lot from lectures which might not seem relevant at the time.'

Darren tried vainly to remember what he had been

dreaming about, in the hope that he might be able to get back to sleep. 'Yeah?' he said, unenthusiastically.

'Sure thing, buddy.' Christ, he was even starting to pick up the vernacular. 'Lectures that you don't want to go to can actually be very rewarding.' Darren was forced to agree. Some of his favourite lectures ever were ones he hadn't wanted to attend. Mainly, in fact, because he hadn't attended them, and had done something more interesting instead. Richard switched to squat-thrusts. 'For example, the lunch seminar today is on bio-informatics, and while that isn't something I know too much about, apart from, you know, the obvious . . .' Darren couldn't think of anything particularly obvious about bio-informatics, but nodded reluctantly anyway, 'it's being given by the guy who published that paper last month in *New Scientist*.'

Richard continued to stretch his body and tire Darren's mind, describing in great detail a gene he had never heard of, which acted in a way he couldn't grasp, through a mechanism he didn't understand. In the meantime, he tried to recall the exact moment he had realized that sharing a room with Richard was not going to be easy. His boss Dr Adams had introduced him to a lanky figure in glasses, who shook hands with painful ebullience. It quickly became clear that, thoroughly nice bloke though he was, Richard was going to be a handful in a confined space. He was like a butterfly collector of facts. He caught great earfuls of information, talked about it at length, and then stuck it away somewhere for future examination. His ears themselves were huge and protruding, and scanned the vicinity like radar as he turned his head to catch a new piece of data. Richard's mission in life could be simply stated: To Know Things. Or, if you lived with him, To Know Things And Tell You About Them. All The Time. At 5:53 a.m. In The Fucking Morning. In Excessive Detail. In retrospect, however, things had begun to go wrong even before his incarceration with

Richard. In fact, it had more or less been downhill since birth, and even that hadn't been particularly successful, given that his parents had desperately hoped for a girl. Now, though, thoroughly male, and lumbered with the hastily chosen name Darren instead of the eagerly anticipated Deborah, he found himself in another of a long line of unpromising situations, and one which, no matter how hard he tried, he was unable to attribute to his roommate.

Verve and Sloth

It had started with the weather. Darren had been quite unprepared for the heat. The heat, on the other hand, had been more than prepared for him. It assaulted him, explored him and surrounded him, like a clinging nylon sheet. It wasn't a breathless heat, though. It was a thin, high altitude heat, arid and unforgiving, making his lips feel instantly chapped, and his sweat free to evaporate copiously into the prevailing dryness. On the first afternoon of his arrival, before the conference had begun, Darren had hired a car and driven into the Colorado mountains. Once there, he put Plan Ultraviolet A into operation. He removed his T-shirt and exposed his etiolated flesh to the high Colorado sun. The tactics were simple. Two hours front, two hours back, an hour on each side, continue until thoroughly burnt. Time it right and he would still look badly blistered on his return to Manchester, which would, he hoped, mark him out as an international traveller amongst the pale masses of the city. Over the course of a couple of minutes, however, innumerable flies came to pay his pale torso a visit, blinded, maybe, by the severity of his whiteness. Swatting merely encouraged their interest in him, and the more Darren swatted, the more they were attracted by the commotion. With each successive landing of an insect on his body, he imagined three or four more, and for every one he saw in front of him he assumed thirty or forty were making an attack from the rear. Pretty soon he was unable to sit still, and had whipped a merry band of flies, bugs and mosquitoes into a frenzy of buzzing and crawling. He watched as one rusty-headed insect marched along his arm, negotiating the dense undergrowth of hair, occasionally buzzing its wings in contentment, running its proboscis up and down like a yo-yo, tasting the salt of his skin. As he observed it, another came to join in the fun, and another. They didn't seem to be biting him, but he wasn't entirely convinced. Finally, unsure of whether he was being savaged or merely licked, was itching or just scratching, he swore and put his T-shirt back on. Fuck it. A farmer's tan would have to do. He returned to his car, returned the car to the hotel car park and returned himself to his room, where he remained, steadfastly insect-free, luxuriating in the air-conditioning and awaiting the arrival of a considerably larger parasite. Richard, who had caught a separate flight, arrived a couple of hours later, having achieved more and slept less than Darren. He lugged his cheerful sense of accomplishment into the room, shook hands vigorously and began to unpack and iron his clothes with an unpalatable vigour. Darren watched him, appalled, his own still-packed and tatty case lying heavily next to the bed, where it was set to remain.

Throughout the following days, a pattern became established which couldn't entirely be blamed on Richard. Darren noticed that he and his roommate were beginning to feed off each other to get what they wanted. The lazier Darren was the more enthusiastic Richard became. And the more enthusiastic Richard was, the firmer apathy's shabby grip on Darren. He was quite sure that if he accompanied Richard to every lecture he attended – and he really did attend every lecture – Richard would soon tire and lose interest in the conference. Conversely, if Richard started to spend his time kicking around the hotel room, Darren would be compelled to visit more sessions. Richard was consuming Darren's torpor, and Darren was justifying his own lethargy against the backdrop of what was quite clearly unhealthy eagerness. In a way they were also competing, and in their own specialist field; Richard in verve, Darren in sloth. It was a close call during the early days as to who was winning, but in quiet moments of reflection, whilst Richard embarked upon another quota of squat-thrusts or leafed through the abstract programme memorizing key sections to impress fellow delegates, Darren imagined that he might just have the edge. Attendance at a conference was, after all, the easy bit. Non-attendance, that was tricky. It required perseverance. Sitting in a small room reading about the things you should be doing was no easy matter. The brain is always happiest when fooled into thinking it is doing something constructive. When it knows it is quite clearly doing nothing of the sort, it starts to invent its own fun. Darren decided he had to get the hell out of Colorado. As if additional encouragement were needed, there was also the presence of Sarah to deal with. Darren bumped into her on the second day. She was standing in a corridor, flicking through her very tatty, well-thumbed programme with some irritation.

'Darren. Where are you heading?'

'I'm not completely sure. You arrived all right then?'

'Ah, there it is,' Sarah said, ignoring the question. 'Lecture Two, Parallel Session Four, the main atrium, four thirty. Lorwitz on co-factors. Sponsored plenary. Could be hot.'

Darren stared at her, wondering what the fuck was she talking about. She seemed to have lapsed into some sort of conference pseudo-speak. She also appeared tired. In fact, Sarah looked knackered. For her, the conference had doubtlessly consisted of lecture after lecture, network after network, question after question, grabbing facts like bubbles about to burst. For the sake of appearances, he felt he ought to say something intelligent. Sarah was, after all, slightly more senior within the department. 'Yeah,' he managed to muster with some difficulty.

'But first I want to check out some new amazing stuff in the Advanced Topics section. Got to run. Don't want to miss anything! Coming?'

Darren didn't know whether he was coming or going. He mumbled the word 'Coffee', and Sarah headed purposefully and alone towards the series of lecture theatres which crouched at the rear of the enormous convention centre. Or center. Darren couldn't remember. His brain wasn't particularly enamoured of being awake so early and so sober, and for such a poor reason. He slunk off towards a room serving hot drinks and tried to avoid as many of the delegates as possible. The only thing worse than the conference itself, he mused, picking up a cup, was the people who went there. Particularly the ones from your own department.

Belongings

I glance back at Darren. His eyes are flickering as if he's dreaming. His mouth is open, and he fidgets from time to time, seemingly unable to get comfortable. I think suddenly of Marcelo, and how easy it is in the right circumstances to step into someone else's life, to slide yourself into someone else's skin. Darren has made it simple. No need to cough up any money this time, except the 200 quid I have lent him. Lost luggage is my gateway to becoming Darren. Not long now, either. The flight is almost over. The man on Darren's right is singing along to something on his headphones, unaware, a headphone version of singing deficient only in melody and lyrics. There is another sound. It takes me a minute to pin it down, but I realize that I am singing as well, a kind of alien, high-pitched squeak which is audible only to me. It reminds me of childhood fear and I stop. The pilot has just announced that we are beginning our descent. This feels oddly apt. I am tense, gripping the armrests, thinking of how the flight has mirrored my last few years. The ascent, the slow oblivious progress, the come-down. Now I am about to become somebody else. In an odd way, this feels good.

The problem is that I used to like myself most of the time, but now I'm not so sure. Being somebody else for a while may well be an improvement. Before, I had always imagined that I relished my own company.

Then I spent a long time alone with it. Finally, I could see what everybody had been complaining about all these years. Sometimes with friends or lovers in my former life I had craved an evening by myself, a few hours on my own, space to visit my thoughts. Sure, when Sue left me, I did live alone for several months, but I never felt entirely abandoned. She was still with me in the house – her smells, her discarded possessions, her photographs. And again, I had work. Not that there was anyone there who was even remotely approaching good company, but I did, none the less, share my office with someone, which was a cohabitation of sorts. And although there were times I felt pangs of isolation, there were still enough people around me to furnish the impression of, if not popularity, then at least acceptance.

It was only when I first moved to Nice that I finally understood the meaning of alone. Alone isn't a place you retreat to for a couple of hours when the cacophonous world around you is wailing in your ears. Alone isn't staying in by yourself and having an early night. Alone isn't taking a long bath with the door locked and the radio on. No, alone is finding yourself in a foreign country, surrounded by people who speak an indecipherable language, bereft of possessions and empty of friends, with no hope of returning home in the near future, on account of the fact that your former employer and perhaps even the police may be more than a little interested in talking to you.

Sue once said to me, 'Being with you makes me feel alone.'

It was the saddest thing anyone had ever said to me. It still is. But it wasn't until I left England for good that I fully understood her words. In France there were people I spent time with whose company served only to remind me of friends and family I missed. Being with them made me feel alone. Such people weren't necessarily different from my old friends, they just weren't quite the same. The reminder didn't come from things they said or jokes they told, it came from the fact that they weren't my friends. I came to the conclusion that friends, true friends, have some intangible quality which you couldn't sum up if you tried, as if you speak an invisible language which can't be translated by outsiders, no matter how welcoming and fun they may be. For my French friends were good people. Bertram, Mimo, Alain, Katrina and Marcelo all invited me to their collective bosom. Katrina even invited me to her private bosom on a couple of occasions. But no matter how much time I spent with them, I knew they were never going to be any more than temporary companions. And the longer I was with them, the more I craved my old, more permanent friends. I felt more isolated when they surrounded me than when I spent time alone.

Sue also once told me that when I held her it was as if I was holding her minutely away from me. Not as if I was grasping her to my chest, more like keeping her at a safe distance. Almost there, skin to skin, but not quite. A few hairs touching, maybe, but that was about it. My friends abroad made me feel like this as well. They were holding me close, but not close enough to feel anything.

Now, though, I have a new friend, and someone who is going to be more use than he knows. I turn my head towards him. A steward comes round to check that his seat belt is fastened. Darren rubs his eyes and mutters under his breath. He has woken up and is stretching, yawning and grumbling. The captain announces, 'Cabin crew to landing positions,' and the plane begins to bank and dip towards a small piece of tarmac several miles away on the surface of the earth.

Customs

The worst thing about travel, aside from the travel itself, is the checking. I suffer badly from this. I am a checker. I check things, and then I check them again. I am also a searcher, and a poor one at that. If I lose my passport, for instance, I will search the obvious places. Then I will check my searching. If I could search my checking, I surely would. I can occupy hours like this. Sometimes, in the course of a search, I will be reminded of another object which has gone missing and will start to chase its tail instead, and maybe even latch onto another one, until finally I forget what the first lost object was. It is a nervous affectation with its roots firmly planted in the million or so times I have failed to arrive somewhere with the desired or necessary object in tow. Before I left my apartment in Los Angeles, I watched as I carefully placed my passport, tickets, insurance and currency into my hand luggage. Then I sat and fidgeted for a while, before watching myself carefully remove the items from the bag for a recount. I generally require a witness in such circumstances. I will ask them again and again until they are thoroughly sick of the whole palaver whether they are sure that they saw me pack the required valuables. First I doubt myself, then I doubt them. If I had the apparatus, I would film myself packing, so I could play it back to settle any disputes I have with myself. Now, though, without the benefit of a video witness, I found that my passport was missing. The plane was stationary on the tarmac, and passengers throughout the cabin were unfolding themselves and standing up, opening overhead lockers and having minor items of baggage and duty-free fall on their heads. The window had lost its patch of condensation, and I monitored the outside proceedings with interest. Workers and small vehicles swam around under the hull of the aircraft like pilot fish picking parasites off an enormous whale. I glanced at Darren who was rounding up his possessions, his passport securely in hand. For an apparently shambolic person, he seemed distressingly more organized than I was. My passport was nowhere. I began to become a little frantic.

'Well, thanks again.' Darren pushed his hand forward, half-heartedly, having located all his effects. 'And don't worry about the money – I'll make sure I get it back to you. Just drop me a line when you know where you're staying.'

I shook his hand weakly, unsure of whether the slight dampness trapped between our palms had leaked from me or from him. The doors were secured, and we were allowed to traipse off the plane ahead of the bulk of its passengers, but a respectful few moments behind First Class. I had a final panic and then spotted the passport on the floor by my feet. Christ knows how it got there. I picked it up, chucked it in with all the other assorted travel-crap and walked off the plane.

Darren's parting gesture seemed a little premature, if anything. We had the variously elongated corridors and walkways to negotiate before we even reached the Arrivals lounge, and the likelihood therefore was that we would probably end up walking side by side, slightly awkward with each other, having already said goodbye. However, this proved not to be the case. Darren surged on in front with no luggage to claim, in a good position to clear the airport quickly. I walked more slowly, eventually being overwhelmed by the plane's remaining passengers, whose jaded momentum carried me along to Customs.

I had rehearsed a few answers on the plane. The chances were that I would be all right, but it pays to be prepared. Even though I doubted Customs would know who I was, I was nervous. This was the first big test of whether my scam had been detected. Presumably, since the money had continued to flow into my various bank accounts, I was still safe. However, an imagined fear can be every bit as distracting as a real one, often more so, difficult as it is to disprove. The queue shuffled forward and I fished around for my passport amongst a plethora of boarding cards, tickets, visa forms, boarding card stubs, ticket stubs and visa form stubs. I examined the assembled detritus. Air travel seems to be characterized by an obsessive desire on the part of travel agents to confuse you with various pieces of paper. Even the most seasoned travellers can find themselves drowning in the compulsory paperchase that always results from air transit. The passport finally retrieved again and the photo briefly grimaced at, I was ushered forward to a vacant booth.

'Purpose of visit?' the Customs man asked.

'Holiday,' I said.

'Holiday? But you're a UK resident, are you not?'

'Yes.'

'So you're entering your own country of residence for a holiday?' He looked up at me, half smiling. 'We usually tend to find it's the other way round.'

This wasn't going well. 'Er, yeah. I mean *returning* from a holiday.'

'And where have you been?'

'Los Angeles.' He was leafing suspiciously through my passport. 'And Nice.'

'And you left the country in, what, October 1997?'

'That's right.'

'Some holiday. Three years, nearly. I'd like a holiday like that.'

'Well, when I say holiday, I mean, you know, travelling.'

'And where exactly did you travel?'

'As I said. Nice and then Los Angeles.'

'Not exactly a lot of travelling then, sir.' It struck me that he was beginning to enjoy himself. 'Hardly a world tour.'

'No.' I faked a half-hearted laugh, which probably sounded more like a nervous affectation.

'You didn't have a US visa, then?'

'No.'

'Let me see. Nearly thirteen months. Should have got yourself a visa – could have stayed there legally.'

'Yes.' One-word answers were my only hope. Presumably it was of no concern to him that I hadn't been staying there legitimately.

'And how long will you be remaining in the country?'

'I don't know. For the foreseeable future, I suppose.'

'Guess you must be knackered after all that travelling,' he said, smiling at me, and handing back the passport.

The Customs man had had his fun. It was good to be back in England, where even people in authority had a sense of humour. I grinned and walked on. This fleeting and inaccurate thought, however, would probably come back to haunt me.

My cases were eased off the plane and thrown heavily onto the conveyor belt. I loaded them onto a trolley whilst other passengers watched anxiously for their own belongings to make the ungainly plunge down the luggage chute. Darren's luggage wasn't scheduled in until tomorrow. I took a taxi and headed for the dearest and nearest hotel.

Nothing to Declare

Darren checked his watch. Nearly three o'clock. Eight in the morning Colorado time. With no baggage to claim, he would be able to clear the airport in minutes. A growing sense of achievement dawned as he headed towards the exit via the Nothing to Declare channel. However, as he picked up his pace, he began to feel that something wasn't quite right. More accurately, he felt that something wasn't quite in the right place. Darren glanced down and realized that he was, much to his horror, in the company of an unwanted and very much uninvited erection. This was foreign territory. Why on earth his body should have chosen this moment to revisit the teenage torture of public erections, a good decade past his sexual peak, and in the very process of attempting to stroll casually past Customs officers trained to sniff out the merest whiff of discomfort, was, to put it mildly, a teaser. Darren stooped a little and continued. Presently, he put his hand luggage down and readjusted his trouser baggage. Pulling his jumper over the offending region, he limped on, partially upright, and finally figured it out. This was a morning salute, an eight a.m. greeting to the day that lay ahead. Only it didn't lie ahead and he wasn't in bed. It was the middle of the afternoon and he was shuffling in a suspicious manner through the Green Lane. Penises, after all, don't understand time zones. Erogenous zones often, but not time zones. He was a sitting duck and knew it. Please, not a strip search, Darren said to himself. A guard stepped out of line. It was all over. And to enliven the sense of occasion, Darren thrilled to the realization that his underwear had seen a solid, or not so solid, twenty hours of duty since he got out of bed in Colorado.

'Would you care to step to your right?' a humourless male officer asked. Actually, Darren didn't care to step to his right at all. He cared very much to make an undignified dash for it, proud erection leading the way, embarrassed bearer bringing up the rear. But as it wasn't really much of a question – more of a demand impersonating a question – Darren felt that it would be rude not to obey. The Customs officer indicated a table, and told him to place his briefcase on it. 'Now you are aware that you have come through the Green Lane, which indicates that you have nothing to declare?' Darren nodded. 'And I am obliged to ask you at this point if you have anything which you would like to declare.'

Something stirred in Darren. And this time well away from the trouser region, which nevertheless showed little sign of abating. A quote from somewhere. The officer's words echoed a phrase he had heard. An image flitted in front of Darren's eyes. That was it! Oscar Wilde at New York Customs. Have you anything to declare, sir? I have nothing to declare but my genius!

The officer asked him again, this time with less patience. 'Do you have anything to declare?'

Darren yawned and stretched, his tired mind wandering off on its own little journey. 'I have nothing to declare but my penis,' he muttered. Then he froze, realizing what he had just said. Fuck. It had just slipped out. He snapped back to reality, and his eyes darted guiltily down to his trousers. That at least hadn't slipped out yet. The guard stared at him with amazement.

'Your *what*?' he asked incredulously.

For about the thousandth time in his adult life, Darren was on the verge of committing verbal suicide. He adjusted his jumper as subtly as he could, well aware that he was blushing. A strip search was one thing, but a strip search with an obvious erection was asking for trouble. It was time to think clearly and strategically. Ill-equipped for such action, Darren remained silent.

'I want to know what you just said to me,' the guard demanded, stepping closer to him.

Darren continued to trawl his addled brain for anything which might save him from the mess he was in. The guard bore into his eyes. People were staring. Darren wished he was dead. And then, as he once again examined his erection for signs of subsidence, he spotted something on the floor. 'Peanuts,' he said, triumphantly.

The officer glared at him. '*Peanuts*?'

'Yes. Peanuts. I have nothing to declare but my peanuts.'

'And what exactly do you mean by that?'

'Nothing. Just that I, you know, dropped one of them on the floor.' Darren pointed with his foot at the nut he had spotted. 'Just wanted to let you know about it in case it was dangerous or something.'

'Dangerous? A peanut?'

This wasn't necessarily the winning idea he had hoped for. 'Someone might trip . . .' Darren left his words hanging in the airport glare.

'Right,' the Customs officer said with unhealthy relish, 'open your case.' Darren opened his hand luggage to reveal an almost entire absence of possessions – particularly of the nut variety – to the watching world. And they *were* watching, Darren noted unhappily, sauntering merrily past, like drivers overtaking a stranded motorist, revelling in the fact that he had been pulled out of line for inspection whilst they were free to drag their cases crammed with fags and booze into the sanctuary of the Arrivals lounge. The officer rifled vigorously through the small percentage of possessions that Darren had managed to hang on to since leaving Colorado, and, as he did so, Darren wondered idly whether Oscar Wilde got strip-searched for making an arse of himself at Customs. A clever remark like that nowadays would guarantee nothing less than a full anal investigation. Maybe that was Oscar's plan, Darren thought to himself. However, he appreciated that if he had to spend a day rummaging through other people's dirty underwear he would probably be delighted if he got the chance to humiliate the occasional poor sod attempting an ill-advised stab at wit. Still, things could have been worse. He shuddered at the questions that might have been asked if he hadn't lost his suitcase. One or two of the items he had bought in Colorado really *would* have taken some explaining. Maybe it was a blessing after all that his luggage had been lost.

Later, on the train, the trauma of the erection long since departed, Darren sat and leafed once more through the healthy wad of notes he had managed to amass. £165, he said to himself with some satisfaction. And this was proper money – an English mile from the indiscriminate, promiscuous currency of America, where ones, twenties and hundreds could only be told apart by their dental records. Indeed, Darren had spent a good deal of his time in Colorado under the happy illusion that he was carrying a lavish amount of cash around with him. As he flicked through the wad of sterling, Darren finally understood why so many years had been devoted by the Royal Mint to the goal of making different notes appear dissimilar, and why this had been time well spent. In America, someone seemed instead to have hit upon the idea of making all notes virtually identical, with the aim of persuading foreigners that they were actually fairly wealthy, despite obvious evidence to the contrary. A sandwich, a drink, some oversized and overpriced crisps and a couple of magazines, and still the wad was thick. Archie had been very generous, surprisingly generous, to him. And such a sum of money would be very useful. Checking out of the Colorado hotel, Darren had been presented with an ominously long catalogue of his mini-bar expenditure. For such a small bar, he had managed to do some substantial damage. Darren had demanded a recount, and had stood at the check-out desk while the past week of sleepless nights was detailed in the form of an extensive list of consumed miniature bottles and barely adequate cans. $418. This wasn't going to look good when he got back to Manchester. But now, with over half that sum in his hands, he would be able to soften the blow. He could pay it into his bank account and claim modest expenses from the department. And the great thing was that it represented free money. Having given Archie a false address and telephone number, Darren was, he hoped, virtually untraceable.

Upgrade

The real pisser about air travel, Darren tutted to himself, isn't the amount of time you spend cooped up in a narrow space breathing other people's disease, but the amount of time you waste hanging about on the ground breathing other people's disease. Air travel itself is usually the easy bit. At least you are moving, and with some speed. No, on a foreign journey, the real damage is done pfaffing about in airport lounges, counting down the torture to departure, sitting on the runway, enduring protracted periods of sub-pedestrian taxiing, and then, at the other end, sweating on stationary planes waiting for a man and his glorified ladder to let you off, grinding teeth as empty conveyor belts slouch past without your luggage, queuing at Customs, trying vainly to catch buses, trains and taxis, lugging dead-weight suitcases with you all the while, and essentially doing everything possible to ruin the magic of having just made 600 mile per hour progress on top of the world. On the way back from a foreign country, the real pisser is that you know exactly where you should be going and how to get there, but the destination remains stubbornly unattainable, a relatively slender number of miles away in the grand scheme of things, with only National Distress coaches or fucking privatized trains doing their damnedest to prolong your journey.

For about the fourteenth time in quick succession,

Darren checked his watch. It was becoming reflexive, and the closer he got to home the more time he spent looking at his watch and sighing. The actual length of the journey had become irrelevant; surreal, almost. It was now an endurance event, and glancing at his timepiece was merely a symptom of the torture. Finally, almost twenty-one hours after leaving Colorado, the taxi rattled into his street and came to a dangerously sudden halt, the driver having failed to hear Darren's first weary request to stop.

Outside his house, he tried to view the building as a long-lost traveller might, but was disappointed to note that it was as identically dilapidated as ever. It had, he was forced to concede, only been a week. A dog week, perhaps, with at least forty or fifty days and even more nights, but a week all the same. For the sake of effect, Darren rang the doorbell, rather than just letting himself in. Karen opened the door. Jesus, you look terrible, she said. Nice to see you as well, Darren answered, before asking her why the hell she had never returned his messages. After reluctantly ushering him in, Karen told him why.

'I've just been dead moody,' she said over a cup of tea. Home equals tea, Darren thought to himself, mulling over her words. 'I even burst into tears once when I heard your message.'

'Christ, I thought I was dull, but never *that* bad. But where's the moodiness come from?'

'You know, going on the pill. And I don't think my job is helping.'

'Early days though – things will get easier.'

'Yeah, but it feels like a lifetime already. Why is it when you start a new job the first weeks seem like decades?'

'Dunno. I'm not sure that changes.'

Later, as they undressed, other, more pleasing side-effects of the pill became apparent. 'They're magnificent!' Darren exclaimed, pulling Karen's blouse away from her cleavage and gazing in awe at her recently swollen breasts. It hadn't taken surgery or exercise, simply a burst condom on a miserable Saturday a couple of weeks before he left, and an uncomfortable visit to the local health centre.

'You may notice a small amount of mammary swelling, but this is perfectly normal,' the family planning matriarch had warned Karen as she handed over three months' worth of pills. 'And next time you might not be so lucky if you rely solely on condoms.'

And, Karen told him, she *had* noticed some swelling, some not inconsiderable swelling. It was an upgrading, Darren suggested, from Jaffa to Grapefruit class. Of course as he climbed into bed he said that it didn't matter, that he had hardly noticed, that other things were more important, especially now he was home. But Karen couldn't help thinking that if it had been a downgrading to Satsuma, maybe Darren would have noticed and maybe he would have said something. Still, as things stood, and they certainly did stand of their own accord, the situation could be worse. But there was still the question of mood swings. 'You know, this is terrible,' she said as she shifted into bed beside Darren. 'I've got these great swollen breasts, which I'm more than certain you can't wait to get your hands on, and all I feel like doing half the time is crying. And from what I've heard from friends on the pill, even my arse is going to get bigger.'

'Really?'

'Yes really.'

'Oh well,' Darren said. 'Great contraceptive.'

Karen frowned and picked up a book. 'Anyway, you must be exhausted,' she said, fishing, half hoping that he would be.

'Knackered. Too tired to sleep, even.'

'Yeah?'

'Mmm. You know I flew back in Club Class?'

'How did you afford that?'

'I didn't. I got upgraded. But it was great. You get your own TV and you get to choose your own film! In Cattle Class, they force any old shit on you. In Club Class, you get to choose your own shit. A brilliant step forward.'

'But how much would you have had to pay?'

'I was talking to this bloke, and apparently it's two and a half grand, almost ten times as much as Standard. I mean it's good and everything, but if you've got that sort of money, why not just buy an entire row of seats in Cattle, and really spread out. Fuck six extra inches of width in your seat, when you can have six extra feet.'

Karen yawned and said, 'Yeah.'

'And if you're the sort of person who feels important sitting in Club with your Buck's Fizz while everyone else struggles past to the back of the plane,' Darren continued, momentum building, 'then think of the filthy looks you'd get as you lounge across four empty seats. They'd *hate* you. Think how good that would feel! And the food! Four trays to yourself, four glasses of wine, four cups of coffee, four miniature sets of crackers – almost a normal-sized meal!'

'I thought you were tired,' Karen said, hoping Darren might shut up and let her read her book.

'I am. Really tired.' He ran his fingers down the side of her neck, over the small prominence of her collar bone, in search of her newly upgraded breasts. 'Too tired.'

Karen slammed her book. The previous days had been a luxury of sleeping alone, eating alone and reading alone. She had moved most of her life into bed with her, the evidence of which lay in the toast crumbs, magazines, clothes and remote controls which littered the immediate vicinity. The holiday was over, she sighed, turning out the light and rolling over to face Darren.

Next Day Collection

This wasn't proving easy. I repeated the address. The woman shook her head again. 'That isn't the address you gave us when you booked the ticket, Dr White. So I'm afraid I can't release your luggage. If you had some ID . . .'

'As I told you, it's in the case.'

'Or a lost luggage ticket?'

'I left it on the plane.'

'Then we can't help you. Security reasons – I hope you understand.'

I understood all right. My plan was already fucked. I was back at the airport the day after arriving and busy discovering that, for some reason, Darren had given me the wrong address. I had to think of another way. 'Look,' I pleaded, 'I can tell you exactly what's in my luggage if you care to open it up. Maybe that would convince you.' She shook her head and smiled. And then I had an idea. 'I think I know what the problem is,' I said. 'My ticket was booked through work. They must have the wrong details on file. I'll get in touch with them and see if that's the case. I'll be back in a couple of minutes.'

I made my way to a phone. The situation was soluble. 192. 'Manchester University, please.'

The number I required was, 'Oh . . . one . . . six . . . one . . . four . . . seven . . .' I hung up before she repeated herself. Then I put my credit card in the slot and dialled the number.

After a very long wait, a female voice eventually greeted me. 'Manchester University.'

'Department of Genetics, please.'

'Just putting you through.'

'Department of Genetics.'

'Oh, hello, I wonder if you can help me. Could I speak to Dr Darren White, please?'

'He's on extension 3916.'

'Could you put me through?' And then go back to charm school?

'Hang on.'

I blame TV and films. No-one ever says hello, goodbye, please or thank you in fictional phone conversations. It's as if script writers are too lazy, or want their characters to be the sort of thrusting, dynamic go-getters who simply don't have time to begin or end phone calls with polite words. If it happens enough on TV, it becomes the norm. There is an inevitability to it. Life imitating art imitating life. As the receptionist sighed whilst putting me through, I resolved that if ever I became a writer of anything more interesting than computer programs, my film characters would spend half their fictional lives saying hello and goodbye, just to redress the balance a little. The phone was answered.

'Hello, Darren White.'

It was time to fake a voice. I should have practised. I had a fairly blunt stab at a Cockney accent. 'Yeah, all right. Heathrow here. Lost luggage.' I pronounced Heathrow with an f, which, to my untrained and recently exiled ear, sounded authentically *EastEnders*. 'Your case's arrived. The thing is, Heathrow Security insist we double check all forwarding addresses.' More fs. So far so good.

'Right. It's 124, Wilmslow Road, Withington, Manchester, M12 8DH.'

'M12 8DH. Lovely.'

'So you're sending it today?'

'That's right.' That was wrong.

'And when should I get it?'

'Oh, tomorrow or the day after.' Or never.

'Great.'

'Well, sorry to disturb you. Goodbye.'

'Goodbye.'

'Bye.'

'Bye.'

I thought I had made an admirable start at redressing Manchester's aversion to saying goodbye. Cheered, and now with an accurate address, I returned to the lost luggage desk. The same person served me, the addresses matched and I was in possession of a rather shabby brown suitcase of the canvas variety. I dragged it into the Gents and examined its contents in a cubicle. One of the items, wrapped up in a black plastic bag, took me by surprise and made me wonder about the sort of activities Darren might get up to in his spare time. I pocketed a particularly anorexic wallet which housed a couple of bank cards, a photo ID and very little else, and closed the case. A few minutes later I left the airport without Darren's luggage and went about the fraught task of trying to get a taxi back to my hotel. On my way there, I wondered whether I should have taken the rest of Darren's possessions with me. One more case would mean three in total. Overnight, I would have gained 50 per cent more life than before. I decided, however, to try to manage with what little I had.

Shunting

The impetus for Darren's recent move from the Sheffield Institute of Medical Diagnostics to a reciprocal institution in Manchester had come largely from his boss Professor Graham Barnes. 'I think it would do you good to move around a bit, try another department, learn some new tricks . . .' he had said. Darren had been suspicious from the start of the sentence, due to its lack of deviation, which suggested it had been rehearsed, and probably several times. 'I have a colleague at Manchester who might be able to help you. Funding isn't quite so tight there, and he's a bright guy. And then maybe in a couple of years, *or so*, you could rejoin us here in Sheffield.' *Or so* had been emphasized in a way which served to add at least a decade to the suggested period of time. For the second occasion in so many years, Darren was about to lose his job. This wasn't quite a firing, though. It was more of a shunting, a nudge from an institution that knew he was useless to another which had yet to find out. This was often the way in academia. In business, if someone isn't pulling their weight, they get the push. In universities and research establishments, they are shunted. And pushing and shunting are vastly different processes. Shunting simply moves the problem elsewhere, whilst pushing removes it from the system altogether. There seems to exist a whole favours network of shunting useless personnel around the country's academic departments. Darren began to see where he might fit into the general scheme of things. Recently, Manchester had sent Sheffield a highly promising researcher, who had promised highly and achieved nothing. To level the score, Sheffield was probably now hoping to palm off someone of equal ineptitude on Manchester, and, looking down at his feet, Darren quickly appreciated his part in the payback. For in the present day, where research is competitive and good departments are rewarded with good funding, it is often easier to drag rival departments down to your level than raise yours to meet their lofty standards. And the easiest way to do this is to thoroughly recommend your shoddy members of staff, in the forlorn hope that, while they reduce the productivity of a competing group, you might get someone decent back in the process.

Professor Graham Barnes cleared his throat and smiled, obviously pleased with his speech. Darren sat and mulled over the implications of what had been said. A colleague of Prof Barnes's. Funding wasn't as tight. These were the two real issues. A colleague. Frightening. Darren had no idea that Prof Barnes had colleagues. Anyone suicidal enough to count him amongst their cronies should probably be avoided, as they were suffering enough as it was. And funding. In all other spheres of employment, people who consistently fail to do what they should be doing are told their employment is about to be terminated. In research, you are told that there is insufficient funding to keep your post open. This is a gentle way of saying we don't want to waste any more money on you. Often, and somewhat tellingly, it happens despite an influx of new personnel who all presumably have to be paid somehow.

'So who's the colleague?' Darren asked.

'Mike Adams. Decent character. Used to work here, actually.'

'And what's the score with funding?'

'He's got a three-year grant going, which might be right up your street.' By right up Darren's street, Prof Barnes meant any street in Manchester, and not in Sheffield. Three years though. OK, so the guy might well be a lunatic judging by the company he kept, but three years was thirty-six months, and thirty-six months was thirty-six pay days, and if any department was short-sighted enough to offer Darren such a substantial period of their time and money, this was the sort of department he wanted to work for. In fact, he would be foolish to overlook them, particularly as Sheffield was a rapidly closing door. 'Look, why don't you pop over and see him this week, have a chat . . .'

It had all sounded reasonable enough. When Darren did meet Dr Adams later that week, he was somewhat taken aback to discover that, although not entirely sane, he was by no means the madman he had envisaged. In fact, as they talked, it became apparent to Darren that Dr Adams was fair and even reasonable company. Of course, at this early stage, he was yet to reveal to Darren his skills in front of a crowd. Those had to be seen to be believed.

Show Time

All in all it had been a good conference, Darren felt as he strode confidently into his new department yawning the jet lag away. This was in strict disagreement with the way he had felt at the time, but that was the benefit of a long distance and a short memory. In fact, thinking back, it had been such a good conference that Darren hadn't bothered to go to very much of it at all, which had only served to improve the situation. This could well be the key to enjoying future trips. Surely, he reasoned, the only bad thing about a conference, apart from its delegates, was the conference itself. The rest of it was fairly pleasant and hardly an inconvenience at all. By the time he turned into the main corridor, Darren had managed to muster a reasonable degree of self-assurance about the whole trip. Having taken the advice, and, later, money, of Archie on the flight back, he had memorized key sections of the conference programme and felt sufficiently well armed to face the superficial level of questions he hoped to face from colleagues. The only minor concern that he had yet to dispel, aside from having very little in the way of clean clothes and even less in the way of clean underwear, was that Sarah might remember the proceedings differently. Richard, the roommate from hell, was less of a problem, having continued his journey on to a destination filled with fresh people to annoy. Darren entered the communal lunch area, which doubled as a seminar room, and was mildly put out to see that a lecture was about to start.

'Well, this *is* good,' Dr Adams exclaimed as Darren walked into the room. Darren remained unconvinced by the show of enthusiasm, and his shallow self-assurance slunk away as readily as it had come. Sarah was standing next to Dr Adams and was smiling confidently. Darren decided he should throttle her if he got the chance. 'Both attendees here, and just in time for the departmental lab meeting.' Panic began to set in. He had a whiff of what was about to happen. 'I've just had a super idea.' Darren doubted it. 'Why don't both of you fill us all in at the same time on what you've picked up from the States? And we'll have the meeting afterwards. It'd save a lot of time in the long run. That's if you don't mind?'

'Well . . .' Darren began.

'Delighted,' Sarah said, cutting him off before he had a chance to try to reverse out of the nightmare which was rapidly unfolding. 'Maybe Darren could start, though. I made some extra notes in my programme booklet, which I'd just like to go and get.'

'Great,' Dr Adams enthused. 'Darren? I see you've got your programme there, so if you have no objection to starting the meeting off? Can't wait, and I'm sure I'm not alone. I'll just give you a quick word of introduction.'

Darren's only hope had been to give his version of events after Sarah's, albeit a strangely coincident version of events. This looked increasingly unlikely as Sarah took her time returning. Thirty or so members of the department chatted idly away and Dr Adams cleared his throat.

'Right then,' he said. 'Show Time!'

This audience warm-up didn't unduly add to Darren's growing apprehension, and neither did it remotely stir the interest of the assembled mass. Dr

Adams always started this way, and was, as a consequence, known universally throughout the department as Show Time Adams. Nothing of even the slightest entertainment value ever followed his opening pronouncement, which was the main reason for its popularity, for Dr Adams was one of the world's greatest proponents of the art of overstatement. Show Time! had become a departmental catchphrase, which staff used to announce any dull event they were about to embark upon. Walk through the institute on any given day and you would hear Show Time! shouted out as someone bent down to do their laces up; Show Time! as a technician counted 500 pipettes into a bag; Show Time! as a bearded researcher dunked a teabag in his mug and Show Time! as a receptionist lowered her head onto her desk and tried vainly to get some sleep. And, dullest of all, in Dr Adams's vocabulary Show Time meant 'I'm going to stand here and mumble for what will seem like an entire lifetime.'

With the build-up almost complete, and the audience stirred to a new level of indifference, Dr Adams muttered words to the effect that Darren was now going to bring everyone up to date with US research and stepped modestly out of the spotlight. Expectation stared up at Darren from every face. This wasn't just the anticipation of new information, though. Far from it, in fact. This was the joy of watching someone else squirm uncomfortably on the spot, thankful that it wasn't you, safe in the knowledge that you could sit on your backside whilst some other bugger sweated away for your benefit. Aware that Sarah still hadn't returned, Darren thought the time was ripe to begin his fictionalized account of a conference he had never really been to.

'Well, I'd like to thank Dr Adams for this opportunity to speak to you.' If he was going to do a lot of fabrication, it was as well to start off on the right foot. He glanced up, suddenly anxious. 'So,' Darren opened the conference booklet, 'a question of where to start.' He was about to be swallowed by stage fright. 'A lot of lectures . . .' This wasn't going to be easy. These were, for the most part and with some notable exceptions, intelligent, enquiring minds. He was also aware of a slight tremor in his voice. This was bad. When you can hear the terror in your own voice, you know you're really fucked. It is positive feedback. The more nervous you are, the more your voice betrays you and the more obvious your nervousness becomes to you and everybody else. Darren spotted Sarah entering at the back of the room. She smiled encouragingly. Now he was truly in trouble. Utter fabrication is one thing, but in front of a witness it is quite another. Darren took a deep breath and began. 'Right. Well the first thing to say is that co-factor work seems a hot area. A lot of sessions, you know, some convincing, some not so, but overall . . . co-factors were pretty cutting edge.' That didn't seem to go too badly. Sarah was still smiling. No-one had thrown anything yet. 'But specifically, the first plenary on' – Darren flicked through his booklet and scanned the title – '"Interactions Away From The Nucleus" wasn't particularly well received.' This was true, at least from his own point of view, since he had actually made it to this lecture and promptly fallen asleep. 'Not really what you might call stimulating data.' A few researchers nodded sagely. Darren congratulated himself on a good guess. The next might be a bit more tricky. Having failed to understand even the title of the subsequent talk, he had sloped off to do some shopping, and, as a result, had tossed a coin over whether it had been interesting or not. Tails. Boring data. 'And as for the retinoic acid side of things, I think I can safely say that we should be shying away from any work in that particular field.' He glanced up. Again, no-one seemed interested in pursuing the matter, and Sarah was still smiling in support. This might just work out after all. 'So then, in the afternoon, one of the parallel sessions dealt with semi-quantification of first strand messenger RNA. Great stuff. This really seems to me to be the way forward for RNA analysis. I mean, the precision . . .'

'You mean *second* strand, surely?' Dr Hibbrets, a new arrival from Edinburgh, interrupted.

'Er . . . yes. Second strand. Sorry.' He had been led to believe that Dr Hibbrets was in fact a shuntee, and therefore implicitly useless. Darren had no idea of the difference between first and second strand RNA and little interest in finding out. He decided to persevere. 'But anyway,' he said, reading wholesale from the abstract, 'quantification can be achieved with only—'

'Semi-quantification, surely?'

Dr Hibbrets was beginning to get on Darren's tits. A topic he obviously knew something about had been raised, and he was going to extract as much value from it as possible. This was often the way. In academia it is possible to be judged solely on the questions you ask, rather than the answers you provide. Not understanding, but doing so in an apparently intelligent way, can make you look brighter than if you actually have a clear grasp of what's going on. And asking the right questions at the right time in front of the right people shows that you are at least awake.

'Semi-quantification, yes,' Darren agreed, again having little idea of what the distinction between the two might be. 'But anyway . . .' He stopped and caught Sarah's eye. She was beaming, and for a second Darren had the uncomfortable impression that she was enjoying the spectacle. So much for conference solidarity. 'Er, the main thing is . . .'

'Surely semi-quantification is on its way out, though, Dr White? Didn't you read this month's *Nature*?'

Darren didn't read any month's *Nature*, so he was able to give at least one honest answer. 'No, I didn't, I'm afraid.'

'Well, I don't understand the apparent contradiction. The talk, I presume, was given by Prof Eastman?' Darren read the name of the author at the top of the abstract and nodded glumly. 'And yet he publishes an article rubbishing the technique in *Nature*, of all places. I mean, are you sure of your facts, or has Prof Eastman begun to get confused in his old age?' This raised a slight titter, and a few members of staff who, until this point, had been having undisguised difficulty remaining conscious began to perk up. Finally, after months of dull lectures which had been vastly oversold by Show Time Adams, here was a fight.

Darren glared at Dr Hibbrets, who wasn't so much playing devil's advocate as Satan's best friend. 'Well, I can only give you my impression of what was discussed . . .' he said, shifting uneasily, placing his weight on one foot and then the other.

'This isn't a subjective opinion we are talking about here, surely.' One more surely and there was going to be trouble. 'This is more of a yes or no. And you're saying yes *and* no.'

Darren began to panic. He could see no way out. Members of staff shuffled eagerly forward in their seats, hyenas at a lion's kill, hungry for some of the second-hand action. It would be suicidal to confess now that he had patently not bothered to attend the session having just stated that he had. He scanned the lecture theatre wildly, searching for a way out. A physical means of escape presented itself. There was a door at the side of the room, if all else failed, and it did look increasingly as if it would. Show Time Adams stood up. It could be all over bar the mumbling. He appeared to have an idea, though, which was an excursion into unfamiliar territory for him. 'What about Sarah?' he asked. 'You were there, what was your impression?'

Sarah smiled. She always smiled, an in-control sort

of smile that irked Darren no end, and now might finally sink him. 'What Darren has failed to mention,' Sarah said, as Darren closed his eyes, 'is that Prof Eastman stated that he had maybe been a little harsh in his *Nature* article, and that he was now prepared to see both sides of the coin. Under the correct set of circumstances, he said, semi-quantification can be every bit as accurate as any other measure, as long as you pre-define your conditions. That, I think, is the point.'

Darren opened his eyes again, and a few members of staff closed theirs. The fight was in danger of ebbing away. But Dr Hibbrets wasn't quite finished. 'And Prof Eastman advocates the use of melatonin in time-change studies. Would that be your sentiment too?'

'Yes,' Sarah said, beaming.

'But surely melatonin has been shown to induce testicular cancer in mice? How could you possibly go along with that?'

'Number one, Dr Hibbrets, I am not a mouse. Number two, as I'm sure you will have noticed, I don't have any testicles.'

A polite academic titter became almost fully fledged sniggering. By scoring the loudest laugh, the point had been won and Dr Hibbrets reluctantly conceded. Really, Darren reflected as the audience settled down, comedians should give up their evening jobs and become scientists. Looking around the room, maybe some of them had. But they would win medals. For a start, the lectures of comedians would be enjoyable, which was half the battle, the other half of which they could achieve by simply being funnier than their critics. As far as Darren was concerned, the science was neither here nor there. Entertainment was what really mattered.

Darren seized the opportunity to pick up where he had left off, taking a couple more guesses at random topics, referring a few questions to Sarah and giving Dr

Hibbrets the odd hard stare. Easy, he whispered to himself as the seminar ran out of momentum and Show Time Adams did the necessary rounding up, with another flurry of overstatement.

Darren finally caught up with Sarah in the corridor outside the seminar room after most of its occupants had dispersed. There was something he needed to ask her. 'You didn't go to that lecture, did you?'

'How would you know?' she retorted.

'Or any of the others.'

'Whatever gave you that idea?'

'Because *I* knew I was talking bollocks. You, on the other hand, were only guessing.'

Sarah remained silent for a couple of moments. 'Maybe,' she said, making eye contact for the first time. 'Or maybe not.'

She smiled and walked away.

Murray Walker

Sarah had been keen to attend the first conference session of the day. She was tired, and events were taking their toll. Her body clock was still struggling to work out what time it was. It had been a long, long trip to Colorado. With so much to attend, she really ought to pace herself. The session would have coffee, the coffee would have caffeine and the caffeine would kick-start her brain. That was today's mission. Drink coffee, sober up, get ready for another onslaught. Also, she was eager to bump into Richard or Darren. At this rate, people were going to notice her continued absence. A quick hello, get her face clocked by the small number of attendees who knew either her or her boss, and Sarah could be back at the hotel relaxing by the pool, preparing for another long night of getting pissed and laughing, thousands of miles from all her troubles in Manchester.

The first night had been a dead loss. Nothing. Downtown Colorado Springs had little to offer the international traveller outside painful bars where everybody drank and sighed, and strip joints where everybody drank and cheered. She spent a gloomy hour and a half combing the streets for signs of action before getting a cab back to the solitary confinement of her hotel room. The second was better. She had bumped into a fellow delegate in the bar. He was Kamal, and was, in ascending order of importance,

Libyan, married, fragrant, charming and ugly. But a riot, all the same. Kamal had discovered a tequila bar on his first night. Tequila was one of the few foreign words Kamal had mastered, and he had certainly got it down to a fine art. He even said it as a Mexican might, particularly if they had spent a protracted period in Libya and had a shaky grasp of English. Te-key-a. Bring me te-key-a, he would say, before grinning and giggling like a schoolboy. They had drunk and laughed into the early hours, with seldom an intelligible word passing either pair of lips. Tonight was going to be different. Kamal had heard about a piano bar which opened until four. Sarah knew this because Kamal had done a sort of Ray Charles impression and repeatedly held up four fingers and pointed to his watch. At least it might be a piano bar. On reflection, it might also be a four-hour finger-drumming marathon, but that was the very point. It was a Murray Walker night. Anything could happen, and it probably would.

Later, by the pool, Sarah leafed through her tattered conference programme. She had managed to drop it into the water on the first day as she stood up for a swim. It was still alive, but had come out wrinkled as if it had been in the bath too long. She ticked off all of the lectures she had missed, and as she did so pictured Darren and Richard sitting resolutely through rigid scientific presentations in darkened theatres. This gave her a warm, fizzy feeling as she sipped her bubbly wine in the sun. In fact, she had run into Darren earlier. He was wandering about in his slightly vague manner, gently smiling, lost in thought. That was the thing about Darren. Always thinking about something which never quite made it to the surface, his green eyes in a daze, his mousy hair unintentionally ruffled. Still, on the scale of things, she would infinitely rather be lumbered with him than with Richard. Richard was plain scary. But tonight would be fun. Singing, dancing and boozing – the three laws of the international conference.

Back to the Old House

Everything was as I had remembered it, only shabbier and more faded. Mind you, this accounted for a fair proportion of the England I had encountered during the two days I had been back. Birmingham itself hadn't changed much, though, and three years didn't seem to have substantially damaged my house. In reality, probably nothing worse than a plague of Jehovah's Witnesses and double glazing salesmen had assaulted its empty walls. I had continued to pay the mortgage by direct debit, despite virtually writing the property off when I realized I had to leave the country. And although I had never envisaged coming back, here I was, turning the key in the lock, feeling it give reluctantly, seeing the repairs my friend Martin had made to the doorframe, pushing against a small mountain of mail and other letterbox dandruff, smelling a cold damp reminder of the house's odour, and walking past the epileptically flashing answer machine into the lounge. As I stood with hands on hips surveying the dusty room, I recognized that I shouldn't have returned. The memories were still too strong.

Lurking in the faintly decaying smell of the house were traces of my history. The two thugs I stitched up. The sleepless nights of planning. The final computer scam. That bastard Archie. The last days I spent in this house before they chased me abroad. Some of the dust my fingertips picked up as I ran them over various surfaces must have been floating around in the air of September 1997, preserving the physical atmosphere of that time as an everlasting film. I might even have exhaled some of this dust before I left the house, turning round to sprint out of the back as Archie and the thugs smashed the front door open, the dust rushing out to spiral down and colonize the floor, the sofa, the breakfast bar, the stereo, the traces of red still visible on the carpet.

I walked through the living room and tiptoed upstairs like an intruder. It was almost as if I was paying a visit to someone I used to know, a long-lost friend or distant cousin, sneaking silently around in their house in the gloom of the early evening. I was, in short, visiting a half-forgotten version of myself. The bedroom made me shudder. All those wasted nights. I opened the wardrobe which was, as it always had been, emptier of clothes than the floor. The Birthday Morning Album was there and I flicked through its sequentially numbered pages, from 21 to 29, each one housing a single Polaroid portrait taken on the morning of my birthday. On successive pages I looked pale (21), glum (22), innocent (23), happy (24), blissful (25), smug (26), relaxed (27), bored (28) and finally, at 29, fucking awful. As I reached the empty pages entitled 30 and 31, I took two photographs from my inside pocket and inserted them under the cellophane which served to keep photos and memories trapped against the paper. The new pictures made me look smug again. I flicked back to the last time I had a similar expression. Twenty-six. This was no longer a mid-twenties smugness. This was a different kind, an older, wiser, wealthier, suntanned smugness. Sure, the hair was still dark, albeit with the occasional grey invader; the eyes still black enough to swallow their pupils whole; the jaw still straight enough to almost look rugged, particularly in poor lighting; the smile still white enough to appear convincing – but the new photos were somehow more unnerving than the older one. This was the now – this was what people saw when they looked at me. I sighed, had one final flick through the album and then replaced it under a folded towel in the wardrobe. I crept down through the house towards the front door and unplugged the phone. After a quick pick through the more interesting items of post, I once again left my house for ever. On the way out, I encountered my elderly neighbour. Garden's a bit of a mess, he said, before shuffling back into his house. Three years' conversation condensed into a single comment. The old fucker had failed to notice my substantial absence, which I guess had saved a lot of time in the long run. The taxi was still waiting. I got back in and asked the driver to recommend a hotel near the centre of town. It seemed a supreme irony that I wouldn't be able to live in my own house in the coming months. A hotel would, however, save me from doing any gardening. We set off in an unknown direction. I smelled the odd mix of plastic and diesel which haunts the interior of black cabs. On the underneath of one of the comedy fold-down seats was a small plaque. I read it. 'There are over *12* passenger safety features in this taxi,' it announced. I thought about it as we trundled towards a hotel. Over 12. What was so special about 12, I wondered? And then I twigged. There were *13* safety features in the taxi, and they didn't want you to know. I imagined the Black Cab Safety Team spending months improving the cab, and getting together for a final meeting. 'So, a quick reckon up – ten, eleven, twelve . . . oh, bugger, *thirteen* safety features. One too many. We'll have to lose one.'

'Sir, I have another idea.'

'Yes?'

'We don't tell them about number 13.'

'And what is number 13?'

'Let me see. Number 13 is side impact bars.'

'So we don't mention the side impact bars. We

keep them quiet. This taxi does not have side impact protection.'

'Yes, sir.'

'And why on earth should we bother doing that?'

'In case anybody counts.'

'Counts?'

'Yes. Then they'd know there were thirteen safety features. And that wouldn't do.'

'But do you really think anyone is going to go to the length of counting?'

'Well, sir, there is one particularly anally retentive individual from the West Midlands who might be tempted to try—'

'This OK for you?' the taxi driver asked, interrupting a conversation which probably never took place.

'Fine,' I said. And it was fine. I needed somewhere fine. I had a job interview to prepare for.

At the hotel, and in the absence of anything else to do, I sat down and thought about things. Big things and small things. Tomorrow was an important day, and I felt inadequate. I stared out of the window at the expanse of life in front of me, before closing the curtains and nosing around the interior of my room. I wondered whether I could have done things differently, and concluded that I probably could, if only I'd had a sense of perspective. Had I been advising someone else, I would have been able to steer them well clear of all the pitfalls I hadn't seen coming, because like most people I have a highly developed sense of perspective which seems to apply to everything but my own life. It is the easiest thing in the world to see another person's lunacies, contradictions and fallacies, but your own are another matter. Turned on yourself, the viewpoint is shifted, magnified, distorted, like looking through a murky fish tank. Small things look big, big things look small, and you can never step back far enough to get a decent view without stepping off the edge and into oblivion. For this reason, perspective is an overrated commodity, more likely to benefit others than do you any good. But seeking reassurance from other people can be equally unsatisfactory. All you get in return are bland encouragements and thoughtless platitudes. Moving country. A cinch. Avoiding the law. A breeze. Assuming a new identity. Simple. Getting a new job. A doddle. Of course it would all be easy. That's the very nature of reassurance. Everything is easy when you are the one sitting on your fat arse giving advice, while I befriend passengers, steal suitcases, assume new identities and check into dwarf hotel rooms.

So far so good, but now was the tricky part. I needed a job. Not just any job, but one which would enable me to move house and country, and, with a bit of luck, permanently this time. After a couple of awkward phone conversations with ex-colleagues who were still curious about my sudden disappearance, I had managed to find a company which might be interested in my services. One more call and I had arranged an informal interview for the following day.

Human Resources

He is forty-five maybe, past it certainly, and has an annoying habit of shuffling papers which, I know for a fact, having had a good look at them while he organized a cup of tea for me, have nothing to do with the job. He asks me my name. Darren White, I tell him. And where have you worked before? Int— I stop myself. It wouldn't be good to mention Intron UK. A quick phone call and they'd realize that Darren White had never been anywhere near Intron UK. Also, I was well aware of the need to maintain every distance I could from my former workplace. Although the money continued to flow into my bank accounts, I couldn't be entirely sure that my illegal programming hadn't been detected. I change direction and tell him about the place in America instead. He raises his eyebrows so I elaborate. And were you specifically Symbiosis? Yes, but I also had dealings with other programming, I tell him. A few more dealings and I might not be in this mess. I would be hanging out in SF or SD or LA or some other similarly abbreviated Californian city, driving large spongy cars around the place as if I virtually owned it. And you're dNTP conversant? he asks. Oh yes, I tell him in the first purely honest exchange of the interview, and not just from my side. I know that he's been talking bollocks as well. This is, after all, an interview, and he is going to tell me what he thinks I want to hear, while I tell him whatever will get me the job. Truth rarely enters the interview room. He is obviously crying out for all the help he can get, and can afford to pay me substantially more than he is offering. I am pretending I don't really need the job and couldn't scrape by on the suggested salary. In short, he is pretending to be doing me a favour, whilst I, for my part, am trying to encourage the idea that I am doing him one. In other spheres of work, an interview for the interviewed usually consists of trying to fake an interest in the job and not the money. I want the job because it interests me, and because I am interested, I will work hard and be glad of my employment. But this is different. This is work in a financial institution. The ethos here is I want the job because it pays well enough to buy my loyalty to the company. So I know he is lying when he says that he can only offer me thirty quid an hour; he expects me to beat him up. Not to be greedy will give out the wrong signals altogether. No haggling and he will doubt my credentials.

'The going rate for our Symbiosis programmers is thirty an hour,' he tells me again.

I feign a look of hurt. 'Thirty? I was hoping you might make me a better offer than that.'

'Like what?'

'I'd be looking for at least forty.'

I can tell he is more interested in me now I am playing ball. 'Forty?' he says, trying to appear shocked. 'Well, maybe if you were in London. But here in Birmingham thirty-five is the highest that any of our guys go. And that's the real cutting-edge boys.'

Again, I fake disappointment. A quick reckon-up says that thirty-five an hour is 70K. Not bad. A bit of a pay cut, admittedly, but not too shabby, all things considered. For a horrible second, I think about ditching my plans and staying entirely legitimate. Then, snapping back to reality, I tell him, 'Thirty-five is the minimum I would go for, and I will also need an advance on my salary.'

He seems about to say something but doesn't, just nods his head slowly. 'You're living locally?' he asks in the way of conversation.

'Manchester. But the commute shouldn't be too bad.'

'Good luck, Dr White,' he says, standing up and offering his hand, 'and welcome to Spartech. Just pass your address and bank details to the Human Resources Department. My secretary will point you in the right direction. We'll talk soon.'

On my way there, it occurs to me that the real Dr Darren White is about to get a pleasant surprise when he checks his bank balance, until I can figure out a better way of getting my hands on my wages. Six grand a month, or thereabouts. Not that it will do him any good. He is, I fear, about to discover the first universal law of money, a law I learned some time ago.

The First Universal Law of Money

Money ruins a person. This is the first universal law of money. And it probably ruined me for a year or so of my stay in France. Not that I was particularly upset about the situation at the time. In fact, as I sat and thought about it in my air-conditioned apartment, I realized that if it had spoiled me, and the signs were fairly healthy, then this was no bad thing. If I had become more of a wanker than I was before, I resolved simply to find more wankerish people to call my friends. Besides, what makes friends quicker than a pile of cash? And it wasn't as if there were any other options. I wasn't about to give my new-found wealth away on the premise that to do so would make me more likeable again. Maybe I wasn't that nice in the first place, and money just helped me express the wankerdom that had always been lurking behind the politeness of my poverty.

The first universal law of money is also the first universal law of music. Pop stars who suddenly find large sums of cash falling into their laps always lose the plot. All of them. Two years after their last hit, they wake up from a particularly desperate final coke and Jack Daniels session, with a bill from the Inland Revenue for half a million pounds, a sore head, an aching cock and an utterly empty heart. And the reason is not that pop stars are particularly foolhardy people – although examples are too numerous to mention – it is simply that getting a large amount of money in a short amount of time through a small amount of effort is a recipe for disaster. Money has to be earned. It cannot be given. We are all, to some degree, cursed by a work ethic which tells us that we cannot enjoy the fruits unless there have been labours to be miserable over in the first place. Take away the labours and what have we got to enjoy? There is no aching satisfaction of honest achievement, no contentment of watching our efforts being gradually rewarded, no fulfilment of nurturing an acorn to a fully grown oak tree. So if, like me, you are suddenly presented with a fully grown oak tree for little more effort than a bit of rudimentary gardening, the easy-come-easy-go philosophy is rapidly going to overwhelm any lingering common sense you were lucky enough to have been clinging on to. A fortnight's labour was all that it had taken to spoil me. Two weeks' work which were very much against my will. Two sleepless weeks and one idea.

It was like the Lottery. The previous year, it had made 238 new millionaires in the UK. I knew because I kept track of the statistics, and with good reason. I felt an unwelcome empathy with all 238 of them, because the only parallel I had, the only sense of scale, was with Lottery winners. I began to wonder whether these people were fundamentally happy now that they could buy anything they wanted. I avidly read all the tabloids I could get my hands on in the hope that they weren't. Most of them, it transpired, still bought Lottery tickets. As I followed their stories, it became apparent that there were obvious categories of winners. There were the It's Not Going To Change Me brigade who stayed in their modest jobs and maybe just paid off their mortgages. There were the Spend Spend Spends, who invested heavily and unwisely in Ferraris and helicopters. There were the New Squires who left their council flats and bought tasteless mansions, chrome-bull-barred four-wheel drives and a brace of labradors to live out the lord of the manor fantasy. Nowhere, however, were there any Dodgy Computer Programmers From The West Midlands Now Living In Nice And Slowly Losing The Plot Through Being A Bit Homesick types.

When I left England, I had no idea how much money I had. As a sensible measure against getting too carried away, I had arranged to take £8,500 from the bulk of my earnings every month. Very soon, however, this didn't seem like nearly enough. I could be sitting on two or three million for all I knew, and here I was, spending a fraction of the proceeds. I began to calculate on those warm French nights when I should have been missing friends and relatives. If I had say three million, even at derisory rates of investment, I should be making £200,000 a year on the interest alone. And here I was, only spending £100,000! I endeavoured therefore to increase my allowance and, in doing so, proved the second universal law of money – that whatever you have will always be slightly less than you need, no matter how much that might have been in the first place. This explains why the rich keep working, millionaires keep striving and, despite massive indifference, the likes of Sting, Cliff Richard and Phil Collins continue to foist ill-advised records on the general public. It is the perpetual belief that just a little more money will make you happy. And whilst I could see the inherent problem with this logic, I was powerless to do anything about it. In England, I had suddenly seen my income rocket to £8,500 a month, and yet as soon as this had become the norm, I realized that it was not enough. I was eaten away at night wondering how I could get my hands on more money. Greed was not the only factor here, though. Through the shallow quest for excess an inherent practicality suggested itself. The money I had fraudulently obtained through my slightly dubious computer programming was by no means safe. There was a real sense of cashing in while I could. It would only take a thorough audit by the financial house which employed me or the intervention of my former workmate Archie, and the money would disappear as instantly as it had come. So I set up a couple of bank accounts in France, and endeavoured to save anything that wasn't frittered away. It didn't amount to much.

Bit by bit, a plan had stitched itself together. I bought a fax machine and checked into a new hotel under an assumed identity. I'd always quite fancied being Luke Skywalker so I tried that on for size for a few days. After all, as dull mediocre names went, Ian Gillick was fairly much sought after. No-one in the hotel seemed remotely interested in my choice of new persona. Presumably a lot of L. Skywalkers passed through French guest houses on a regular basis. During the day, I used the room purely to fax and phone the various banking bureaucrats whose permission would be needed to change my original arrangement. I had to explain why I couldn't return to England to sign the papers (a dying relative in France) and had to haggle and plead no end, sending replica faxes with replica signatures to endless banking jobsworths. But ultimately I had to face a partial defeat. I had planned to try to double my income, but there was simply no way the investment house would significantly change my financial commitments over the phone or by fax from another country. In the end, I forced a compromise. They increased the monthly sum to just over £10,000, tax free. This meagre amount would have to suffice. Bureaucrats everywhere celebrated. I drowned my sorrows in champagne. But as well as wearing other people's names, I discovered a new hobby during this time. One night I entered a casino with a fair slice of my new pay rise and lost it all. It was brilliant. I was hooked. In England, I had always been indifferent to gambling, at best. I had never won so much as a raffle, and could see little point in transferring luck like mine into hard-earned cash. But it seemed to make perfect sense that I should do it now. This was one of the very points about going away – to leave my rigid, calculating behaviours behind, in order to discover new rigid, calculating behaviours, like gambling.

Nullability

Starting a new job is bad enough. But starting it a) after three years of lounging about in the sun, b) in a workplace stuffed full of computer programmers, c) when you're not exactly sure what you should be doing, d) in Birmingham, e) in the rain, f) at eight in the morning and g) with a frightful hangover is not good at all.

I was shown around and introduced to staff by a senior manager. Right hands were proffered as lefts continued to tap away at keyboards, Catch up with you at coffee mumbled into monitors. There was, I sensed, a degree of hostility to my presence at Spartech. Throughout the day, the picture became clearer. Spartech was predominantly a rabble of ex-Y2K programmers, who had strung things out for as long as possible into the new millennium tidying up the few mistakes they had made in the last. The gold rush had appeared dangerously close to petering out, until Symbiosis had come along. Symbiosis was what every contractor dreamed of – a new computer language. It might only last a couple of years, but if you were there at the beginning, one of the first to learn its grammar, you were a valuable commodity. Time it right, particularly in London, and you were talking two or three hundred thousand. In Birmingham, maybe sixty or seventy, but still a very good living. Symbiosis had just hit the West Midlands, and the two main financial programming companies in Birmingham – Spartech and Intron – were crying out for people with my sort of experience. Inside such corporations, however, workers showed less enthusiasm towards new employees, and hence the vague hostility I encountered on my first day. The reason for this was that every new master of the language who came along diluted the specialty of those already using it. And the fuller the boat, the more quickly it would sink.

Spartech was using Symbiosis to create new architectures for banks, who were busy laying off as many people as they could to make way for Internet banking. Many of Spartech's staff were ex-bankers who had foreseen the trend and were now earning significantly more money encouraging the very thing which was killing their former profession. There was a sick logic to it, a kind of joining the enemy and then really putting the boot in. Overall, though, the company had a plan. Symbiosis was to be installed on all of Spartech's networked machines. At the same time, existing code was to be edited. This might well have been a leisurely pursuit in different circumstances, but there were now real grounds for urgency. And the reason was Catch 21. The name was a typical programmers' joke – slim on humour but deadly on intent. Catch 21 is the Catch 22 of the computer world, and this is how it works. Databases need null values. Where you don't want to insert a value into a database field, or there is no number available to input, you have to insert something. Zero isn't an option – it has an intrinsic value, particularly if, for example, you average a set of figures. So programmers began to come up with null digits. 9999 was one of the first to be used, with its appearance simply meaning 'Ignore this entry in the database'. All of which caused a massive panic on 9 September 1999. Whole datasets had to be edited to stop programs recognizing 9/9/99 as a null integer. When the date is indistinguishable from a number designed to mean literally 'I do not exist', the repercussions for programs which monitor stock market trading are frightening. Another common nullable number was 010101. 010101 was peppered through thousands of databases on millions of computers across the world. Once again, the number that was never supposed to happen in real life was about to do just that. The first of January 2001, or 010101 to its digital friends, was becoming daily more imminent. If you were a computer programmer, you were likely to refer to the problem as Catch 21, given that 010101 was 21 when translated from binary into proper numbers. You were also likely to do a number of other dull things, most of which are of little relevance here. But if a computer went around thinking that the date was irrelevant, all sorts of mayhem would ensue. So people were nervous, and programming had to be done with a genuine sense of urgency. 010101 null values had to be painstakingly edited out of existing code at the same time that Symbiosis was installed. All the applications which Symbiosis could run alone were safe, but older programs which it merely complemented had to be rewritten, and before the first of January. This included older programs like those responsible for the Original Swindle.

The Original Swindle

September 1997 and I was being taken for a ride at Intron UK. Two undesirables persuaded me to use my lowly position within the world of computer banking to make them some money. As an incentive, they held a colleague of mine called Archie captive. I did exactly as they instructed me, except for one minor point. I ripped them off. To do this I had to perform some fairly tricky programming, which is where my knowledge of banking came in. If you work with these things you will know that financial institutions are composed of two 'offices' – Front and Back – which mediate the input of information and the flow of money. The Front Office doesn't hold real currency, but acts as a shop window, where balances can be checked and transactions monitored. The Back Office is where the real money exists, and represents the true position of the bank. Between the two entities resides a host of software which governs the flow of data between both. Control the Front Office and in theory you control the Back. Control the flow of numbers and you can control the flow of money.

In order to pull my swindle off, I set up a Ghost Account, to act as a holding point for the cash I created by turning digits into dough, and then installed some hidden lines of programming to transfer the ill-gotten numerical gains of my parasites' account into mine. At the time, setting it up had been a major achievement.

Accounts were strictly regulated, were administered elsewhere and were required to hold a minimum of £250,000. I therefore had to enter the regulatory architecture at Intron and install code which would allow the system to recognize my empty account as a bona fide one. This amounted to many nights' work, several screenfuls of text and a couple of nervous breakdowns. Without the Ghost Account nothing else would have been possible. It was the pillar on which everything else rested. Take it away, the system would collapse and I would have no further income. Which is what had happened. The Ghost Account code, which sat happily between the soft digits of the Front Office and the hard cash of the Back, was peppered with inappropriate nullability. In other words, it had so much 010101 coming out of its arse that it would have been spotted by a dyslexic blind man with no aptitude for computer programming. And that was why my money was about to run out. A dangerously myopic anorak was virtually guaranteed to spot it during the installation of Symbiosis, would probably not know what it was, and, given its dated syntax, would either move or delete it. The lump sum would still be there, though, somewhere. The account as such remained relevant – no-one was going to tamper with what appeared to be actual money – but the programming which had created it and told other programs what to do and how to talk to it was about to disappear, with little chance of ever being retrieved. My database programming, which happily provided for my selfish needs, was at best about to fall apart, and at worst set to be deleted by some over-zealous Draylon-clad Catch 21 de-bugger. Hence I was in Birmingham, and on a mission. I had a few months to rescue my code, or I would once again have to face the reality of working for a living.

Balance

'Have you seen this?' Darren asked excitedly, waving a letter at Karen. She informed him curtly that she didn't read his mail. 'Something funny is going on.'

Karen looked a little taken aback. 'Don't tell me they've finally found your luggage.'

'Fat chance. No, it's from the bank. There's been some sort of fuck-up. They've put nearly six grand in our account. Six grand! We're rich!'

Karen prised the letter from Darren's rictus grip. It was only real when she had seen it with her own eyes. 'Jesus. Six grand.' She tried to whistle, but ended up with a noise which fell just short of a raspberry.

'So what do you want to buy?'

Karen frowned. 'We can't spend it,' she said.

'What?'

'I'll ring the bank, tell them there's been a mistake.'

'You're joking.' Darren grabbed the statement back. 'There's six thousand pounds here. Paid in by something called Spartech, Birmingham, whatever that is. But anyway, who's going to know? We'll spend it, and if they pursue the matter, we'll tell them we thought it was ours.'

Karen grabbed the statement, continuing the letter tennis, and told Darren not to be so stupid, which annoyed him slightly. 'And what do we do when they ask us to repay the money?'

'I don't know. Plead poverty. Which isn't too far from the truth. Come on, let's have a little fun.'

Karen appeared to be considering the proposition. 'Look, I'm not sure where we'd stand, you know, if they found out and demanded it back.'

Darren sought to undermine her resolve. It was time for some underhand tactics. 'I just thought it might be nice to buy you something.'

'Bribery will get you everywhere.'

'So what do you say?'

Karen paused, thinking. 'Well, I don't get any money 'til next week. I suppose we could just spend a bit to tide us over, and then replace it as soon as we get paid.'

And with that a decision had been made. Darren ran his mind over some of the purchasing possibilities that awaited him in various high-tech, low-value shops in the centre of town. His meagre scientific salary and abundant mortgage were ruining them. Karen's part-time wages hardly required a wheelbarrow for transportation purposes. A large sum of money might not be everything, but it sure beat the pants off protracted debt. They were, Darren smiled to himself, about to spend themselves happy.

Customer Services

Karen had found a job several weeks after they moved to Manchester and Darren started his post at the institute. Sitting at home had become something of a dangerous occupation, and she had found herself teetering on the edge of daytime TV psychosis. The job was a grim bus ride in the direction of town, at the less than glamorous offices of Onco Insurance Services, but at least it dragged her away from the mind-bending worlds of Oprah, Springer, Ricki et al.

Karen was responsible for giving telephone assistance to people caught up in one of a wide range of minor catastrophes they had insured themselves against. The hours weren't too bad, the salary was almost acceptable, and her workmates were generally good-natured and approachable. However, as she sat on the bus one afternoon after her shift, she realized that something was wrong. It was becoming increasingly obvious to Karen that she didn't like the general public. Having dealt with them for the best part of four weeks, she could now say this with authority. As Karen saw it, being exposed to normal people for most of the day went firmly against the principles of being human, which mainly seemed to involve isolating yourself from all but a tiny fraction of the planet's population. The fact that she couldn't stomach the general public wasn't a realization she was particularly upset about, until she started to think about the wider consequences. If she felt this way about the majority of the population, and yet was also part of this mass of people, didn't she in some way hate herself? Also, if all her friends and family were, to the best of her knowledge and giving some of them a very generous benefit of the doubt, part of the normal populace, didn't she by implication hate them as well?

Karen worried that living with Darren was making her less tolerant, and that maybe she was just getting carried away. She asked her colleagues at coffee break the next day. Disturbingly, it appeared that none of her fellow workers was overly in love with the general public either, and none of them saw the apparent contradiction.

'People? Load of tossers.'

'Idiots.'

'Arses.'

'Dickheads, most of them. One or two are all right though.' This was about the most constructive opinion on offer.

'And what does that make us?' Karen asked, almost pleading for enlightenment.

'Customer service personnel,' the Customer Services manager answered.

'So we're not members of the general public?'

'Technically, no.'

'But if I complain about my washing machine to customer service people at another company, surely I am.'

'I suppose. So what are you saying?'

'Well, if we're all members of the general public, and we all hate the general public, then we all hate ourselves and each other.'

'Ah, you see, there's a flaw in your argument.'

'What?'

'You're thinking like one of them.'

'Like one of who?'

'The general bastard public.'

'But I *am* one of them.'

'Not here you're not. Look, take your example. If you complain about your washing machine, you inevitably become one of the general public, to the person dealing with your call. But that's a different general public than the one we hate. In fact, there are many general publics.'

'Yeah?'

'Yes.'

'And what does many general publics make?' Karen asked.

'I dunno.'

'It makes a population. Surely we can't all hate all of the population?'

'No,' the Customer Services manager agreed. 'But we can have a bloody good go.'

Karen sat and pondered further after her coffee break, but didn't make a lot of progress beyond the fact that humans were essentially likeable creatures, as long as you didn't have to deal with them very often. They tried to use you as much as they could, and you tried to use them when you didn't think they'd notice particularly. When she got home, Darren was unpacking a mysterious box which seemed to house a gadget of some sort. Having had a bad day, she saw it as her duty to inflict at least part of it on Darren. There was little point in suffering alone when you had a boyfriend you could harass. Particularly one who was seemingly incapable of even hanging on to a suitcase for a few days.

'Good day?' Darren asked as Karen walked through into the kitchen. By the look in her eye Darren could see that he had just made an enormous error. She was going to tell him about it. He concentrated on the box in his hands, which represented the first of what he hoped might be many such purchases, praying it would be brief.

'No.'

Darren would have been happy to leave it there, but sensed that Karen was seeking further questioning. Attempting not to sigh, he asked, 'Why not?'

'I just feel so used,' she said.

Darren looked up. 'But that's what you're there for, isn't it? You know, to help people.'

'It doesn't mean they have to take the piss. I don't mind the using so much, it's the abusing which gets me.'

'What do you mean?'

'The abuse that some of these bastards give you.'

'If it's not making you happy, maybe you should give it up. It's not as if we need the money as badly now.'

'Look, no matter how bad it gets, it still beats sitting at home.'

'So what's your point?'

'My point is that as soon as someone offers to help you, it becomes an opportunity to try and get what you can out of them. You hear it in their voices. As soon as I say that we'll be happy to help them, their tone changes, they start rubbing their sweaty palms together and it's almost "Well, they're offering to do this, what else will they do for me?" '

Darren finally extracted the bubble-wrapped gizmo from its protective polystyrene shell. For a waterproof, shockproof, sandproof go-anywhere Sports Walkman, they certainly weren't taking any chances. 'Pass me the scissors, will you?'

Karen walked into the kitchen and retrieved the necessary tool for Darren to open his purchase. 'And the thing is, when we point out we can only do so much, they get all petulant and arsey, like we're trying to take their sweets back off them.'

'Ah,' Darren answered, plugging the earphones into his ears, trying them for size, 'that's the general public for you.'

Karen looked as if she was going to say something, but instead took a bottle of wine from the fridge and poured herself a dangerously large measure.

The First of the First of the First

New-language programming was the ultimate get rich quick job with no future. Learning a new language because it was new, and ditching it before it got old, was no indicator of a lifetime career. In fact, quite the opposite. It was a virtual guarantee of imminent unemployment as languages came and went. Despite the glaringly transient nature of the work, there were still employees at Spartech who bravely spent their money as if the job was going to last for ever. I had an awed respect for the sheer reckless myopia of these people, who would turn up in Porsches and drive home to fake Tudor houses. Although the very nature of what I hoped to achieve meant that I couldn't stay at Spartech particularly long, I ached to be around when the Porsches were traded in for Polos, and the Tudor houses swapped for terraces, as the next code came along and rendered their current skills obsolete, until they could learn their way back to prosperity.

James was one of the workers at the cutting edge of this spending technology. He did differ slightly from the others, though. James had a knack for accomplishing things quickly. In fact, he wasn't just quick, he was a miracle-worker. He could install Symbiosis and adjust the existing code of two or three machines in the time it took me to botch one, and without ever appearing in the remotest bit stressed. For this, he was both widely praised by the management and universally unpopular with his co-workers. The latter, and I was one of them, were unhappy at the shadow his prodigious progress cast over our own meagre efforts. We began to look bad. Managers would ask us why we couldn't keep up with James, so we decided to take turns in badgering him to let us in on his system. For several weeks, James had more free lunches than he knew what to do with. Occasionally he even had to eat some of them. Often, people would ask him if he fancied a quick bite and he would have to tell them that he was already being taken out by Bob or Jan or Mike or Mary, so that he could eat for free and not tell them anything about the method he had developed. Removing James from the office for a protracted lunch also fulfilled another function. With James out of the frame, even for an extra hour or so each day, his overall productivity declined marginally, and we all benefited from not looking quite so lazy. But there had to be a system. We all knew he had found a short cut. There was no human way of carrying out all the programming he did by any conventional method. James never told anybody, though. And, as he asked time and time again over increasingly superfluous lunches, why should he? Spartech awarded a £50 incentive for each machine fixed before Catch 21. James was making enough on incentives alone to buy the lunches he wasn't paying for by not telling anybody how he was making so much money. If he let us in on the scheme, he reasoned, everybody would soon be as rich as he was, and where was the fun in that? And worse still, given that he would then have to buy his own food, he would actually be losing money on the deal, which was a prospect he considered to be in bad taste.

People aside, however, Spartech was quite different from any other computer company I had previously worked for. Intron, my former employer in Birmingham, had been a drab two-storey affair with drab two-dimensional people. Spartech, by comparison, stretched to an almost extravagant five floors and employed, in addition to the compulsory legions of the dull, a small number of relatively interesting people, dotted about like pot plants, seemingly there to liven the place up a bit. Although the total acreage was probably very similar for the two buildings – Spartech merely representing a vertical version of Intron – there was a perplexing hierarchy about my new workplace. Any right-minded capitalist institution sprawling over a number of floors is arranged in the following manner. Ground floor – reception, lifts, lobby. First floor – secretaries, coffee areas, rooms for meeting the general public. Second floor – office staff, programmers, workers. Third floor – middle management, plusher closed offices. Fourth floor – executive suites and toilets, smoked glass partitions, thick carpets, a floor only visited by general workers about to be fired or promoted. But Spartech had turned this on its head. The more senior you were, the lower your office in terms of altitude, and, conversely, the higher the lift took you from the ground floor, the further you could watch your salary plummet. I wondered whether this arrangement might reflect a pervasive laziness on behalf of the upper management, but one popular theory was that it was an efficiency initiative. When the building had been designed, an ergonomics consultancy suggested valuable savings in time expenditure by allowing senior bosses almost instant access to their offices as they rushed in and out of their workplace to and from important meetings. Clearly ergonomics shares little ground with common sense. Most staff were yet to witness a senior manager rush anywhere, let alone into the building, though many had seen them make rapid exits at one time or other, particularly on Fridays. In fact, senior managers rarely hurried at all, except where free drinks were involved, and even then it tended to be more of a waddle than a rush. No, a more plausible explanation was the fear factor. Sneaking home early or staggering back from lunch a couple of hours late was a much less attractive proposition when you had to do so in full view of the management.

It wasn't just the geography of the place which was troublesome. Spartech also had a plan. This was rare. Certainly, working in business before, I had never come across a company with a plan, or at least not one which made sense. And Spartech's plan made sense. Everyone was subdivided into groups of eight individuals. Each group was called an Octet. Each Octet had a team leader. Each member of each Octet was accountable only to the group. Once a week, at a dreaded and predetermined hour, Octet members had to stand up in front of their colleagues and explain exactly what they had achieved in the previous seven days. This was purgatory. People expected results, and got upset if you didn't achieve them. You were holding the rest of your team back by slacking. No longer was I freewheeling in a structureless organization. Spartech expected me to actually do some work. I was now burdened with goals and responsibilities and targets. If I'm honest, a small part of me craved this, lapped it up even, rose to the challenge, worked with strident optimism, desperate to fulfil the goals set out for me. However, it was only a small part, minute in fact, and soon began to rub the lazy rest of me up the wrong way. I was at Spartech for a reason, I had to remind myself, and didn't want work getting in the way.

Less is More

On the way home from work, Darren veered into town. His wallet, which had previously brought nothing but bad news, was burning a hole in the back pocket of his jeans. It was a new wallet, one of the first purchases he had made after the fantastic realization that a large sum of cash had strayed into his bank account. His old one had been lost with his luggage, and Darren had been forced to have fresh cards issued. New wallet, new cards, new happiness. Darren smiled in the rear-view mirror. He turned into Deansgate and dumped his Polo in a urine-soaked multi-storey car park. What was it with the stairwells of car parks? he wondered, making his way towards the exit. Surely there were better places for urination. Like urinals, for a start. He picked up his pace. He was on a mission. The music press had been urging him for some time now to buy an album by the group Less is More, who, having disbanded a year ago owing to musical differences, had now got back together for tax reasons. In fact, they had virtually been begging him. There had been adverts, reviews and special offers, and all with the single aim of persuading Darren that the only additional thing he needed for his life to be worthwhile was this one product. Having nobly resisted for several weeks, he felt it would be rude to continue to shun their advances. Surely with all their experience they knew what was best for him, as well as what was best for Less is More. He headed grimly towards HMV, praying that they still had the CD in stock. He wasn't disappointed – there were shelffuls of it. Standing at the counter, Darren felt a wave of what Americans might call closure. In the absence of an English alternative, Darren also felt closure. The CD purchased, the small carrier bag safely in his hand, the tax man happy, he left the shop and headed back to the car, feeling somehow victorious. But as he passed an expensive-looking hi-fi shop, a disturbing thought came to him. He didn't own a CD player, let alone a stereo. Darren entered the shop. He was not about to be defeated by an absence of equipment, and approached a particularly smug sales assistant.

'Can I help you?'

'Yes,' Darren said, 'I'd like to buy a CD player.'

'Right. What sort of cash can you spend?'

Darren could spend a lot of cash, but decided to go easy. 'Average.'

'What's average?'

'I don't know. One hundred, two hundred, three hundred?'

'Well, we've got the Marantz T2300, 16 bit, multi-access for two nine nine.'

Darren examined the sleek black box with its sleek black buttons. It certainly looked as if it should sound good. He had a quick reckon-up while the assistant straightened his tie. Three hundred quid from a £6,000 lump sum. Five per cent. Karen would hardly notice. With a distinctly unnatural flourish, Darren pulled his wallet out and said, 'I'll take it.'

'Great. If you just pay at the counter, I'll grab you one from stock.'

Darren paid and then nosed around the shop for a couple of minutes while the assistant struggled back with an impressively large box. As he ran his fingers over the many pieces of enticing hardware which lined the shelves, an uncomfortable thought began to form. 'I know this might sound daft,' he said, 'but this CD player doesn't have a inbuilt amp, does it?'

'You don't have an amp?'

'No. Will I definitely need one?'

'Well, it will tend to be a bit on the quiet side otherwise.'

'How quiet?'

The assistant lifted the box up towards Darren. 'Here. Put your ear against the box.' Darren did as he was told. 'About that quiet,' he said.

Darren had money and wasn't going to be put off by a cocky shop worker. 'OK. Point proved. How much will an amp be?'

'How much can you spend?'

'Look, just show me a good one.'

Two hundred and eighty pounds later Darren had another shiny piece of equipment to his name. He was just about to leave the shop with the duo of boxes when another unwelcome idea came to him. Speakers. Fuck. He made another quick calculation. Ten per cent of the sum had gone already, and any further expenditure was likely to get him into trouble. But to pull out now would be a mistake. He had come this far and without speakers still wouldn't be able to satisfy the music media's obsession that he should listen to the CD. Sheepishly, he tackled the sales assistant again.

'I was thinking, I might buy some speakers while I'm here. You know, replace the old ones.'

'And what type were the old ones?'

'Oh, you know, just, um, average ones.'

'Right. Average ones here start at a hundred and seventy.'

'Pounds?' This was getting out of hand.

'Yes, sir. Pounds.'

'Right. Fine.' Thirteen per cent. 'I'll take a pair.' This would take some explaining when he got home. He had better leave the shop before they wanted a kidney.

Darren signed the third in a succession of money-sapping receipts, and the assistant dumped the speaker box on top of the amp box, which itself sat heavily on top of the CD box. Darren surveyed the pile. This was like some sort of World's Strongest Man challenge. Only he was now going to be an entrant for the World's Deadest Boyfriend competition. He bent over the boxes and was about to attempt a clean and jerk, which sounded like a dubious thing to do in public, though not as bad as a lift and snatch, when the shop assistant went in for the kill.

'You OK for leads?' he asked casually.

'Leads? What do you mean, "leads"?'

'You know, to attach everything together.'

Darren straightened and took the CD out of its bag. 'Look, is there anything else I'm going to need to play this bloody album?' he demanded, waving it about.

The assistant read the name of the band. 'Less is More?' He let out an annoyingly knowing smirk. 'If I knew you were going to play that sort of rubbish, I'd have flogged you something cheap.'

Having bought a large amount of stereo equipment, along with attendant paraphernalia, and having spent a correspondingly large amount of cash, Darren left the shop swearing under his breath and headed for the car park. If he couldn't bring the stereo to the car, he could at least bring the car to the stereo. In a parking spot close to the shop, Darren opened the hatchback and cleared some room, while the assistant stood in the doorway and monitored proceedings with some interest. Eventually forcing the boxes into the back of his car, Darren came to the conclusion that money, whether free or not, wasn't necessarily all it was cracked up to be.

The Unpopulars

There is a constancy about labour, an inevitability. Sometimes this is bad, and at Intron I had certainly disappeared into a black and white nine to five routine. Now, a period of stability appealed to me with real urgency. I almost welcomed the dull ache of apprehension on a Sunday evening, the prospect of another working week eating the last few hours of freedom away. I got excited by the thought of lively discussions over lunch about football, news and music. I positively rejoiced at the thought of sharing an office with fellow computer programmers.

It didn't last.

By the end of the first week I decided isolation would be preferable. By the end of the second, that an Uzi would be better still. By the end of the third that I wouldn't make a fourth, and by the end of the fourth that I might as well just give up on my scheme and live in poverty in some corner of the country where programmers weren't allowed to loiter in awkward groups.

My Octet, Octet F, had the usual unpopular types, but also two or three apparently normal people as well, who avoided me like the plague. Abandoned to the dullness and eccentricity of my Octet's Unpopulars, I spent a few weeks getting to know them. Each programmer had their own quirks, which whilst not especially debilitating in the grand scheme of things had certainly contributed to their status as Unpopulars. Unpopular Number One was Bob. Bob would have been OK but for the fact that he had no concept of either time or distance. Ten Bob minutes might occupy a long hour of most people's time, and a couple of Bob miles might account for a tankful of petrol. Admittedly, little consequence would result were it not for the fact that Bob's inability with the basic measurements of life seemed to coincide with any occasion when you needed to travel a given distance and arrive there punctually. The chances of achieving this dual feat in the hands of Bob were barely measurable. But Bob had a knack of persuading you they were, and this was the real downer about him. Just when an imminent departure to an assuredly close financial institution was on the verge of happening, he would neatly insert a last-minute spanner in the works. For a man with no sense of time, he certainly had an immaculate sense of timing.

Unpopular Number Two was Jan. Jan had you logged. You were up there in his filing system. In the absence of the ability to interact naturally, Jan had constructed a series of conversation cards for each of his colleagues. I was on file as Football. He would see me, pull my file out and start talking. So how are Leeds doing? he would ask, every time. I would say fine. Next, he would ask what I thought of the manager. I would tell him good or terrible. And that was it, until the next occasion I saw him. At first, I mistook his questions for genuine interest in a subject with which he was familiar. I used to return the favour, probing him about his team, before I realized that he didn't support one, and even if he did he would have difficulty distinguishing a football from a fromage frais. These ghost conversations began to irritate me and I would find myself making up statistics just to see if he was paying attention. They've been relegated to the Sunday Part Time Ovaltine

League, I would say, and their manager is now a successful racehorse.

But at least Jan's conversation cards were brief, which was more than could be said for Unpopular Number Three, Mary. Mary could always say more than should have been said about anything. Mary would talk all day if you let her. This seemed to be her primary reason for visiting the office, as work itself certainly didn't seem to get much of a look in, except maybe when she paused for breath. Talk is fine. No-one can object to talk. But Mary didn't talk. She conquered. She would open her mouth and the most overwhelming tide of nothingness would gush forth, drowning everything in its path. She didn't talk in words or sentences or paragraphs. Mary talked in *pages*. Every thought you might have, every idea, every memory; all of it would fall foul of Mary's mouth. To call Mary's conversation minutiae would be doing a disservice to the trivial. It was on a level of interest inaudible to the naked ear. Donkeys had been known to quietly hand their back legs over to Mary before she opened her mouth, limping off miserably into the distance. This, then, was the level of Mary's conversation. They're building a new Kwiksave in Dullsville, near the spot where our previous next door neighbours' son used to moor the caravan he had before he traded it in for a mobile home. (You have never been to Dullsville – except with Mary – or known the person who for some reason was suicidal enough to buy a caravan, let alone his mother, and have never even thought about expressing an interest in the location of Kwiksaves.)

Finally, bringing up the rear of the Unpopulars, was Interesting Dave. Everything was interesting to Dave. In fact, I was unable to find a single thing which failed to interest him. And Christ knows I tried some dull topics. My computer isn't very fast. Interesting, he would say. Some people collect coins, you know.

Similarly interesting. Christmas is on a Wednesday. Interesting. Crown green bowling. Interesting. I also tried some exciting topics, just to even the score up a little. I have set light to the back of your jacket. Interesting. Mary has just given birth to Siamese quadruplets. Interesting. Your car seems to be doing handbrake turns in the car park. Interesting. I have just shagged your wife. Thank you.

Amongst such people I felt relatively together. I sat at my desk and watched the interactions of the virtually autistic, which kept me entertained. When I wasn't watching I was thinking and remembering. Observing the occasionally comical actions of my colleagues reminded me that I couldn't spend the rest of my life working in computers. I had to sort things out, and quickly.

Unpopular Coffee

I was sitting at my desk trying to figure out what the hell I was going to do about the imminent loss of my earnings when he passed again. He was familiar and belonged to Octet B. There was something jaded about him and I spent a while fretting over where I might have met him before. It was a couple of days before I sussed it out. He had worked at Intron as a Permie during the time I was there. If memory served me right, he was called Alan. I got talking to him one afternoon. He told me that he had made the jump from Permie to Tractor – that is, from underpaid permanent member of staff to distinctly overpaid contractor – when Symbiosis took off in the West Midlands. We chatted about people we knew at Intron and what they were doing now. Mostly though we talked about how much they were earning. There was an Americanization about contractors these days, I noted, a willingness, an enthusiasm even, to discuss salaries. Thirty, thirty-five and forty an hour were thrown about like proud boasts of conquest. This would have been vulgar but for the fact that hourly rates avoided the need to talk in terms of the permanent, final quotient of what a person is truly worth – the annual salary.

More than just a genuine eagerness of curiosity and boastfulness was the underlying truth of modern programming. People talked money because that was the single criterion by which they could be judged. Their worth was literally their worth. And although we all knew that thirty p.h. meant sixty grand p.a., talking in hours rather than years somehow kept it abstract, away from the personal. Alan was on twenty-five, he told me. Settling for twenty-five would have taken some doing. Only a Permie could hope to negotiate such a mediocre salary in times of severe programmer drought and a vastly imminent hitch. However poor his salary, though, Alan wouldn't be giving very much of it to the Inland Revenue. Tractors and tax loopholes went together like Tories and sleaze. For the sake of not rubbing it in, I told him I was on twenty-five as well.

Away from money, the conversation was edgy. I was acutely aware that Alan could hardly fail to be conscious of my dual identity. At Spartech I was Darren and I commuted daily from Manchester. At Intron, where we had both worked in the late 1990s, I was Ian and I slouched in from Kings Heath. Whilst programmers of Alan's ilk didn't tend to be over-endowed with curiosity, I still had the general impression that he was summing me up. He asked me what I had been doing since Intron. Travelling, I said. He had heard a similar report, and this seemed to placate him a little. He told me that most of the old crew were still at Intron – Jamie, Archie, Simon et al. I asked if they were all the same as ever. He had heard that Archie had become even more obsessive recently. More, I asked? More, Alan nodded glumly. It was the first time I had heard direct mention of Archie, and I was quiet for a while. There was an element of a former life about hearing his name. Archie. The man whose identity I had been using before I met Darren. The dullest and potentially most dangerous person in my world. Not exactly hazardous on his own, but in the company he kept, lethal. The conversation petered out and I went off to join the lively and surreal conversation of the coffee room.

'So how're Leeds doing?' Jan asked me, as I sat down with my cup of tea and tried not to think about Archie.

'Terrible,' I told him. Yesterday it had been fantastic and the day before average, despite the fact that they had failed to play a single game in nearly two weeks. I felt I was at least giving his conversation cards some value for money.

'My aunty used to work for Rowntrees in a factory just outside Leeds,' Mary announced to no-one in particular.

Interesting Dave took the ball and ran off with it. 'Interesting,' he said.

Mary drew breath, capitalizing on Dave's apparent attention. 'Well, her husband was working on a new Kwiksave there. Enormous place it was . . .'

She was about to get some momentum up, but Bob chipped in, 'Does anybody need a lift anywhere? I've got to head off, literally in a minute, the car's only fifty yards down the road. Anyone?'

There was a distinct lack of takers. Half an hour later and Bob was still there. 'And the manager,' Jan continued, shuffling his cards and returning to me. 'How do you think he's panning out?'

'Brilliant.' I couldn't remember how that tied in with my earlier answer, but decided to go with it anyway. Jan nodded sagely.

'Still, the weather's been OK,' he said to Mike, a man of no discernible personality.

'Yeah. Hotter than expected.'

'Mind you, Sainsbury's, to give them their credit, put disabled car parking in well before the others. Then Tesco's. My mum, you see. Can't walk very far . . .'

'Interesting.'

Bob was shouting. 'Take the M40 clockwise, or anti-clockwise, for a mile or two, past a junction with the A11 on your left, maybe right, or is it straight on? M21, could be. Either way, you'll be there in no time.

Twenty minutes max . . .' Some poor sod was receiving misleading directions through Bob's mobile phone.

'So come on, James, what's your system all about? Spill the beans.'

'Jan, if I told you, I'd be proportionally poorer. Surely you understand that? Remember, greed is good, and avarice makes you richer.'

'Yes, forty or so miles . . . maybe sixty . . . twenty minutes should do it.'

I felt the need to point out the error of Bob's time and distance estimation. 'A hundred and eighty miles an hour?'

'I'm trying to have a telephone conversation, Darren.'

'. . . although they're building a new Gateway's in Stirchley. I mean, I don't know why they're bothering. There's a perfectly good one in Yardley . . .'

'Interesting.'

'Sixty miles in twenty minutes? What's he driving, a fucking rocket?'

'You see, I know I have a system, and I know you know I have a system, so why don't we leave it at that? I'm getting rich, you're being kept on your toes, so everybody's happy.'

'No, not you . . . I said I'm trying to have a conversation here. I'll only be a second.'

'Global warming, I reckon. Be warm in November soon.'

'And the garden, Mary, how is that?'

Jan came over all glazed as Mary told him, leaving no stone unturned. I stood up. This was very unfair. These bastards were driving me back to work.

Ear Wax 2000

Archie sat at his desk in one of the many anonymous offices at the headquarters of Intron UK and stared at the empty seat opposite. It hadn't always been this way. He used to share his room. Not the kind of sharing where either person benefited in any way, but a sharing of sorts all the same. The office hadn't changed much since his solitary confinement began. A calendar with time measured out in biro crosses, a pen holder holding pens, a couple of shelves bearing the weight of some dusty books. Three years ago, Archie had even invested in a new plant. It was thriving. He glanced at it and smiled, but his good humour quickly faded. A memory snapped him back to the awfulness of his life, and he stood up irritably and paced around the room. As he did so, the calendar caught his eye – a Wednesday had slipped by unnoticed. He plucked a biro from its holder and erased the offending period of time. Slightly more satisfied, he sat down and resumed his work.

Later, as Archie counted the nasal hairs he had managed to pluck during what had been a successful afternoon, the phone rang. He was deliberate with his movements because he had lined up the day's hairs on a piece of A4 paper in ascending order of size, and didn't want to disturb his handiwork. The Sellotape was on the wrong side of the desk, and if he brushed the line-up on the way to answering the call before sticking everything down, a fair amount of measuring and placement would be needed to get back to his current point of progress. And progress there was. Some of the hairs were particularly long specimens, so long in fact, when Archie thought about it, that they must surely have been growing in his brain. He glanced across his collection at the phone, which was still ringing. At the near end languished blonder, more slender examples, from the inner grazing surfaces of his septum. These had been the most painful and were therefore the most prized. Slowly, Archie stretched for the telephone, which promptly stopped ringing. Unfazed, he changed direction and picked the Sellotape up instead. When he had finally attached his collection to the piece of paper, labelled it with the date and filed it away with an impressive wad of similar entries, the phone rang again. Archie answered it more promptly this time.

'Hello?'

'Archie?'

'Yes.'

'It's Alan.'

'Alan who?' Archie asked.

There was a slight sigh. Alan was tempted to ask just how many people of his name there were amongst Archie's meagre acquaintances, but refrained. 'You know – I used to work with you there at Intron.'

'Oh,' Archie said. '*Alan*.'

'So, how are things in Permie Central?'

'You know. Pretty hectic.' Archie partially opened his drawer and gazed with some satisfaction at the folders within. 'Made some good progress this afternoon.'

'Good. Look, I'll keep this brief. Thought you might be interested in someone who's just turned up here at Spartech.'

'Oh yeah?' Archie tried to sound inquisitive, but it wasn't in his nature, and he didn't make a good job of it.

'Ian Gillick. Your old friend.'

'*Really?*' This time, Archie didn't have to fake an interest. In fact, so excited was he that he shut the Nasal Hair 2000 drawer with something approaching gusto. Had Ear Wax 2000 also been open, he would surely have shut that as well. 'When did he get back?'

'He's been here five or six weeks. Think his round the world thing must have ended because he seems—'

'And you only just rang me now?'

'I didn't think you were that close. I only mentioned it because of something you once said about him.' Alan was on the defensive, seriously wondering whether he should have bothered ringing in the first place.

'What did I say?'

'You know, that you needed something from him. I don't remember exactly.'

'Look, Alan, do me a favour. Don't mention this to Gillick. I do want to meet up with him, but I want it to be a surprise. You know, get a couple of friends in on the act, if you understand what I mean.'

Alan did understand. He had heard about parties and such. People getting together and not discussing work much, apparently. 'Yes, of course. There's something else though.'

'Yes?' Archie asked.

'He's not Ian Gillick any more. For some reason, he's calling himself another name.'

'What name?'

'Darren White. *Dr* Darren White, actually. And he's living in Manchester.'

Archie pushed two fingers into his temple. 'Why would he . . . Look, Alan, thank you for calling. It was good of you. I'd better go. Bye.'

'Bye.'

Archie stood up again, this time with real purpose. Things were going to get a lot more interesting. He picked up the phone again and dialled a number he hadn't used for over a year.

Family Values

I sat and stared at the monitor after another harrowing coffee-time conversation with the Unpopulars. This was no good. I was going to need a revelation of some sort to get anywhere. Although little had changed in the way of programming since my departure, I found myself unable to see an easy way of changing the code I had written. Time was passing. As leaves tumbled to the ground I saw my opportunities dwindle. I was going through the motions at work, treading water and thinking. January was looming closer every day, and I realized, rather belatedly, that I should have saved some money, just in case. Accessibility was going to be the problem. I had imagined that by practising some of the ins and outs of Symbiosis programming I would be able to come up with a way of mending my existing code and therefore resuming my postponed lifestyle. So far so good. However, the real issue now was getting my hands on the stuff. It was in the machines of another company, a company I was too scared to work for again, on account of my illicit opportunism. The only way would be to gain access to Intron illegally and hack into their systems from the inside. All right in theory, but a bugger in practice.

I interlocked the fingers of my hands behind my head. As risks went, entering an old workplace and pfaffing about with its computers was hardly Great Train Robbery stuff. In fact, all things considered, it was a very reasonable proposition if you were given to that kind of thing. If, however, you were a slightly nerdy computer programmer from the West Midlands who had once accidentally pulled off a digital swindle, the proposition was totally unreasonable. Still, it would have to be done, and soon.

Later, as I grew tired of thinking, I glanced around the office. Only Interesting Dave was still at work, hammering frantically away at an unlucky keyboard. I watched him for a couple of moments. He always sat there, night after night, beavering away, occasionally looking up to stare at the photographs of his wife and children on his desk, which were arranged like some sort of mini-altar to family life, before smiling and returning to his work. Time and time again I wanted to ask him why the hell not just go home? Why not pack up your paperwork and drive home to your children? I imagined them in a reciprocal arrangement, sitting around in the house, staring longingly at a montage of photos of their father taken at work, bent industriously over his terminal. I decided I had to ask him. I mean, it was understandable that I should hang around after everybody else had turned out their lights and slunk off. I had no-one to go home to and hence no pictures on my desk. But Interesting . . .

'Dave.'

He was once again peering through his glasses at the photos of his family. 'Yes?' he asked eagerly, looking up and sensing the opportunity for some riveting conversation.

'Why don't you just go home to them?'

'Who?'

'Your wife and kids.'

'What do you mean?'

'Well, you're here late every night, banging away on that keyboard . . . I mean, why not take your stuff with you and go back to your family?'

He gazed at the photos and picked one of them up. 'Because of one interesting and important thing, Darren.'

'What?'

'They annoy the fuck out of me.'

'What?'

'Staying late is the only way I can get any peace.' He stretched back in his chair. 'You don't think I'm here just for the love of the job, do you?'

'I'd begun to suspect that maybe you were.'

'Jesus no. This is a win win situation. I'm getting paid not to listen to my kids screaming and playing up all the time. By the time I get home, they're all in bed and my dinner's on the table.'

'But what about your wife?'

'She annoys me as well.'

'No, I mean, doesn't she mind you never being there?'

'Don't think so. It's interesting, but I think I rub her up the wrong way too.' He put the photo down. 'Perfect arrangement.'

'Perfect,' I said quietly to myself. Hotel life might be shite, but not as shite as perpetually avoiding your nearest and dearest. Perhaps they didn't find him so interesting. I wondered whether the pictures on his desk were for the purposes of identification, just to remind him what his family looked like.

'And I'm making a mint,' Interesting continued. 'An absolute mint. Can't be doing so bad yourself?'

I smiled. Money. All that mattered. All that we were striving for. All that I had run towards with eager hands, only to find that the tighter I clasped my fingers around its shiny coins, the deeper the indentations it left in my flesh. It was still something which unnerved me, particularly since I had discovered what life is really worth. A revelation, the first and probably only one of my life, clear and overwhelming. Everything else had slipped suddenly away into irrelevance. It started with a sign – a dark African girl dressed in rags on an otherwise dull night in Nice. In a second, although it took several hours for me to fully appreciate what had happened, my life changed for good. And it *was* good.

The Revelation

I had been walking out of a casino in St Raphael, two-thirds drunk, fully broke, bitterness welling, my ration for the night gambled and lost. Normally, I wouldn't have been particularly upset. Numbness had set in some time ago. Numb when I won, numb when I lost, numb when I arrived, numb when I left. Gambling was no longer about the thrill of money. It was just something I did, a protracted experiment into the numbers of chance. Tonight was different. Tonight the casino had refused me credit. I was losing heavily and the establishment had refused to help me win my way out of the streak that had swallowed my evening's early success. I was livid. They had taken my cash and refused to lend it back to me. My own money, for fuck's sake. Furious at the injustice, I stumbled past a homeless black girl and into the street in search of a taxi. The girl followed me and stuck her hand out for change. I had seen her before somewhere, and I tried to ignore her. I had problems of my own, and a lot larger than the ten francs she was begging for. Tonight had witnessed the demise of nearly £1,200. But the sum of money was irrelevant. I lost this sort of sum several times a month. It was the snub, the indifference shown by the manager. I decided to waste my money elsewhere from now on. The presence of the girl made me even more irritated. She stayed silently by my side, and then suddenly threw out her arm and pushed something into my hand. I stopped and looked at her. Dawn was stretching, yawning and thinking about breaking into song, and only the deliberately reckless were still awake. I moved on, glancing from time to time at the small strip of paper as I made my way towards the nearest taxi rank, cursing her, cursing the manager, cursing everybody. There were four or five paragraphs, which made little sense to me as I struggled to focus. Then, near the bottom of the page, I realized that each chunk of text was in a different language. English was third, after French and Italian. I had a go at reading it, but it didn't sink in. Then, a few paces later, I stopped and tried again.

What are we worth?
How much are a human life?
How many dollar?
The answer? Human life are worth $15.
$15 will keep a child alive for a month.
YOU can afford to save a life.
PLEASE save life today.

And that was it. A few poorly typed lines of text with dubious grammar. The revelation had come and gone, and had thrown a switch somewhere. Nothing changed immediately, though. I caught a taxi home, flopped into bed, swore at the chattering birds and slept through to eleven o'clock. From here on, however, everything I did was doomed to clash with a thought I had as I read the leaflet.

Ridiculous Spending Priorities

Overnight, a new currency had entered my life. It wasn't a currency I had spent before, or even considered spending. Money now had a frame of reference, and this was a dangerous thing. The one great thing about money is that it is an entirely abstract concept. A bundle of paper in your hand has no intrinsic value, and yet it can persuade people to do things they wouldn't otherwise do, can take you places you couldn't otherwise go, can feed you, clothe you, spoil you; can, and this was the real nightmare for me, keep people alive who would otherwise die.

Sure, like most people, I was well aware that I had ridiculous spending priorities. This had never been in doubt. I would gladly blow forty quid on a Friday night out with my old football team, while spending a good proportion of the next day weighing up packets of spaghetti in Sainsbury's, trying to decide which one might save me forty pence. I would spend thirty quid on CDs in Virgin, only to skulk past a tramp outside, telling him I had no spare change, all the time rubbing my fingers over warm, familiar coins in my pocket. As a student I would spend evenings in the pub during winter convincing myself that I was saving money by not staying at home with the heating on. When I started work, I was well aware that I could spare enough money at the end of each month to make a modest donation to any number of charities, but I never did. It was as though I just got lost in my daily life. I did, however, notice a trend. I was considerably more egalitarian when I had a little than when I had a lot. It is always easy to be generous when you only have a small amount to be generous with. The more money I amassed, or was amassed on my behalf, the less inclined I felt to give any of it away. And I had managed to drag this ridiculous state of affairs with me even when I had over 10,000 tax-free pounds a month to dispose of.

The morning after I read the leaflet, I continued to pursue the mind-occupying trivialities of my life as if nothing had changed. I collected a picture I had purchased the previous week from a gallery. Eighteen hundred francs – 16 children alive for a month. In a fit of vehicular desperation I took my Jeep to the garage. The gearbox was fucked. A new one would be 70 children; 42 for the part and 28 for the labour. I filled the Jeep up with petrol while I considered. Four children. The gearbox did seem to be getting worse, if that was possible. I left it with them, with an 8-child deposit. Later, I ate a hearty and unhealthy breakfast at a nearby hotel. Settling the bill with half a child, laziness prevailed and I decided to catch a taxi home, visiting the supermarket on the way. Three children. This was starting to get out of hand. And then worse. I turned things on their logical head. If it cost $15 a month to keep a child alive, and no-one else coughed up, not paying $15 was killing a child every month. By spending roughly $15,000 on items other than children, I was effectively killing 1,000 of them. And so began a circular argument which I had no chance of winning. The logic was faultless. I had money, a lot of money. I could use that money to save people's lives, but failed to. Everything I didn't spend on saving lives meant that children continued to die. My lack of concern was actually killing people! This was by far the most harmful apathy in the history of determined indifference. Of course I knew that I wasn't alone. I thought of other people. Did they give their money away? Did they fuck. And I was only modestly wealthy compared with a lot of them. But all the same, it gnawed away at me and I could no longer enjoy spending my ill-gotten gains. As this was about the only pleasure I had, my life took a down turn. I found myself thinking increasingly about the African girl, and after a couple of guilt-laden days I decided to try to find her. I wanted to help the girl, but I also needed her to help me.

There was more to my unhappiness than the realization of what I could have done with my money. The homeless girl struck a chord with me. I realized that we were in the same situation. To all intents and purposes, I too was homeless. I was living abroad, away from everything which had been my home for all of my life so far. I was an English vagrant, bumming around with no particular destination in mind, the one place I wanted to be more than all others denied me. For the first time in my protracted isolation abroad, it was clear to me that homelessness and isolation amounted to the same thing. I continued to wallow in the despondency of the situation as I combed the streets for her. But when I finally caught sight of her in a street close to the casino, I suddenly felt ashamed. My miserable self-pity sickened me. I was a matter of a few hundred miles from the UK, not a few thousand from Africa. I had an apartment of some style, not a sleeping bag of some holes. I had notes in my pockets, not coins. I was disillusioned, not destitute. I wasn't homeless, I concluded, just soulless.

I watched her from a distance as people staggered by, occasionally taking leaflets, generally dumping them when they had read the words. I wasn't exactly sure of what I wanted to say. It just didn't seem right that a skinny homeless girl should be hanging around the streets in the early hours trying to help people less fortunate than herself. Somewhere, some balance was needed. I decided to ask her if she wanted to come and stay in my apartment. After a degree of persuasion in a language which was alien to both of us, she agreed, and we caught a taxi. At home, while I sat silently, unsure of what my misguided guilt was trying to achieve, the African girl started to undress, unprompted. At first, I watched. Seeing her naked arms was a shock. They were flesh and bone, just like a normal person. Homelessness was just the grime that clung to her clothes. Underneath, her skin looked as if it had spent as many nights in clean, warm bed sheets as anybody else's. When she was naked, I turned away, only glimpsing her ebony form out of the corner of my eye. She was completely without shame for her body, which suddenly made me feel awkward about mine. Next to her beauty I was pale and skinny. She walked over to me and smiled. I stared into her face. She took one of my hands and placed it on her breast. Her skin had a sort of coolness to it. Not a clammy coolness, more a marble-smooth finish, which made me want to run my fingers over it as if I were caressing a statue or sculpture in an air-conditioned museum. She took my other hand and placed it on her other breast. There was even an element of morbidity about her skin, and I found myself wondering if this was what a dead person would feel like, as I held her cool body in my sweaty hands. And then I removed my grip and stood up. The girl was offering herself to me like some sort of sacrifice. This was not what I wanted. There had been a genuine desire on my behalf to befriend her and protect her, not to fuck her. I walked into the bathroom and returned with a dressing gown. She appeared unsure at first, and then a little upset. I tried to tell her in my pidgin French that it was OK, I just wanted her to have somewhere to sleep for the night, but I couldn't help feeling that I had let her down somehow. It was almost like the law of the streets – I was going to do her a favour, so she had to do me one. Later, she cheered up and we talked and drank into what slender portion of the night remained. When I awoke in the morning, she had already let herself out. As I nursed my brain from its brittle hangover towards some sort of pleasant cloudiness, I found myself wondering whether the girl had ever really been in my apartment. And try as I might, I never saw her again, despite hanging around the streets from time to time in the early hours. I did see a lot of prostitutes, gamblers, drunks and street cleaners, but no African girls distributing leaflets. This bothered me because the piece of paper I had gave no indication of where to send donations. It simply read like a statement of fact – people are starving to death and *you* are doing nothing about it. The longer I went without finding her, the more she burrowed beneath my skin. I continued to search, and felt a growing ache of dissatisfaction at being denied something I wanted. I craved her because I couldn't find her. And, for the moment at least, my reckless spending was on hold.

Hotel Life

I headed down Broad Street and back to the hotel, telling Interesting Dave I was off to catch my train home to Manchester. Doubtless he was still hammering away, looking at his watch and counting down to his children's bedtime. Broad Street failed to live up to its name. Its relatively narrow pavements weren't choked with women of a dubious nature. Instead, young attractive females and males stumbled between bars, shivering and laughing, immune to the cold. 8:17. Time was becoming immaterial. I was finding ways of killing it, chewing it and spitting it out. Had the weather been a little less bitter I would have loitered amongst other people's cheerfulness just to use up some more minutes. As I watched Birmingham's jubilation swaying past bouncers arm in arm I realized that the world's best way of wasting time was being denied me. Love was the real thief of the hours and the days. Without it, I was sitting around alone in hotel bars and lobbies, empty arms holding nothing more than a watch, whose hands caressed the minutes they should have been racing past.

In my room, I kicked off my shoes, pulled my tie until it was loose enough to drag over my head, snagging only nose and ears on its journey, and threw my jacket on the sofa. As is the norm in hotel life, I turned the TV on and tried to ignore it. Slowly, inevitably, it dragged me into its company. MTV was on and I lay on the bed and watched a band who were already well past their peak following a career of almost a year. Evidently, I concluded, the modern purpose of talent is purely *achieving* fame, rather than *sustaining* it. The world is full of stars who have burst their bubbles in the effort of reaching the surface, only to find themselves gasping for breath once they get there. I made a cup of tea while the video struggled on. Pop is a particularly pertinent example. Five years spent writing songs, trying to get a deal, playing shitty gigs to mediocre punters, practising, hoping, posturing . . . and then, the signing. All the best songs stitched together for the first album. The tours, the promotions, the interviews, the difficult second album. And it *is* difficult. A year of flitting around the world on a high, and suddenly there is no material. Whereas the music started out angry and was born of frustration, now it is slower and happier. After all, maintaining a deep-felt sense of injustice when you are sitting on a pile of cash, surrounded by ever willing and seldom clothed members of the (sometimes) opposite sex, is no easy matter. I tired of the song and surfed channels. The posher the hotel the more the channels. The more the channels the wider the choice. The wider the choice the greater the torture. This is the reality of ultra-short-term accommodation. The loop of forty-seven channels ate up about a minute. I continued. Each loop was completed without the appearance of a single programme of interest. Loops extended, endless and uninvolving, into an enormous linear quest for something more entertaining than the last programme. It is never there, of course, but with the continuous lure of forty-six other options, pure optimism is going to tell you that there must be a better programme on, if you can only find it.

I managed to persevere until 9:11 before changing and heading for the bar. This was becoming an incarceration. It isn't possible to be normal in such circumstances. As I waited for the lift, I reflected that spending time alone in hotels is a voluntary form of solitary confinement. Hotels are prisons with their own rooms, keys, exercise yards and bars. Public bars admittedly, but bars all the same. You stay for a fixed, predetermined period isolated from your loved ones, whether you like it or not. Time is largely irrelevant. OK, you are free to come and go, your slopping out is done by someone else and dropping the soap in the shower is a minor inconvenience rather than a major catastrophe, but you can't help at times feeling the burden of captivity.

For creatures of habit, though, and I counted myself very firmly amongst their number, there are a few good points. A hotel room is a self-cleaning paradise of well-timed convenience. The contents of breakfast can be stipulated to the nth degree and promptly delivered to your door. Rooms are miraculously hoovered, swept and dusted in your absence. Your clothes can be washed and pressed, your shoes shined, your luggage unpacked. In short, shite though they may be, hotels represent order in a disordered world.

The bar, when I reached it, was far from busy, and I charged a drink to my room. At least I still had sufficient funds entering my bank account from the scam to afford a drink and a packet of crisps. I could have walked outside and bought a beer for half the price, but that's the thing about hotels. They charge what they like because they know you are incarcerated. Abroad, I had occasionally stayed at the kinds of places whose prices were beyond the point of taking the piss. In fact, so far had they exceeded the point of taking the piss that they were openly laughing at you. But they knew no-one would ever refuse to pay. The whole point of staying in such places was to prove that you could afford to do so. No matter what they threw at you. It was like a test to be endured, and on the other side you passed out, throwing your wallet in the air, celebrating that you had enough money to be openly taken to the cleaners and not care.

I drank a couple of miserable beers and slouched back to my room significantly skinter. The door was locked and I fumbled with my key-card. Stepping into the gloom inside, I had a powerful sense that I was not alone. That, or someone had been here. I turned the lights on and swept my eyes around the room. Nothing appeared any different from when I had left. The bathroom door was closed, though, and this made me nervous. I couldn't remember whether I had shut it. Always the bathroom. I approached the door, turned the handle slowly and then kicked it open. There was a sharp crack as the door slammed into the corner of the bath and sprang back towards me. But no-one was there. I relaxed a little and sniffed around the room. There was a mint on the pillow, where a maid had given the room its final clean of the day, and I could smell a faint odour of smoke. I kicked my shoes off. Such jittery behaviour had almost become the norm, stemming as it did from three years of pursuit.

Porcelain and Enamel

From the outside, Marcelo's old apartment is dark, but apart from that looks very much as it did when I left in the morning. The windows are open and the shutters pinned back. I instruct the taxi driver to wait in the small side street while I enter the gates on foot. The courtyard is busy with the sounds of living, which seep through apartment walls and drift around the enclosure. I walk briskly up the single flight of stairs which leads to my front door. Everything appears normal. The door is still locked and I turn my key and push it open. I stand still and peer into the hallway, listening.

There is no sound. I switch the lights on and enter. The hallway opens into the main room, with the first two bedrooms on the left and the kitchen to the right. I edge down the corridor. Having already turned the lights on and announced my arrival, there seems little point in stealth, but I lack the courage to walk briskly into the living room. Eventually I reach the door, which is half open, and peer through the crack between the door and its frame. It is semi-dark, and shadows from the hall light stretch the furniture across the carpet. Again, everything appears normal. I reach round and put the light on.

No-one has been here. I relax a little, but only a little. The drawers at the far end have my passport, some cash and some more necessary effects. I fill my pockets and think what else I might need. In the bathroom, I grab a handful of toiletries. The harsh white tiles with their faint etchings of mould catch my eye. Porcelain and enamel, a recurring nightmare. Teeth smashing into tiles, face slammed into the wall. Always when I piss in public toilets, I have this dream. Brittle teeth crashing against the merciless veneer of the tiles. I leave the bathroom, my mouth on edge.

A door in the main room hides a storage space and I open it. Inside is a suitcase, which I slide out from a tangle of empty boxes and other debris. I open the case and . . . the living room light goes out. I see a rapid movement across the door frame and into the gloom which surrounds me. The hall light has also been extinguished. The only light is from the courtyard.

He is here. Somewhere, he is breathing the same air as me. I am not nervous, just alert. My nerves were spent in the hours after I ran away from him, pacing the streets fretting what to do. I have no doubt it is him. He has tracked me down through the expat network, through the streets of Nice and now to my apartment. Nothing stirs. He is enjoying this. In his way, he is playing with me, stringing it out, hoping I will shit myself.

The floor is wooden. I imagine I would hear him if he is edging towards me. I strain my eyes. Nothing. My ears report a similar lack of information. A wooden floor. Slippery. I have trainers on. He is in Doc Martens, size thirteen. There is something to my right. A few feet. There is only one option. I sprint for the hall.

He catches my arm. He is unexpectedly close. I push through. A dead weight against my shoulder. I am trying to take him with me. A struggle. I feel the breath of a punch which misses my head by inches. Maybe he slips a little. Then I am free, accelerating. Through the open door. Whip the front door back, dash through, dead-leg still aching, slam it. Pull against the door as he reaches it. Force my key into the lock and turn it. Leave the keys and run for the taxi. Get in, tell him Le Airport, staring out of the back window. Urge him 'plus vitesse'. Possessionless, and now properly homeless. We stop at an autoteller and I withdraw my daily maximum of cash. Pay him. Departures. Looks as if the world tour is about to enter a new phase. Air France. Need to go somewhere quick. I take my platinum card and passport, breathe deeply and approach the desk.

Little and Large

Darren was quite unprepared for the welcome he received as he stepped through his front door. In the messy passageway loomed a man of excessive bulk, and behind him, literally in his shadow, a man of excessive unpleasantness. Both stiffened as Darren shut the door behind him and asked who the hell they might be. No-one moved.

The shorter one said, 'Don't worry who we are. You have far more serious things to think about.'

Darren remembered something about the front door. It was just like normal. They hadn't forced their way in. Karen. Shit. 'Where's Karen?' he demanded.

'She's resting.'

'From what?'

The shorter man glanced at the larger. A practised look of conspiracy passed between them.

'Just resting,' the smaller man said.

'Karen!' Darren shouted. 'Karen, can you hear me?' The two men turned round and walked through the door and into the back room. There was no answer. Darren followed them. Karen wasn't there. 'Look, what the hell is going on here?' he shouted. 'Why are you in my house? Where's my girlfriend?'

The smaller of the duo remained on his feet, whilst his companion rested uncomfortably, half sitting, half standing, against the arm of the sofa, his leg-wide arms crossed in front of him. 'No need to panic, son,' Small said. 'There's a couple of things puzzling us as well. Maybe you can help us and we can help you. Now, you're Darren White, aren't you? Dr Darren White?' Darren nodded warily. 'And can you prove that?'

'What are you, the police?'

'No.'

'Well then fuck off. Look, this is crazy. You can't just come into my house. I'm ringing—'

Big stood up and walked over to the phone. 'You're not fucking ringing nobody.'

'I asked you if you could prove it,' Small said. Darren decided to give the phone a miss. He stood and stared at the man's weaselly face. Mainly bone, with tight, pale skin straining across its rodent angles. 'Well?' Darren reached irritably into his back pocket and dragged his wallet out, extracting a much-folded driving licence. Small unfolded it roughly before examining it. 'Speeding,' he said, tutting. 'You see, me and my friend didn't believe you were a doctor from the first time we saw you. Scruffy bastard like you. There's no fucking way, I thought . . .'

'You mean you've seen me before?'

'Oh yes. Many times. My friend has been following you to work for the last couple of days.'

Darren glanced at Big, who winked menacingly back at him. 'What? Following me?'

'And keeping a spy on this shit hole of a gaff,' Big added.

'I'm decorating,' Darren said, in defence of the mess.

'So you see, we do have some business being here.' He folded the driving licence up again to wallet size, more carefully this time, and put it in his pocket. 'Now, you are who you say you are, and you live where we thought you lived.' Small cupped his face in his hands, which were equally taut and bony.

'Can I have my—'

'Shut up,' Small interjected. 'I'm thinking. Your friend is using your name and address, and you've given him access to your bank details . . . Now, what does that say?'

'This is crazy. I want you to leave.'

'You're not following me.'

Darren looked at Big, who also appeared puzzled. 'Please,' Darren beseeched, 'leave my house and tell me where my girlfriend is.'

'What you are not following is that your friend Ian owes us a lot of money. He needs an identity and you lend him yours.' Small took a big step towards Darren. 'You help him and you become an enemy of ours.' Big repeated the manoeuvre from behind. Darren became a Little and Large sandwich, which, although far from pleasant, was at least better than the Sid and Eddie pantomime variety. 'Now we want to know why he's back and where the fuck is he?'

'Who? I don't know anyone called Ian.'

Darren could feel Big's breath on his neck. 'Don't fuck us about.'

Small was in his face. 'Out with it.' He put his hand around Darren's neck. 'Now.' Big gripped his arms from behind. 'Come on, you shit.' Small gripped harder. 'Where is he?' Darren felt the bony fingers digging into his windpipe. 'Why is he back?' Big began to force his digits into Darren's biceps, muscles jarring against bone. 'Tell me!' Small screamed. Darren gagged on the words, fingers cutting their passage through his throat. 'Tell me now or we're going to fuck you over.' Darren tried to cough, but the hack got stuck in his lungs. Suddenly, his windpipe was open. He gasped and began to cough reflexively. Big spun him down and forced him onto the sofa, his face wedged into the seat cushions.

'OK,' he mumbled, tasting the stale dust of his second-hand furniture. 'OK.'

'So?'

'So . . .' An idea had occurred to Darren. 'My bank details?'

'What?'

He was allowed a little breathing room. 'You said he had my bank details?'

'Yeah.'

'And address?'

'Yep.'

Big relaxed his grip and Darren turned his face to the side, the rough pattern of the sofa scratching against his cheek. He was thinking. Now seemed a good time for his brain to help him out. Bank details. A nasty thought was piecing itself together. For a moment, Karen, the two thugs and his throat were forgotten. He had given his address to only one stranger recently. Admittedly a false address, but maybe not false enough. And the bank account was performing weird tricks. The cards had been lost with his luggage, which he had told the man on the plane about. 'The guy on the plane. Jesus.'

'What plane?' Small snapped.

'I'm just thinking. What does he look like?'

'He's *your* mate. You tell us what he looks like. Don't piss us about.'

'I'm not. What does he look like?'

'A cunt,' Big offered in the way of a description.

Small filled in some of the remaining details that Big had glossed over. 'Five ten, skinny, ex-fucking-student, dark hair . . .'

'That's him,' Darren said quietly. What was his name? Rich bastard. Andrew? Angus? 'Archie!'

Small shrank back. Clearly the name meant something. 'Archie?' he repeated, exchanging a quick glance with Big.

'Yeah, Archie.'

'Archie, indeed.'

Big joined in the surprise. 'The wanker!'

'Hang on,' Small said, walking over to Darren. 'You met Archie on a plane?'

'Yes.'

'Where?'
'Coming back from America.'
'Boring bloke dressed in nylon?'
'Well . . .'
'Droned on about computers?'

Archie certainly had mentioned that he was a computer programmer. He wasn't the dullest person Darren had met and hadn't been overburdened with man-made fibres, but then again, it was all relative. Compared to Big and Small he suddenly didn't seem too interesting either. He tried the words placed in his mouth for size. 'A bit, yes.'

Small and Big conferred. 'You don't think Archie's playing a fast one? I mean, we've only got his word for it that Ian Gillick is back working at Spartech. What if he's lying? What if he's figured out how to get the money and is using Gillick to throw us off the scent?'

The name Spartech rang a bell with Darren.

'Dunno,' Big answered.

'What if . . .' Small paused, his eyes squinting slightly. 'What if, indeed.'

Fame Whore

I should have known what Los Angeles would be like. After all, it was forever appearing in its own films, and therefore should have been familiar territory. What the city fails to bring to its many screen roles is any perception of its size. LA is vast. In fact, lower case letters don't do it justice. It is VAST, and the all-consuming hugeness of the city overwhelmed me in the days after I arrived from Nice via Paris.

In my panicked search for anonymity, I had ended up in the one place where quite the opposite was worshipped. With every poster I passed, every billboard, every advert, it was hammered home to me that anybody could be famous here. Even people on the run from Brummie psychopaths. But within the vacuum of the city's thin atmosphere I sensed an air of desperation, a pervading misconception that being popular with people who don't know you is somehow a substitute for being popular with people who do know you. There is a Californian phrase for this. Fame Whore. And LA appeared to be a breeding ground for such people. It was, in short, the Fame Pimp of the world.

As time passed, though, my alienation began to ease in the incessant sunshine and I got on with the job of living. I found an apartment in West Hollywood, between parallel scars across the city's shallow surface known as Fairfax and La Brea. It was a transitional area, where the gay quarter ended and the Russian began. Gay Russians, I imagined, would have felt particularly at home here. Fitting neither category, I felt a little confused at times. One block would see you go from pumping disco to laboured waltzes, via pumping waltzes and laboured disco. The apartment itself was just off Sunset Boulevard. Although 'just off' could, I found, encompass several miles in LA, I did actually live within a few yards of the infamous strip of faded tarmac. A few *more* yards might have been desirable, for, like many American streets, Sunset Boulevard was a bit hit and miss, with the distances between hits and misses often surprisingly small. Nice had been simple. Good areas and bad areas. But in LA, three or four blocks often saw a road plunge from slick offices and seemingly inaccessible apartments to sticky sidewalks and all too accessible inhabitants. Still, I was entrenched within an excellent neighbourhood – not that I ever saw any of my neighbours, which was probably one of the reasons for its excellence. I did meet one person, though, who also seemed to be moping around with very little to do. Greg had an apartment a few doors down from mine. We began to spend a little time together. The first thing I noticed about him was a distressing level of sobriety. Greg had sensible written all over him, from his short curly hair past his clasp-buckled belt down the creases of his trousers to his flat leather shoes. But just as continually taking left turns leads you right, Greg had taken sensible to the edge of crazy. He was extremely sensible, zealously so. As I got to know him, I started to sense that something was amiss. Greg was trying too hard. He had even developed a system. I had been there, I knew what systems could do to you. He had a diet, a regime, an outlook, a philosophy almost. But the system meant sacrificing many of the key elements of life which keep the majority of us sane.

Sleep, for instance. Greg told me he didn't believe in

sleep. Sleep was where sense deserted you. Sleep was where you dreamt, tossed and turned, and performed the random actions of senseless brains. Greg had whittled sleep down to four hours a night. The obvious paradox for me was that not sleeping was inherently senseless, but Greg had seemed to square it somehow. Another thing which wasn't sensible was Greg's Toyota Four-Runner, which he was more than happy to sell to me, and, on account of my undeniable laziness, I was more than happy to buy from him.

In this city, of all cities, I needed transportation. Performance-wise, the enormous vehicle was a mouse in man's clothing, which would happily have lost out to a milk float in a straight race, had America needed milkmen, and had such people been willing to subject themselves to the indignity of driving anything powered by batteries. Rarely, though, for someone selling me a car, Greg stuck around, which also didn't seem sensible, certainly not by Marcelo's standards. Surely, from pure superstition, he should have tried to lose contact with me. Even I could see that the car was about to fall apart. But there was an air of suffering about him which had never troubled Marcelo. He wanted to be there when things went wrong. And, to his lugubrious joy, he was, and many a time.

But amongst undependable machinery and maniacally sensible people, I gradually became desperate during the weeks that I sat around licking my wounds and missing Nice. There was simply too much to do in LA. In the face of such an impossible wealth of opportunity, I panicked and did nothing. I began to hang around in parks, malls and bars soaking up the business of others. I was becoming a slacker, and was getting perilously close to uttering the d-word. Yo, wha's up, du— *Very* close. Too much loitering in the southern Californian sun was fucking with my brain. I was one step away from bleaching my hair and talking endlessly about doing reps or catching air. The only thing I was catching was restlessness. I craved Birmingham's rain clouds. In the absence of such unhappiness I decided I would do the next most miserable thing. I would get a job. And that was where I first encountered Symbiosis.

Advert Lies

Greg had a brother called Carl, who ran a small computer firm in the Valley. Carl was almost famous, having acted in a series of commercials as a child. He had even once been mentioned in the same breath as Brad Pitt. Greg said it had been a particularly long breath, during which the subject had changed several times, but it was a breath all the same, and that was what mattered to Carl. He was very different from his brother. Carl had confidence, and always came armed with friends, like amicable bodyguards, lending weight to everything he said, supporting every statement he made. They hung at his sides like guns, restless and silent, waiting to be pulled from his holster. He rarely lost an argument with such support. Greg recommended my services to Carl and his omnipresent friends, quite unaware of what those services might be, and I got the nod. With Greg's help they were developing the use of new software which allowed easy processing of credit payments to Web-based companies.

Carl's headquarters was a large rented office in a large rented office block just off Ventura. The drive was mainly downhill on the way, past car washes with slogans like 'Keep LA Beautiful: Wash Your Car', and uphill on the return, past posters advertising for 'Real People' to be extras in films, as if real people were a rare commodity in the city. The more I saw, the more I realized this was the case. Either way, it was a mercifully short trip across LA's tarmac. For LA was, it seemed, just one great big lump of tarmac. It was practically drowning under the stuff. Every conceivable square inch that could have been tarmacked had been. If it weren't for the palm trees, which reminded me of weeds poking through gaps between paving stones, LA would look like a concerted effort to annihilate a huge area of natural vegetation.

But the palm trees, like many things in this great city, provided a false impression of fertility. Another false impression of fertility came in the shape of Carl's girlfriend Toni, who ran the office's administration. Her breasts, she proudly told me, were essentially false, but in the absence of such inside information appeared fertile enough to mother an entire maternity ward.

I worshipped Toni from the first moment I saw her, and I was in good company. She had probably never spent a single day since her easy adolescence when she hadn't been the desire, the possession, the everything of a man somewhere. You had no chance of just waiting around for such a girl to be on her own. For every man standing vainly in line there were ten others in the background itching to take his place. I decided to join the queue anyway, just in case two or three thousand of them suddenly decided to give up waiting. Toni wasn't without her problems, however. In England she would have been fine – likeable but unobtainable, and gently questioning of her identity. In America, she was a pain in the arse. Or ass. She knew what she was, and that was the danger. There was no shy insecurity to counter the weight of her beauty. She flaunted it, made an item of it and drew attention to it as she flicked her hair. Of course, I knew I stood no chance, but it didn't stop me trying. Over the months, I remained excited about the possibilities contained within the near-faultlessness which was

Toni. Although I had never bought the advert lies about the perfect car, the perfect washing powder, the perfect breakfast cereal, the perfect chocolate bar or the perfect pint, what I had bought, and abundantly, was the perfect woman. And Toni – personality, nationality and plasticity aside – was the perfect woman. I adopted a half-hearted-but-still-obvious sort of approach, which ultimately began to annoy even myself. I found I was turning into Hugh Grant in any one of the plethora of movies he has appeared in as a slightly crap Englishman saying daft, ineffectual things to American women. In my case, however, I left it there and headed home each night alone towards the dusty green of the Hollywood hills, rather than the Divine Brown of Sunset Boulevard.

Pointless girl-chasing aside, my efforts were absorbed in the struggle to adapt to American work practices. It wasn't as if there were complex rules to understand. American work practices were easy, and could be summarized as follows: Work hard all the time. There were also various subsections to be adhered to: Idolize your boss. Talk only about job-related matters. Show unhealthy enthusiasm for the sort of hours which put your father in an early grave at fifty-five. Volunteer for weekends. Do unpaid overtime. Compete. Be afraid. Never admit to weakness, but always appear tired – tired equals long hours, and long hours equal success. Dine with clients. Drink with colleagues, but not too much. Network. Strive. Be first in and last out. Die early, the earlier the better. Be utterly, utterly humourless about your job. And take the piss mercilessly out of any Limey unfortunate enough to come your way.

But even the hours and the seriousness would have been fine had it not been for my boss, which was not, I knew, an unusual situation in the world of employment. Carl employed a management ball-crusher called Phil Mannox to run the office. Under Phil M's beady gaze, Greg and I were exploring Symbiosis, a new language specifically designed for the transfer of encrypted information in the financial world. As such, it functioned more or less as an operating system for banking. It had been created to co-exist happily with other, less cutting-edge programs, while at the same time increasing the stability of their activities. In the abstract sense at least, Symbiosis represented the late Nineties/early Zeros ethos of caring capitalism. Here was a program that, rather than immediately rendering others obsolete, actually helped them, whilst also helping itself. Given its fail-safe mode of action, people were becoming less wary of transferring money across the unregulated mess of telephone wires which made up the Internet. It was clear even from our preliminary dealings with it that banks and businesses across the world were going to need this language. And having worked in financial institutions, I became quite excited about the possibilities.

Greg and I meanwhile spent a fair proportion of the time we weren't learning how to use Symbiosis frequenting mock Irish pubs and drinking imitation beer. Our reasons for this behaviour were quite different, however. I was happy to maintain any illusion, no matter how shallow, that I was doing what I would have been doing at home. Greg, on the other hand, was happy to find an added excuse to eat anything scientifically proved to be devoid of nutrition. His capacity for crap was boundless. While we drank, Greg was able to munch a variety of foodstuffs which were more stuff than food, and with a good conscience, for the bars we wasted our evenings in were hardly arenas dedicated to the pursuit of a balanced diet. On Greg's scale of dietary intake, doughnuts positively oozed fibre, corn dogs were dripping with goodness and pretzels came dangerously close to harbouring vitamins. For Greg, beef jerky, chips and pistachios were appetizers, to be followed down by large volumes of beer. All perfectly acceptable behaviour, were it not for the great Californian health dichotomy, to which he also subscribed vigorously. He would pump iron, take supplements, read the right magazines, eat organic produce, memorize long sections of books devoted to aerobic exercise, whilst all the time drowning in snack food, driving everywhere, and welding himself to his sofa for the protracted viewing of snippets of sport sandwiched between extended adverts. In essence, Greg lived the dual LA existence of superficial fitness within an all-pervasive smog to the letter. But for my own part, beer and snacks aside, the city allowed me to avoid the one thing which had posed the greatest risk to my health over the last couple of years – my fellow countrymen.

Expatriatism

There is an acute difference between holidaying abroad and living abroad. Before I began my globe-trotting odyssey, which admittedly only took in two countries, an English accent abroad would have sent me diving for cover. There is something particularly English about not wanting to be burdened with your compatriots when you are holidaying outside your country. Nightmare scenarios could ensue: trapped by a spoon salesman from East Anglia and his fat sweaty wife who itinerize your measly annual escape from work with brass-rubbing excursions and all-you-can-eat suppers in plastic tavernas. True, this had never happened to me yet, but you can never be too careful. Living abroad is different. The normal rules are bypassed. Selection procedures go out of the window in the cause of solidarity. You will talk to someone purely because they hail from the same country, and the majority of the other people around you don't. You might have opposing views on almost everything, be physically repulsed by each other, and yet there is a bond of unity. Us against them. The English united in xenophobia abroad.

After living abroad for only a short time, I found myself pining for English company, in strict disagreement with all previous feelings I had as a holidaymaker. I craved conversations about spoons and brass rubbing, longed for all-you-can-eat fake plastic pubs, yearned to be lumbered with substandard sunburned Brits. And I even found myself missing the things that irritated me before. The rain, for instance. When I first moved to Nice, on the relatively rare occasions it rained, it did so during the night, and I would wake up sighing for the English climate. In short, for the first time in my life, I felt truly British, and began to understand why expatriates formed colonies of resistance in Hong Kong, Singapore, the Costa Brava, Vancouver, Kenya and Johannesburg.

When I finally discovered the expat community of Nice, they were more than happy to invite me into their drinking venues. Only then did I discover the true horror of the term of reference. Expatriatism, I came to appreciate, was like one big ugly anthropological experiment. Throw a large number of people who would normally avoid each other like the plague into close proximity, isolate the group from their natural habitat, place them against an unfamiliar background and then really put the cat amongst the pigeons – deprive them of the trivialities they had based their lives around. Surely this could only end in bloodshed, I hoped.

I was wrong. In the months that I was both repelled and intrigued by the resident Brits of Nice, I witnessed no trouble at all. The reason for the relative harmony was not an enthusiastic camaraderie between Britons abroad, however. It was due instead to the presence of a rigid hierarchy of division. First, the Expats had isolated themselves from the French. Second, and generally the first level of division when foreigners aren't involved, the classes had segregated. Third, the Scottish, Welsh, Irish and English had factioned. Fourth, a strong sense of regionalism had prevailed. Geordies, Scousers and Cockneys frequented different pubs, kept out of each other's way and formed close-knit sects. As an unemployed naturalized Brummie, I didn't fit well into any of the categories, and perhaps this was why I disliked the expat colony so. But there was more to it than the simple ache of not fitting in. The expat network had a fatal flaw. Everybody always knew everybody else and their business, and if someone wanted to find you, this made things considerably easier for them. This was, I assumed, how I had been tracked to Nice. Now, in Los Angeles, I kept clear of the British. The chances that my pursuers knew I was here were slim, but even if they did, with no expat network to open its mouth, I was, I hoped, virtually untraceable.

Miscellaneous Pocket Pubes

A peacock's tail of colour-coded A4 folders fanned out across the living room table. Each was catalogued with a uniquely distressing description. From the bathroom came a series of short, clipped buzzes, occasionally punctuated by ten or so seconds of silence and indistinct mutterings. Presently the buzzing ceased for good and was followed by running water.

Archie emerged from the bathroom with his hands cupped, cradling a pile of dark brown hair, which he placed carefully on a piece of paper by the table. Next, he selected a folder marked 'Head Hair 2000', retrieved an empty envelope from within and wrote 'November' on it. To complete the task, he folded the paper slightly, and used it to ease his hair into the envelope, which he then returned to the folder. Satisfied, he walked back to the bathroom and examined his handiwork in the mirror. A little bit basin-esque, he noted, but more than adequate for the function his hairstyle fulfilled, which was mainly keeping his ears warm.

A thought occurred to him, and he headed briskly back to the front room. From his work bag, amongst a background of generally unglamorous junk like a thermos, some empty Tupperware and a calculator, he retrieved a large computer manual. Archie flicked briskly through its pages until he found what he was looking for – a brown envelope entitled 'Ear Wax;

Work; November 2000'. From the wad of folders on the table, he found 'Ear Wax 2000', and slotted his recent harvest, which didn't admittedly amount to a particularly onerous mass, inside. However, the envelope bulged noticeably more than previous collections, and Archie smiled proudly to himself at the achievement. By systematically neglecting to wash his ears, 'Ear Wax; Work; November 2000' was in danger of becoming the new benchmark for monthly wax collection. Archie slotted Ear Wax back amongst Nasal Hair, Head Hair, Dandruff, Facial Pus, Bogeys With Hairs, Bogeys Without Hairs, Finger Nails, Toe Nails and Miscellaneous Pocket Pubes, and returned the gruesome assortment to a drawer.

Nasal hairs with and without bogeys had been a nagging source of trouble, and had required some thought. Was a nasal hair with an appendage of snot more a hair or a snot? In the end, he had been forced to subdivide them into hairs with and without attachments, but he didn't feel especially at ease about it. Archie was just about to have another reckon-up of the possible options when the bell rang. Opening the front door, he was confronted by two people he had seen very little of for a fair amount of time.

'Archie,' the smaller of the duo said, 'long time . . .'

'Hello, Jeremy,' Archie responded flatly, before nodding in the direction of his considerably larger accomplice. 'Brian,' he acknowledged.

'Mr Magoo,' the big man replied.

Archie was well aware that the presence of Jeremy and Brian was unlikely to bring a lot of sunshine into his life, and the recent satisfaction that cataloguing his various bodily samples had brought him quickly ebbed away. In fact he had managed to avoid them almost entirely, with a few uncomfortable exceptions, since the swindle they had hatched three years ago went pear-shaped and Ian Gillick ran off with their money. 'So what do you want?' he asked.

'We're a bit worried that you might be fucking us around, Archie,' Jeremy said.

Archie was a little taken aback by the directness of the approach. 'What do you mean?'

'I mean that if you *are* fucking us about, Brian is going to break your legs. And then your arms. And then he's really going to get started on you. Do I make myself clear?'

'Yes.'

'Now, after you rang us we went to the address in Manchester you told us Ian Gillick has been using. It took a bit of doing, but what the fuck, we thought we'd sort it out. And what do we find when we get there? Some fucking boffin who reckons he doesn't know Gillick. And what's more, he says the only person who has had access to his name and address is a bloke he met on an aeroplane. And do you know who that was, Archie?'

Archie didn't know, but was sure that he didn't like the way things were heading. 'No,' he mumbled.

'You.'

'What? Me?'

'Yeah. Said he met a boring bastard called Archie on a flight somewhere. Now excuse me if that doesn't sound a bit like you.'

'Boring bastard,' Brian added, in case the evidence was still open to interpretation.

'Of course we only have your word for it that Gillick is back. We're going to pay him a visit at Spartech in a few days. But we've seen nothing of him yet in Manchester. So either he's an elusive wanker, or . . .'

'Or what?'

'Or you're fucking us about. And you know how I feel about that.' Jeremy stood up and sauntered over to Archie. Brian followed as if attached. Jeremy wrapped his bony fingers around Archie's lower jaw and squeezed. 'A lot of people got understandably upset when Gillick fucked us over and legged it to France.

And I personally got a bit upset when the cunt got away from me in Nice. So a lot of people, including me and Brian, still want to see their money back. And if you're planning something, you'd better think again.'

'Look,' Archie said through his pinned jaw, 'I'm not planning anything. Where was this flight?'

'Dunno. America I think.'

'Get my passport. It's in the top drawer over there.'

Brian lumbered over and tipped the contents onto the floor, before retrieving the slim burgundy Euro-style passport. 'Here,' he said, passing it to Jeremy.

'So?'

'Look through it,' Archie implored. 'I'm petrified of flying – I've never even been abroad. It couldn't have been me.'

Jeremy released his grip and examined the unused passport. After a few seconds, he let go of Archie completely and passed the evidence to Brian.

'Fuck me,' Brian said. 'Fuck me ragged.'

'What?' Archie asked.

Jeremy took it back for another look, and began to go a funny colour. 'That's fucking magic!' He caught Brian's eye and the two of them dissolved into giggles.

'What?'

Giggles gave way to loud, uncontrolled laughter. 'Fuck me, four eyes!'

'What?'

It was some time before either of them could give him a straight answer. 'Were you being fucked up the ass in that photo, or does it just look like it?'

'Meaning?'

'Jesus, Archie, have a look.'

'I've seen it,' Archie mouthed flatly.

'I'd sack your photographer if I was you.'

'It was taken in a booth.'

'And so were you by the looks of it.' Jeremy and Brian straightened themselves up. 'OK, so you might not be fucking us about. Which is good, because we've got plans for you while we check Spartech out.'

'What do you mean, "plans"?'

'Take some time off work, Archie. A couple of weeks should do it.'

'Should do what?'

'We've got a job for you,' Jeremy said, putting the passport in his back pocket. 'A nice cosy number indoors. Should suit you down to the ground. You start next week.'

Bullshit Bingo

As time passed, the day to day intricacies of the job began to grind me down. Phil M turned out to be an egotistical, bullying, self-righteous, pig-headed wanker. In short, the ideal American boss. I had stuck it for nearly ten months. When he began to use and harass me in my sleep, I knew it was time to quit. The money wasn't really an issue. I was hard-spending again, though mainly through one of my French bank accounts. Carl paid me a basic salary of $53,000, and with that added to my less conventional income I was even more comfortable than I had been in France. However, in the rush to leave the country, I had failed to wrap up all my financial dealings. The apartment was still being paid for through a second account to which I had no access, and therefore little chance of cancelling. Twenty per cent of my wages from Carl went to help the homeless of LA, and thereby eased the conscience of the soulless of Birmingham. Carl himself would have been appalled to know that the hobos he screamed abuse at through the open top of his car were drinking his money and sleeping in his beds. My interest in Symbiosis was growing, though, and I didn't want to give up on it. I decided that it might be time to change jobs rather than stop working altogether. And I had begun to come round to American labour practices.

Word was beginning to spread about Symbiosis, and

small pockets of need were arising, niches to be filled. One day I got lucky. A fellow programmer at a rival company named Digisat said they, like, needed some people, like totally now, to head up a new, kinda, division. American speech practices, however, remained the work of the devil. One Saturday morning, when Greg and I should have been playing Bullshit Bingo, I met the boss of Digisat. Kai was a man of two-thirds my age and about half my height. A good breath of fresh air would have done for him. Salary-wise, Digisat could give even more tramps a bed for the night, if I started within the month. It was a small company, with a noticeable lack of Phils. The premises were plush, the punters seemed acceptable and I would have my own office. I shook gently on the deal, afraid of crushing my new boss, and went to Santa Monica to listen to the sea.

I spent the next couple of weeks perfecting unnoticed flirtations with Toni, avoiding Phil M where possible, and rehearsing my resignation speech. Although worried about my impending exit, I was basking in the thought of imminent dossing about. Kai hardly came across as a ball-breaker. Bruising would have been a struggle. Work was going to get a lot less work-like. If anything, Phil M became increasingly dynamic during this period, and if he could have sworn allegiance to the company and waved a flag, he would have. Two hundred per cent effort, he would implore in the mornings as I passed his desk, and 200 when I sauntered out at night.

Meanwhile, Greg and I stepped up our daily games of Bullshit Bingo, and when we started gambling for beer most of the rest of the office joined in as well. The rules were simple. Phil M, at some point, had swallowed a dictionary of management jargon, which he regurgitated at any given opportunity. Very little of it made sense to anyone, particularly, we suspected, to Phil himself. For several weeks before the game began,

Greg and I had been collecting Phrases of Phil and writing them on the backs of envelopes. When we had fifty, we had enough to start. Everyone in the office was given ten random numbers, and each number was assigned to one of Phil's key phrases of bullshit. Number One, for example, may have been 'implementing prodynamic motivation', Number Two 'levering top-down paradigms', Three 'counter-conflictive progress' and Four 'opening the envelope of architectural touch-down'. The price per game was the standard unit of a single beer, and eyes down for a full round commenced at nine sharp. Bullshit Bingo soon brought about a change in the workplace. Suddenly, people were paying attention to Phil's utterances. Encouraged, he began to see himself as some sort of guru – his prodynamic strategy of management communication was finally filtering down and his staff were listening carefully to everything he said. He strode around the place and could hardly contain his glee. At last, his methods were paying off. He resolved to push his employees even harder, which only added to the amount of pseudo-speak that gushed from his mouth, and the game therefore gathered momentum. On a good day, we managed five or six sessions. Much to his eternal curiosity, several times a day one of his staff would stand up at their desk and shout 'Habitual Domestic Residence' before sitting down and continuing with their work. Greg had decided that shouting 'House', in the standard Bingo rules, was unbefitting our version, and 'Habitual Domestic Residence' should be used instead.

Whilst the game took my mind off my imminent resignation, I realized that Phil M was still going to be proactively upset. I was about to push the envelope of his wrath. At the prospect of such dynamic personal interface, I was increasingly scared shitless. The man had got under my skin. I could prevaricate no longer. Digisat were expecting me in less than a week. The day arrived. I slouched into his office. Having handed Toni an envelope containing my notice to quit, I thought I ought to tell Phil M in robot. Had he been human, I would have told him in person, but I had to do the best I could with the available material. He was polishing his Employee of the Month plaque. In truth, Phil M was the Employee of the Month every month, largely because assigning such a distinction was his duty, and he despised the lack of dedication of his employees to such a degree that he couldn't bear to hand the award over to any one of them. He glanced up.

'Got the batch code written?' he shout-asked.

I hoped my silence might hint that something was awry. 'No,' I said, after a dramatic pause which was mistaken for hesitation. 'I've actually come to tell you—'

'Right,' he replied. 'Right. Look, Ian, I have to say some things to you today.'

'Yes, but I—'

'Commitment, Ian. You know how I value commitment.'

I nodded. I was going to get a pep talk, and it was preferable to get my resignation over with first, to take the joy out of it. 'I understand all that. However—'

'Just let me speak.' I let him speak. He was American, and if he wanted to speak there was precious little I could do about it. 'Now I love my job. Jesus H. Christ I love my job. And because I love my job, I come to expect certain things. Only I don't get them. You see what I'm saying?'

I shrugged. All this seemed a bit irrelevant now. 'I think so.' He was going to demand 300 per cent.

'And when I don't get the things I need, I get upset.'

Four hundred per cent maybe. 'Right.'

'So things have to change.'

Things were going to change all right. I was about to fuck off to Digisat. 'Mmm.'

'Therefore, and I appreciate your feelings on this, Ian, don't get me wrong, certain things have been implemented.'

'Yeah?'

'Yeah. I've had some very proactive discussions with Carl, and I've got an announcement to make. Something which is going to affect you very directly.'

'What?'

Phil M paused for effect, before clearing his throat. 'I'm leaving. Another company is crying out for users, and they want me to head up a new group they're assembling.' He put the freshly polished plaque face down on his desk before glancing up at me. 'I start a week today.'

I stood and stared at him. 'But when—'

He waved his hand. 'Don't worry. I'm going to take you with me. Think I'll be able to negotiate something. Of course, you'll have to step your commitment up, but your future, from now on, is one word.' Phil M beamed at me. 'Digisat.'

Surely, he was taking the piss. 'Digisat?'

'That's right. Boss is a total pussy. Says he needs someone more, how'd he put it, ultra-active, to get things moving.'

The motherfucker. I tried not to get angry. Phil M spouted some more up-tempo nonsense and I turned round and walked out. Toni held up my letter of resignation and said she'd faxed it to Carl. I ignored her. There was a small Taiwanese man I had to deal with.

Digisat never happened though. Two days before I was due to start, I awoke at 7:43, squinting the sun out of my eyes, the words Catch 21 on my breath. I showered and rang a travel agent before heading into work to collect a few knick-knacks and flick the Vs at Phil M, which I did when he was safely out of sight. I gave Greg the spare keys to my apartment and asked him to keep an eye on the place. I might, after all, need to come back. The following day, I drove to the beach to watch the lazy waves go about their business in glorious indifference to my plight. And a couple of sandy hours later, I was standing nervously at the airport with a debatable excess of luggage.

Delivery

Big ambled back through the open front door with his arm round Karen's shoulder. Clearly uncomfortable with the concept of saying anything nice, he released his grip, shrugged and lumbered out of the house again. Karen slumped into a kitchen chair, and Darren walked over to put an altogether smaller arm round her.

'Did they hurt you?' he asked.

Karen screwed her fingers up against her scalp, making tight fists which sprouted hair. 'No. Not really.' She was shaking and Darren kissed her face.

'What did they say?'

'Just that they were here to deliver something and would I come out to the van to check it was right.'

'Then what?'

'They pushed me inside and told me to be quiet.'

'So what did you do?'

'You saw them – I don't think you'd have made much noise.'

'But you're OK?'

'What do you think?'

'Well, you're shaking and you've been crying, but you're alive.'

Karen was quiet awhile, and continued to tremble under Darren's arm. 'Do you think we should call the police?' she asked.

'Yeah. I'll get the phone.'

'But they said they'd come back if we did.'

'Mmm.'

'So what do you think?'

'I don't know. It's not as if they want to steal anything or are particularly interested in us. But something they said has got me thinking . . .'

A Question of Identity

Picking up the grubby receiver, Darren was forced to concede that there was something distinctly amiss about trying to track yourself down. Generally speaking, you should at least have a vague idea of where you are and what you are doing, which tends to make things less convoluted. Before, in his only other brush with anything remotely resembling detective work, things had been simple. In lieu of anything constructive, Darren had used science to jump to the wrong conclusion about a friend's involvement in a murder. He had been removed, detached, a bystander in the third person. Now, it felt very different. He was the pursuer and the pursued, the hare and the hound, the fox and the beagle. He was very much in the first person. He was looking for himself. He sighed, scanned the number on the scrap of paper and dialled.

'Spartech UK . . .'

'Hi. I was—'

'Your call is valuable to us. Please hold until a representative is available.' The recorded message gave way to music of a brainlessness that must have taken thought. Presently the tinny melody ceased with an unexpected flourish and the female voice resumed. 'Thank you for calling. If you have a touch-tone phone, please press the star key twice now.' Darren swore, picturing a receptionist sitting by a computerized switchboard, sipping coffee and leafing through magazines, whilst an array of hapless punters attempted to negotiate their way through a maze of potential options. 'To review this information, press one.' He found the underused star key and hammered it twice. 'Thank you. If you know the extension you require, please enter the number now. If not, press one, then the hash key, and wait for assistance.' Darren examined the keypad of the phone for anything resembling hash. There was a noughts and crosses button which he had assumed to be largely for the purpose of playing games over the line, but nothing remotely herbal in origin. In the absence of other alternatives, he gambled and chose the noughts and crosses anyway. There was a pause, and then another robot voice. 'Spartech UK. Your time is valuable to us. How may I direct your call?'

'Not a-fucking-gain,' Darren shouted, banging the receiver against the perspex of the phone box.

'Look, this is Spartech UK,' a curt female voice answered. 'Can I help you?'

'Oh, right. Sorry. I thought you were a machine.'

'A what?'

'You know, a . . . Um, yes, I wondered whether you could put me through to Darren White?'

'What company are you calling from?'

'I'm not.'

'And your name is . . . ?'

'Darren White.' Shit. It had been reflexive, a lifetime of answering to his own name.

A sigh. 'Is this a prank call?'

'No. Definitely not. I . . . I got confused. I want to speak with Mr Darren White.'

'I'm afraid I can't actually find anyone by that name.' Even with two people sharing his name, he was still anonymous. 'Do you know which department?' the telephonist asked. Bugger. Spartech had departments. It could be huge. Darren drummed his fingers. After a few seconds, the woman said, 'Hang on, would it be a *Dr* Darren White?'

'Er, yes that's it.' The bastard was even using his title.

'Right. Just hold a second, please.'

The line went quiet and then a voice answered, 'Darren White.'

'Darren? You know who this is, don't you?'

A flat, 'No.'

'Oh, come on, surely you recognize the voice?'

'Er . . .'

'Someone you owe something to. Someone you have taken something from.'

An audible intake of breath. 'Oh fuck.'

'So you know now?' The voice replied unhappily that it did. 'And you realize I know where you're working?'

'Yes.'

'And that things have now got to be sorted. It's time you stopped—'

'Look, what do you want, Archie?'

Darren paused. Archie? So there were two Archies. This didn't seem likely. He must have stolen another identity. But if Archie wasn't his real name, then what was? And while he pondered, Darren remembered that the two thugs had been obsessed with someone called Ian Gillick. Maybe that was it. Darren had been about to demand that the wanker stopped impersonating him, and every other fucker for that matter, but, as the seconds ticked away, a better idea began to form. He would play Ian at his own game. If he was going to assume someone else's persona when it suited him, then so was Darren. If thugs were going to come round and assault him and his girlfriend in their own home, then the rules were going to change. And as Darren saw it, Ian had some reason to be worried about this Archie character, which might do some good. He decided to string him along a bit. 'You know what I want, Ian.'

'If it's a question of the money, there's not much left. A few thousand at most.'

A few thousand? This was interesting. 'It's not just money. It's a question of identity.'

'I'm not sure I follow you.' There was an uncomfortable gap. 'Anyway, you sound different.'

'Maybe because I'm angry.'

'You sound almost normal.'

'So why the change of ID, Ian?'

'Why do you think? I couldn't exactly come swanning back to England to work under my real name.'

'Where did you get the one you're using?'

'Some dull scientific type I met on a plane.'

'Dull?' Darren couldn't help but be a little hurt. 'What makes you think he's . . . was dull?'

'I've met enough boring bastards to know.'

Dull. Boring bastard. This was getting personal. Not only had he stolen his identity, he was abusing it from the inside. Darren tried to step back from getting rattled, but was unable to prevent himself from pursuing the matter. 'Maybe he was an interesting guy who had done a lot of interesting stuff.'

'Doubt it,' Ian said. 'Just a case of any port in a storm. Anyway, Archie, where is this leading, and what do you want? You know I haven't got much of the money left, and you can't exactly go to the police, so I don't see how I can help you.'

Darren attempted to calm himself. If the fucker had caused him enough grief already, he certainly wasn't tired of the notion. Maybe it was time to pay back some of the favour. 'I might be able to help you.'

'I doubt it.'

'No, really, I know what you're trying to do, and I don't think you'll be able to do it without me.' Darren had no idea what Ian was trying to do, but reasoned that any help he could furnish could only be of disadvantage to Ian.

'And what might I be trying to do?'

'I think that's obvious to both of us.'

Ian was quiet awhile. 'Why on earth would you, of all people, want to help *me*?'

'Maybe there's something you can do for me.'

'What?'

'I'll be in touch, Ian.' And, with the feeling that he had accomplished something, though with little notion of what that thing might actually be, Darren put the phone down. This was certainly more fun than ringing the police.

Back to the Future

I sat and stared at the receiver, then took a furtive glance around the office. The phone rang again and I picked it up, slightly panicked. It was a routine work call which I hurried away. I stood up and went to the bathroom, locking myself in a cubicle. This was too close for comfort. Archie now knew where I was working. But something had changed in the interim. He was offering to help me. Obviously he needed something in return. He even sounded different. And if he was ringing me alone, he must surely have parted company with his two large and dangerous parasites. Maybe he had foreseen Catch 21 from the outset, and knew it was only a matter of time before I returned. Perhaps he wanted to share the work and share the money. Maybe we could help each other, and maybe this was a good thing. Maybe. I flushed the toilet for effect and left the cubicle.

Back at my desk, I resolved to try to forget about the call. If I was in any immediate danger, Archie would hardly have rung me to announce the fact. Besides, I had to concentrate. There were other more pressing matters. Today was my turn to take James out for an unwanted meal, to keep the pressure on about his system. So popular had this pastime become, he was now doing afternoon and evening engagements, and, seeing as lunch had already been booked, supper and a couple of pints were on me. And I had an idea I might be able to succeed where others had failed.

'So come on, James, how do you do it?' I asked, when we were safely ensconced in a pub, with our food in front of us.

'I have a system,' he said, sighing and loosening his belt subtly under the table, the extra meals evidently taking their toll.

'Look, we've all got systems, it's just that none of them work. Come on, what's the secret?'

'There is no secret. It's common sense.'

'You've found a short cut?'

'Exactly.'

'Which is?'

'It's common sense.'

'Maybe it's not so common. Help me out.'

'Think about it.'

'I can't. Come on, tell me.'

'Why should I?'

'So I can earn more money.'

'Why should you earn more money?'

I tried a route other colleagues were unlikely to have taken. I appealed to James's hungry greed. 'So I can give some of it to you. I'll pay you a commission.'

'But why don't you just think of a short cut yourself? That way you could keep your money.'

'I'll give you a quarter of everything extra that I make.'

'You're joking.'

'Look, twenty-five per cent of my wages, for doing nothing.'

'No way.'

'All right, a third.'

'No. This is daft.'

'What have you got to lose?'

'It's not that, it's just—'

'Come on, a third of everything I make, just for sitting on your arse.'

He rubbed his recently acquired second chin and was silent for a few moments. 'No. And that's my final decision.'

'Well, give me a clue, then.'

Having made a valiant stab at eating his meal, James placed his knife and fork together and stood up to leave. 'I've got to go. I'll only tell you what I told Mary at lunch, just to keep you lot on your toes. But you'll never get it.' He tightened his belt again. '1972. Right, that's your clue. I'm off.'

As James shuffled out from behind the table, something clicked. '1972?'

'Yep.' He drained his drink.

'Twenty-eight years ago?'

James looked at me intently. As a piece of advice, he should never become a poker player. 'Yes,' he replied, nodding slowly.

'Seven days in a week, one in four years are leap years . . .'

'And?'

'Days and dates repeat exactly . . .'

'So?'

'Well, this year and 1972 have the same calendar, obviously.'

He pulled the chair next to mine out and slumped down. 'Bugger. I didn't think anyone would guess.'

I wasn't exactly sure where I was heading with my reasoning. All I knew was that days and dates are precisely repeated every twenty-eight years. But I was on to something. It was time to call his bluff. 'So that's what you've done, eh?'

'But how the hell did you . . . ?'

'An anorak's intuition.'

'Better get me another beer. That's if you've got enough change in your kagoule.'

I obliged, and with a little further encouragement, James began to fill in the remaining details. I promised I wouldn't tell anyone and James generously offered to split the forthcoming profits with me, on a 90 per cent (him), 10 per cent (me) basis.

'So I was born in 1972. That's what first got me thinking. My birthday is on 15 March. This year, it falls on a Wednesday. I was born on a Wednesday.'

'Obviously,' I said, still largely in the dark.

'And my mother's birthday was on Friday 11 June that year. It also fell on a Friday this year. So eventually I came to realize that 1972 was the last year with exactly the same dates as the year 2000.'

'What was the next step?' I was treading a fine line between encouragement and ignorance.

'I began resetting all the computers to 1972. And hey presto! C21 sorted!'

The penny began to drop. James was concocting a sort of time machine scenario for computers. They were going to go back in time, so that the future wouldn't happen. It was your typical *Terminator 2* meets *Back to the Future* diorama, which have the common feature that the deeper you think about them, the less sense they make. 'You're doing *what*?' I asked, finally displaying my ignorance.

'Installing Symbiosis and resetting the dates.'

'Fuck me! Have you any idea . . . Look, don't you realize what this means?'

'Yes. For all the machines I work on, C21 will be irrelevant for twenty-eight more years. The first of the first of the first won't happen, and I will become very wealthy.'

'Wrong. You are going to be skint. Whole networks are going to collapse.'

'Bollocks. Something else will have come along by then.'

'Look, PCs themselves will function fine and are obviously continuing to do so. But think of the fucking software. It's going to go ballistic. You've got any rigid commands asking for a set date, and not a relative one, and everything's going to grind to a halt. Jesus.'

James went slightly pale. 'But . . . surely, if the machine thinks . . .'

'Machines don't think. If anything thinks, it's the software. And that isn't going to like waking up one morning to find it's living in the early Seventies.'

He began to look sickly. 'You mean . . . Oh, Christ.' Something appeared to occur to him as his eyes gazed into the middle distance. James put his drink down and rushed out of the pub in the direction of work. I wondered whether he had gone to start the Herculean task of undoing all his handiwork, or whether he had simply gone to clear his desk without leaving any forwarding address. I finished my drink and started on his, and smiled to myself. Programming was the get-rich-quick deal of the century, and James thought he had stumbled upon a get-even-richer-even-quicker deal. The sorry reality of the situation, however, was that he was on the brink of securing a get-fired-now deal. And with unhealthy down payments on a German sports car and a mock old-English mansionette to uphold, this was going to be an interesting time for James. I vowed to stick around at Spartech for a while and monitor developments.

Reception

James was nowhere to be found the following day. His desk had a faint air of rearrangement about it, as if a few key items had been extracted from the overall mess. A couple of people commented on his non-appearance. This wasn't just out of idle curiosity. Bob had arranged to take him for lunch, and was understandably upset that if he couldn't buy James's meal, he wouldn't be able to waste time probing him about the elusive system.

'He *must* be ill,' Jan surmised, and a general nod of agreement went around the office. How he could afford to stay at home on his salary was hard to reconcile. Indeed, the sum of money James was losing by not working would bankrupt most normal people inside a week. For that sort of money, writers, actors and even pop stars would consider doing a day's work. As long as it was between them. And tax deductible. And would be on TV. I didn't feel like sharing my information with the team, at least not until it was definite that James wasn't coming back, so I kept my head down for a while and busied myself fouling up a couple of relatively straightforward jobs. James failed to materialize.

Around ten days later, and still no sign of him, we had a visitor. More precisely, I had a visitor. Gazing out of the third-floor window, alternately scratching my head and leafing through a manual to find out what I had done wrong, I happened to half recognize someone entering the building below. It was difficult to tell from above, but it might well have been . . . The phone rang and I answered it.

'Darren White?'

'Yes?' I said, carrying the phone to the window.

'You've got a visitor in reception.'

'Who is it?'

'It's your brother.'

I stared intently at the street below. Sure enough, I was right. A silver van was double-parked across the road. 'Tell him I'll be down in five minutes.'

'Right-oh.' The line was interrupted briefly. 'Says he'll be waiting outside.'

'Thanks. Bye.' I returned the phone to my desk and put my jacket on, before collecting a few small items from my drawers.

'Off somewhere?' Dave asked.

'Got a visitor.'

'Sounds interesting.'

'Yeah. Might be gone a while. Say I'm sick or something. See you later.'

The only other way out of the building was a several-storey staircase which no-one could be arsed to use due to its close proximity to the lift. I walked briskly down the stairs to the heavy door at the bottom, which opened onto an alley at the side of the building. The element of surprise was important here. The alley served the kitchens of a hotel which skulked behind Spartech. I neared the back of the hotel, and as I did so the odour of food became progressively fresher, from the rank stench of dustbins languishing in the winter sun to the enticing smell leaking from the kitchen itself. The more delicious the food smell, the more on edge I became.

The kitchen entrance was veiled with thick vertical strips of once-transparent plastic which might have caught flies if they'd been sticky. I could hear voices and a radio, and see the moving shapes of people within. With no door to knock on, I pushed through the strips and into the kitchen. I approached a thin, unhealthy chef who looked like he should eat more and cook less. 'Can oi help yow?' he asked, guiltily stubbing a cigarette out.

'Yes, I'm a bit lost. I was looking for reception. Can I get through this way?'

The chef weighed me up for a second, and wiped his hands on his trousers. Due largely, I imagined, to the fact I was wearing a suit, he straightened a little and said, 'I'll just show you through, sir, if you'll follow me.'

We left the kitchen and entered a subsequent dining area which was being prepared for a meal. A couple more corridors saw us at reception. The chef nodded to the woman at the desk and said, 'This gentleman was wanting to check in.' I thanked him and he whistled his way back to the kitchens, stopping a couple of times on the way in a vain attempt to cough some unwilling phlegm up. I looked back at the receptionist and smiled.

'Actually, I've changed my mind. Sorry. I won't be staying.'

The woman glanced in the direction of the chef. 'I do hope that Kevin hasn't put you off. He is new, and if he's offending potential guests, we'll have to—'

I needed to get out and fast. I had told the Spartech receptionist that I would be down from my office in five minutes to meet the man pretending to be my brother. 'No, really, he seemed lovely – I've just changed my mind,' I said, walking towards the main entrance. The woman picked up a telephone and asked for the manager. I hoped Kevin wasn't going to get it.

Outside, I had a quick reckon-up. I was at the top end of New Street, where shops gradually softened into council buildings. My hotel was on Broad Street, which was virtually dead ahead via a tangle of subways. Maybe they knew where I was staying. I set off down New Street and headed for a taxi rank which fed off the recently pedestrianized section of the road.

Ten minutes later I was in my room, in fifteen my cases were partially full with the few items I had time to grab, and in twenty I was in another taxi heading for the train station. I was sweating and nervous, and once again bade farewell to Birmingham. Clearly, they knew I was back. First the phone call from Archie and then this. In the many months since France, I had often fretted over just how close my parasites came to catching up with me in Nice. They evidently had resources and information. This time, I guessed that Alan had been their informant, but whoever it was, the effect was the same. As was becoming the norm in my increasingly unsettled existence, I found myself moving on with my two unimpressive cases.

On the way to the hotel I had wondered where I might go. My old house was out. Friends had fallen by the wayside, or had moved to the canalside, since my departure. Hotels were fine, but it was Birmingham that worried me. There was no point in going to work for the foreseeable future, and therefore little to keep me here. No, it was time to pay a visit to someone who owed me some money.

Takeaway

The train to Manchester was late and I was nervous. I couldn't help but feel watched. Amongst so many people, it was still difficult to persuade myself that the two thugs couldn't simply find me at the drop of a baseball hat. Even in customarily drab clothes I felt fluorescent. As an economy measure, I travelled in standard class. This proved to be a mistake. Children were crying, mobile phones ringing, pointless conversations grating ('Yep. I'm on the train. Just ringing to confirm that I'm due in at the expected time'), announcements incomprehensibly announcing, the sandwiches unappealing, the tea uninviting, the company irritating . . . In short, the ninety-minute journey was as standard as they came, and served only to remind me of how panicked I was.

Arriving at Piccadilly station, surrounded by bold Sixties architecture which looked suspiciously like a mini-Bull Ring, only cleaner and with slightly fewer tramps, I had two potential addresses to explore. One of them seemed unlikely, and had certainly failed to match the information Dr Darren White had given the airline when he booked his ticket to Colorado. This remained a mystery. He had seemed a little scatty, but certainly not daft enough to warrant forgetting where he lived. Still, I decided to try it first, just to eliminate it from my inquiries, as it were. The taxi driver was reasonably sympathetic. Can't see any bugger living *there*, pal, he said, smirking, as we pulled up outside 133 Oakwood Street, which proved to be a single-storey Chinese takeaway in Rusholme. 'Hong Kong Suey'? Think you've been had. I nodded graciously and suggested we try option B, the address given to me over the telephone by the elusive Dr White. The taxi driver continued to chuckle, repeating 'Hong Kong Suey' to himself a couple of times beyond the call of duty. Eventually he pulled off, and I watched Rusholme fade into Didsbury, which soon became Withington, seamless houses lining the route, dissolving into new streets in new districts without apparent break.

'No chopsticks, so you might be in luck,' the driver said as we finally approached what might actually have been Darren's house.

'You never know,' I said, climbing out.

The house, though large, appeared shabby. A badly painted door peered over the mess of a cracked front step, which was set several yards back from the road. There was a bell, but it didn't look to have seen any electricity for a number of years. I banged on the door, which was presently opened by a reasonably attractive female of about my age.

'Yes?' she asked, looking me up and down for a clue as to why I might be knocking on her door in the middle of a Wednesday afternoon. Evidently finding none, she continued, 'Can I help you?'

'Maybe. Is Darren around?'

'He's at work,' she answered. 'You a friend?'

'Yes. Kind of. What time are you expecting him back?'

'Who did you say you were?'

I paused momentarily, trying to determine who I was today. 'Ian,' I said, deciding that honesty was the most convenient policy.

'Ian. I'm not sure he's ever mentioned you.' Eventually bewilderment and suspicion gave way to politeness. 'I mean . . . sorry, look, do you want to come in?'

Sitting in the high-ceilinged front room with a cup of tea, she told me that she was Karen, and apologized for the mess, saying that they had only been in the house a few months and hadn't really sorted it out yet. Darren had made a stab at doing the place up, but had recently admitted defeat and employed a firm of decorators. Amongst the chaos I noted a reasonable number of impressive gadgets with superabundances of buttons, and an as-yet not unpacked stereo. They had moved from Sheffield when Darren got offered a new job, she told me, and she was currently working part time. She asked me what I thought of the general public and I said I didn't really have much to do with them. Good thing too, she answered. Yes, I agreed, unsure of the question, and wondering why she was filling me in, a complete stranger, on her life history. If I were a friend of Darren's, surely I would know about her life already. Maybe she just wanted to talk. Certainly, Karen appeared a little frustrated.

'So, Ian, how do you know Darren?' she asked, running out of things to tell me about her life.

'I met him on a plane, coming back from the States.'

'So you haven't known each other very long?'

'A few weeks, really.' There was a shift in Karen's demeanour. It was only slight, and I would have missed it if I hadn't been watching her as I spoke. She was no longer protected by the thought that Darren and I were good friends of some standing. She appreciated now that we were relative strangers, and I was someone her boyfriend had failed to even mention. There was a sliver of panic about her eyes. 'Look,' I said, standing up, 'I guess I'd better be off. Things to do, you know. Would you tell Darren I called around, and that I'll be in touch soon? Thanks for the tea and sorry to dash off . . .'

Shopping

'I met a friend of yours today,' Karen said.

'Yeah? Who?'

'Some bloke. Met you on a flight somewhere.'

Darren stood still. 'What was his name?'

'Ian.'

He remained silent for a couple of seconds, and then swore. 'Shit. Shit. That's the guy. The one those lunatics were after.'

'You're joking. I thought he was Archie or something.'

'That's what he told me. But he seems to be using whatever name suits.'

'Well, if I'd known that . . .'

'Did he ask for anything? Money?'

'No. Why, do you owe him?'

'Look, I didn't tell you, but I did something a bit daft.'

'Yeah? Like that would make a change.'

'This guy lent me some money when my luggage got lost. I'm not exactly proud of this, but he seemed fairly well off and so I kept it. I said I would mail it back to him but never did.'

'Mail it back to him then.'

'It's not that simple.'

'Why?'

'He was going to get in touch with me when he knew where he was staying, but I gave him a false address.'

'What?'

'Look, I don't know what came over me. He gave me the cash, I thought he wouldn't miss it, and I had vastly overspent at the conference. I knew I was going to be in trouble when I got back, and that we didn't have any money since the move. So I gave him the wrong address, thinking I'd never see him again.'

'Oh, great. Now he knows where we live and he wants his money. How much?'

'Not a lot. A hundred. Ish.'

'Ish?'

'Two hundred.'

'Jesus!'

'It gets worse. I actually rang him up yesterday.'

'What the hell for?'

'Something a bit unnerving is going on. He's started to use my name as well.'

'Why?'

'No idea, but it's freaky. It has something to do with the thugs, though. They seem to be after him, and he's passing himself off as me to try and evade them.'

'But why you?'

'Beats me.'

'Forget the two hundred quid then – I call that a fair swap.'

'I'd have thought my name was worth more than that.'

'Really?'

Darren looked her in the eye and decided not to pursue the point. 'Talking of money, we'd better go a bit careful.'

'Why? The six grand can't have gone again, surely? Where the hell is it going?'

'The usual. Doing the house up is eating a lot of it. They've set yet another decorator on. Their top man, apparently. And other stuff, of course.' Darren glanced guiltily down at the Dixons carrier bag in his hand. More gadgets to play with after tea, all of them generously sponsored for a second consecutive month by Spartech UK. He hoped they could afford it. 'Anyway, it's not easy with you only working part time, you know,' he said, in an attempt to shift some of the blame.

Karen looked as if she was going to scream. 'Not easy? You think sitting around for hours on end listening to other people complaining is easy?' Darren was about to venture the opinion that yes, it probably was fairly easy, and at the very worst beat working, but his girlfriend's manner persuaded him to stay silent. 'I'm getting fed up. I want a proper job, like my one in Sheffield.'

'Well, look, if the money keeps coming in, maybe you could give it up and find another one. And in the meantime we'll go and do some more shopping and cheer you up a bit.'

'Shopping? You think shopping makes people feel appreciated and fulfilled?'

Darren again risked a darting look at the carrier bag, which concealed a rather expensive digital video camera, and felt a warm rush of satisfaction about his purchase. 'Mmm,' he muttered absent-mindedly.

'If you ask me, shopping makes everybody miserable in the long run.'

Darren smiled and nodded, running through a very pleasant daydream involving the palm-sized camera. Had he heard what Karen was saying, he would doubtless have disagreed. The very nature of his indifference, however, went some way towards disproving her point. After the dream had ended, he said, 'You're right, of course,' in the hope that he was sounding supportive of whatever the current issue might be.

'Mind you,' Karen ventured after a couple of

moments' reflection, 'we could get the decorator to put a new kitchen in.'

Darren snapped back to reality. 'I'll get on to their finest man,' he said, before sloping upstairs to unpack and worship his most recent toy.

DIY

The doorbell rang. Understandably reticent of late, given the ability of the house to attract an endless procession of oddballs, Darren peered cautiously through the newly fitted spy hole in the front door. The spy hole had, however, been installed by the new decorator, and all was not exactly as it should have been. As he tried to focus, a voice passed through the door saying, 'Hello, it's me, Dr White, can I come in please?'

'It's me who?' Darren asked in response, unable to get a decent view through the hypothetical security feature.

'The decorator,' the voice replied. 'Can't you see me?'

'I can't see anything.'

'Well I can see you as clear as day.'

Darren opened the door and glared at the handyman. A thought had occurred to him and he walked outside and stared through the spy hole, which afforded a panoramic view of the hallway. 'You've put the fucking thing in back to front.'

'What do you mean?'

'Look, the whole point of one of these,' Darren said, trying to remain calm, 'is that I can see out and potential villains can't see in. It's not a lot of use if they've got a perfectly clear view of the inside of my house while I haven't got a clue who might be lurking on my doorstep. Is it?'

The man shrugged and said, 'I guess not,' before walking in to resume his work. Darren watched, and couldn't help noticing there was something a little unsettling about him. For a start, he didn't appear to be able to decorate, which seemed something of a handicap with regard to the job at hand. Added to an alarming inability to do the one thing he was being paid to do was a myopia which didn't so much border on the blind as crash through its walls and stumble vainly around inside. It had been this way since he started, and things showed little sign of improving.

Darren had rung the decorating company and complained, to be reassured not only that Stevie Wonder was the finest craftsman the company could offer, but that they would be happy to do the job for free in the unlikely event that it wasn't entirely to his satisfaction. Spying a potential opportunity to invest even further in black plastic gadgetry with the spare cash, Darren agreed, reassuring his girlfriend that everything was as it should be. He was, however, beginning to regret the decision. All last evening, waves of wallpaper had descended gracefully from the ceiling to attack him while he ate his tea. Although cheered by the thought that at least the home improvements weren't costing him anything, there was precious little evidence of even the remotest improvement. In fact, it had only taken a week for the place to start looking considerably worse. And on top of this, Stevie Wonder was by far the dullest man he had ever encountered, which, given Darren's employment within the personality-crushing sphere of academic science, was saying something. On Friday evening, shortly after the decorator had left, the doorbell rang again, and Darren opened the door, expecting to be confronted by an inept labourer who had taken his toolbox home instead of his lunchbox. He was confronted instead by a very different visitor. It was the other Dr Darren White.

How and Why

'You came a couple of days ago. Why?'

'All will be explained.'

'So you keep saying.' Karen was out shopping. Darren and I were sitting on opposing sofas. Things weren't going well. Although he hadn't exactly been overjoyed to see me, there was an air of resignation about the situation which unsettled me slightly. I had expected more hostility. It was almost as if this was a perfectly natural situation for Darren to find himself in. 'And why did you steal my name?'

'Some people are after me. You know the thugs you said came to see you?'

'Unfortunately.'

'Them.'

'How did they get my address?'

'They got your address because I've been using it as well.'

'Anything else?'

'The money you've been spending? My wages, paid into your bank account. Your suitcase and possessions? I threw them.'

Darren appeared slightly panicked. 'What about the . . . ?' he asked.

'What?'

'Was there anything in the luggage that . . . anything, you know, a bit . . . because it wasn't mine.'

'What wasn't yours?'

'The strap . . .' Darren blurted.

'What strap?'

'Er, just the strap on the suitcase.'

'Oh, right.' Darren was blushing and looking furtive. An alarm bell of recognition rang somewhere, but went unanswered in the heat of the exchange. 'Look, I didn't go through your things. Everything I was interested in was on top of your clothes.'

He took a noisy sip of tea. I hadn't been offered one. 'So how did you manage all this?' he asked.

I told him, mainly truthfully, but with the odd lie thrown in where appropriate. When I had finished he was thoughtful for a while, and then quietly began to discuss habits I might amuse myself with, parts of the male and female anatomy I reminded him of, sexual actions I might perform both with and without a variety of animals, ways I could pass the time of day with my mum, bicycling religious icons, and, for a grand finale, my similarity to a small rodent with a predilection for tangy condiments of a chunky nature.

I suggested that he might like to reconsider some of the issues he had just raised. 'Fuck you. Just fuck you, Darren.' I stood up. 'I think you're forgetting something here. You're not exactly squeaky clean yourself.'

'What the hell does that mean?' he demanded.

'I helped you out on that flight. Two hundred quid! And how did you reward me?' Darren's anger appeared to abate. 'I'll tell you how. By inviting me round to Mr Hong Kong fucking Suey's place.' I stepped closer to him. 'Someone gets you out of a tight spot, and what do you do? You do a runner with the cash.'

'Yeah, yeah. And why did you help me out?'

'Because you were stuck.'

'Bollocks. You gave me the money because you'd already decided you were going to steal my case.'

'So we stiffed each other. I call that a draw.'

'But the point is, you started all this.'

'So go and complain to teacher. Look, I'm genuinely

sorry about what I did, really, I was desperate. I know that's no excuse.' I stared past him at the wall behind, which was shedding a length of wallpaper, at the same time as a piece of wet plaster belly-flopped onto the floor. 'All things considered, you haven't done too badly. I guess the insurance must have more than covered your losses, and you've been frittering my wages around like there's no tomorrow.'

'I see that as compensation.'

'For what, exactly?'

'For having some thugs come and terrorize me and my girlfriend, for a start.'

'Oh yeah.' I scratched my head. 'Sorry about that.'

Darren remained quiet, allowing the apology to hang in the air. After a couple of minutes, he asked, 'So why are you here? Really?'

'The sorry truth,' I told him as I walked over to the sofa and sat down, 'is that I can't think of anywhere else to go. Birmingham's out, and I don't know many people outside the Midlands. Plus I wanted to apologize.'

Again, Darren left the repentance to fester awhile. 'Who are they, these thugs?'

'Never found out their real names. I've just come to think of them as parasites who follow me around trying to suck money from me. Basically, a few years ago, they roped me into a financial swindle at Intron, the company I was working for. They were going to harm Archie, a bloke I shared an office with, if I didn't help them. To cut a long story short, I ended up pulling a fast one, and legged it to France. One of them caught up with me, I panicked and got on a plane to America.'

'So why come back?'

'A programming glitch is about to fuck me over. The code I wrote will become obsolete at the beginning of January, and I'll lose my source of funding. The swindle, as they say, will be history.'

Call a Comedian

The next evening, Darren was on the other couch, and I gained the impression that he was watching me. What's the problem? he asked, as I glanced up. I ignored the question and continued to fiddle with my watch, an Oyster Perpetual Date. It was Saturday, days were rushing past, I was running out of time and my watch ticked the days off as if it was enjoying itself. I used to have a fake Rolex with glued-on hands, which lived rather literally up to its title. Then I bought a real one. It was a way of proving to myself that my former life had been an imitation, and that now I was living the real thing. I used to hold the two together, the fake in my left hand, the real in my right, bringing the watches close, examining them like some sort of spot-the-difference competition. I still had the copy somewhere, but the battery was dead and its wandering hands had given up the chase as well. As I stared into the cold face of my watch, part of me still yearned for the fake.

'Well, do you at least fancy a beer?' he enquired.

I left the lure of my heavy timepiece and gazed over at Darren. He had the look of a captive beast about him. It had probably been several evenings since he last went to the pub. He raised his eyebrows in conspiracy. I sighed and nodded. 'OK. If we must.' He was on his feet and searching for his jacket before I had even put my watch back on.

Karen declined our invitation. 'I'd rather drink with some of my customers than go out with you,' she said. I surmised from this that she was still angry at me.

The pub was an Irish pub, which wanted only the necessary location. As compensation, it was crammed from its fake floor to its false ceiling with suspicious memorabilia that might conceivably have been near Ireland at some point, but probably only on a day trip. The Guinness took for ever and Darren chattered excitedly, evidently glad to be out of the house. I watched the drink settle, bubbles becoming foam, foam becoming liquid, until all was dark and impenetrable. I decided I ought to try to lighten up.

'So come on,' Darren said, 'what's on your mind?'

'Nothing,' I responded, flatly. Not the world's best attempt at cheeriness, admittedly.

'Nothing?'

'Nothing.' A band, which had been setting up at the far end of the room, burst into life, and proceeded to strangle the life out of a couple of covers. It became more and more evident as Darren and I chatted that this group of musicians, Spandau Ballet aside, was possibly one of the worst ever assembled.

'Jesus!' Darren shouted in my ear, as the second song ground to a halt at different junctures and in very different registers according to each musician's whim.

The front man stepped up to the mike and announced, 'We're the One-Eyed Men. Any requests, an' we guarantee to play 'em. Ta very much.' A long-haired beard at the front, whom Darren said he recognized from work, shouted up for some Pink Floyd, and the band launched tunelessly into 'Brick in the Wall'.

'Yes you fucking do!' a man at the side of us screamed during the chorus, as the singer proclaimed that they didn't need any education. '*Singing* lessons for a fucking start!'

That such a shambles could have the blind bravado to step onto a stage, the sheer unwillingness to accept that they were hopeless, and the reckless gall to actually demand money for their services filled us with awed respect.

'You're not in a great hurry to leave?' Darren asked.

'No fucking way,' I told him. 'I'm not missing this for anything.'

'Any requests?'

'What?'

'I've had an idea. Here, hold this . . .' Darren handed me his pint and pushed his way towards the front, through the none-too-eager crowd. The singer stooped down and presented an ear to him. 'We've had a request for some Phil Collins,' he said into the mike, standing up. Darren scuttled back grinning, and the band began to massacre 'In the Air Tonight', which seemed a little unfair, given that the song was already down on its luck. Still, the band excelled themselves and managed to make the song noticeably worse. This was, after all, the true measure of awful musicianship – it is easy to vandalize a great song, but to ruin a terrible one takes practice and commitment. The heckler on our right glanced over at us and winked. Either he was on to something or we had pulled a sweaty bearded man for the night. He similarly made his way to the front, and pretty soon a scandalously out-of-tune version of 'Karma Chameleon' was rattling through the speakers, sounding oddly like 'Call a Comedian', which seemed to fit the proceedings quite nicely. Next, in ascending order of musical crime, came Take That's 'I Want You Back' ('I Want to Pack'), a brave attempt at Wham's 'Club Tropicana' ('Claptraporama'), a misguided stab at Adam and the Ants' 'Stand and Deliver' ('Stand in the Liver') and one which neither Darren nor I could quite pin down, but which might have been an experimental number. Over the next twenty minutes or so, which continued to witness the slaughter of many an already-awful song, we began to talk more and retreat gradually to the back of the pub, where we at least stood a fifty-fifty chance of catching what the other was saying. Whilst bad entertainment can be every bit as enjoyable as good entertainment, and often a whole lot better, it does have the disadvantage that the joke eventually wears off, terrible as it was in the first place anyway.

'So come on, out with it,' Darren said. 'Either you're always this miserable, or something's not right.'

Over the oddly supportive sounds of 'Bring Your Daughter to the Slaughter', I told Darren that my scheme to correct the programming was looking increasingly fucked. I could see no way of sorting it out now that I had left Spartech. For his part, Darren said that Karen still hadn't forgiven me for the visit of the thugs. She wouldn't answer the door any more when she was alone in the house, and only let me in when I first called on Wednesday because, in her words, and he emphasized *her words* as if they contained a gross error of judgement, you looked like a decent bloke. Appearances, I said. Yes, Darren answered, staring straight at me. She even thought you might have been the police or something. I smiled at the sheer inaccuracy of her estimation. Darren continued to look at me and I got the impression he was angry as well, and really I couldn't blame him. I suddenly felt horribly guilty and offered to buy him a drink. Whilst not an entirely generous compensation package, it at least served to dissipate some of the weight from my shoulders. Thus we were both a little happier. Darren was slightly more pissed, and I was slightly less ashamed. Returning from the bar, I asked Darren if he could face telling me exactly what happened a few days ago, and got the impression he was only too happy to have another go at making me feel worse. So far, both he and Karen had been understandably reticent. I wondered now though whether he had sniffed the potential opportunity of another free drink, and imagined him performing the scientific calculation in his head: guilt equals beer squared. Darren began an award-winning portrayal of hardship and terror. Maybe not Oscar calibre, but certainly in with a chance of an Emmy. After setting the dramatic scene, he steadied himself. 'So they're demanding where the fuck this Ian character is, Ian Gillick or whatever . . .'

'Me.'

'If that is your real name.'

'It is. I told you, I'm Ian Gillick.'

'And not Archie or Darren today?'

'Like I said, I needed an identity.'

'All a bit devious.'

'A necessary evil.'

'Mmm,' Darren replied, heavy in preoccupation. He was doubtless planning his acceptance speech. 'I accept this lager, not on my behalf, but for all fellow lager scroungers everywhere.' His short attention span was then once again caught by the band. 'Hang on,' he said, 'the One-Eyed Men seem to be lacking a bit of inspiration. We'll continue this in a minute.' He headed off to put in another request, this time for the Steve Miller Band's 'Abracadabra' ('Have a Kebab-aa'), and I watched him pick his way through the crowd. Lying can be such an unsatisfying act at times, I reflected, peering into my drink. There are occasions, of course, when it is a positive joy. But when you open your mouth with a happy disregard for the truth, only to find your words greeted with suspicion, indifference, disdain even, lying begins to lose its appeal. Lies, like the people who spin them, need company. Allowed to mingle with shady truths and half-truths, they are never more content. A falsehood which suddenly finds itself out in the open, however, will often shrivel in the sun. And as Darren returned and I tried to lie to him again about some of the financial details, amongst a background of otherwise honest candour, I found I was struggling. This was not necessarily an instance where the truth was welcome for either of us, though. He might not be particularly interested in hearing the real story. If I had rummaged through his suitcase, I would undoubtedly know about its contents. Admittedly, these had been playing on my mind. Several unwelcome mental images had plagued me since opening his case. For my part, though, there was no point telling him the full truth of my financial swindle. Large sums of money can change people and betray confidences. If he really sat down and thought things through, as I'm sure he already had, he would appreciate that what was keeping us in each other's company was a healthy lack of honesty. As things stood, then, a few untruths were good for both of us.

'I guess it doesn't make any difference what your name is,' Darren said, grinning at the cacophony the band were making. 'It was still you they were after.'

'Not that you'd have known who I was, of course.'

'No, but I did tell them I'd been talking to someone called Archie on a plane.'

Something extremely pleasant occurred to me. 'You told them I was Archie?'

'Yeah.'

I wanted to kiss him, but quickly changed my mind. There is gratitude, and then there is swapping spit with a stubbly man who smells of beer. And another thought entered my mind. 'And how did they react to the name Archie?'

'Not very well, really.'

Again, I thought about a kiss but decided against it, particularly because the alarm bell which had been ringing from yesterday's conversation had recently been answered, with the recollection of exactly what I had found amongst the contents of his luggage.

Night Fever

Later, after the chip shop, while Darren and Ian sat on a wall and ate soggy pies full of gravy and thin strips of indeterminate meat, Darren proposed a club.

Ian gave up on his own runny mess of pastry and slop and jettisoned the leftovers. 'Could do, I suppose,' he answered. 'Do you know one?'

'Yeah. There's this Seventies disco place just off Canal Street. Took Karen there a couple of weeks ago. It's a good laugh, you know, really camp and everything.'

'I thought the Seventies were out now.'

Darren similarly admitted defeat and dumped what remained of his own pie. 'Back in, apparently.'

'Wish they'd make their minds up . . .'

'Yeah.'

Ian stood up. 'Better get there before they go out of fashion again.'

After a short walk shivering in the sub-zero December air, Darren and Ian found themselves basking in the tropical Seventies. Liveliness abounded, and cheesy music encouraged otherwise reserved Mancunians to the dizzy release of substandard disco dancing. Men who should have known better threw themselves around the place with gay abandon, whilst abandoned gays threw themselves around trying to find men to get to know better. The place was indeed camp, and all the more fun for it. They were here to dance and laugh and enjoy themselves, without the inconvenience of failing to impress any girls. Darren went to the bar with £10 of Ian's money and brought back the necessary refreshment. Ian, meanwhile, was desperately trying to spell YMCA with his body, to the sounds of the Village People. He was intoxicated with a sudden loss of inhibition, and beckoned Darren to come over and join him on the dance floor. Darren declined while he finished his beer and made a start on Ian's. 'YMCA' gave way to 'Staying Alive'. Ian glanced over and smiled to himself. A tall, rough-looking man was chatting Darren up. Ian began to laugh a little under his breath, pointing to the ceiling and then the floor, shaking his hips and lip-synching that it was obvious by the way he walked that he was a woman's man, with little time to chat. Darren continued to converse with his new friend, their heads pressed tightly together due to the volume of the music. Ian wondered whether he should rescue him, but decided to stay on the dance floor and enjoy the spectacle from a safe distance. He twirled round, now announcing that you could also tell by the way he wore his hair, should a second opinion be needed, that he was a woman's man, again without much time on his hands. Ian had never realized before just how much of the decade the Bee Gees had devoted to announcing their heterosexuality. Maybe with hair-styles like that, he thought, smiling at a girl on the far side of the room, they had had some convincing to do.

Had Ian not been thinking about the Bee Gees and singing, and had the music not been so loud, he might have been able to hear the actual conversation Darren was having.

'Hi. I'm Leigh,' the man said, introducing himself.

'Hi. Darren.'

'So, is your friend in the green top available?'

Darren took a deep swig of Ian's drink and considered the question. Judging by his dancing, he was very available and likely to remain that way. 'Yes,' he said.

'And you two . . . are you together?'

'No. We're just friends.'

'So do you think I might be in with a chance?'

Darren smiled over at Ian. 'Oh yes. In fact he came here tonight specifically to meet someone like you.'

'Really?'

'Yes. But the thing about Ian is that he usually plays hard to get. He's like one of those fairground rides.'

'What do you mean?'

'You know – the louder he screams, the faster he wants it.'

'One of those, eh? Plenty of them here tonight. Try to make out they're straight, then it's all you can do to get rid of them once you've fucked them.'

'I know what you mean,' Darren answered, not entirely sure, but conjuring up some fairly interesting images.

Ian, meanwhile, was thoroughly enjoying himself. He was currently in the process of losing his heart to a Star Ship Trooper, an all too easy feat in those days. He glanced over to see how Darren was getting on, and watched with absolute delight as the large gay man bent forward and kissed him. This was fantastic. He couldn't wait to tell Karen.

Again, with more sensitive hearing and in a quieter room, Ian might have heard Darren's new friend say, 'Wish me luck then, Darren.'

'Good luck,' he obliged. 'And remember what I said – the louder he screams . . .'

Leigh thanked him and planted a gentle kiss on his cheek. Darren returned to the bar with what remained of Ian's money and waited in line to get another round in, which he hoped to drink on his own. Eventually refreshed, he had a wander through the club, which had a second, smaller room at the rear. He had a go at dancing, but quickly gave it up in the interest of hanging on to the small amount of credibility he had been born with. By the time he made it back to his spot next to the dance floor some twenty minutes later, a very pale and stricken Ian was eagerly anticipating his arrival.

'How's things?' Darren asked, handing him what remained of a pint of beer.

'We're leaving,' Ian shouted, ignoring the half-empty drink.

'I thought you were enjoying yourself.'

'Put your pint down.' Ian looked shaken. 'We're going. Now.'

'What's wrong?'

'This place . . .' Ian said, unable to describe his ordeal. 'This place . . .'

'What about it?'

'I'll tell you what about it,' he stammered, glancing nervously around the room, and paying particular attention to the area immediately to his rear. 'Those fucking toilets . . .'

'What? No paper?'

'There was plenty of paper all right. And one fucking huge homosexual man assuring me that he knew my type, trying to push me into a fucking cubicle.'

'Yeah? And what happened?'

'He wouldn't take no for an answer. In fact, it only encouraged him.' Ian changed his mind and swallowed some medicinal beer, his hands shaking. 'I was lucky to get out with my trousers on. Christ knows, he had his down.'

'Really?' Darren asked, barely able to contain his glee.

'And not just his fucking trousers.'

'You don't think maybe you were leading him on a bit?'

'What?'

'Well, maybe you caught his eye on the dance floor?'

Ian stared murderously at Darren. 'I was *not* leading

him on. No fucking way. I've got another theory. Someone must have spiked his drink with Viagra – it was the same randy bastard who was chatting you up earlier.'

'Well, if you say so.'

'Yes I do say so.'

Although Darren was all for lingering awhile in the club, Ian was desperate for the toilets and there was no way, and he stated this on several occasions, that he was ever visiting the gents there again. Darren swallowed his drink as slowly as he could manage, before Ian eventually grabbed his arm and marched him towards the exit. Arm in arm and on the way out, they once again encountered Leigh, who was chatting to another man.

'Not so fussy now, are we, luv?' he shouted at Ian as they passed. Ian swore and walked outside into the frigid air, as side-on to his would-be lover as he could manage without actually side-stepping.

'This didn't happen in the Eighties,' he spat, heading for a taxi, while Darren did everything in his power to contain his delight. Besides, he was in a hurry to get home and tell Karen all about their evening. This was payback indeed.

Giant Steps

Catch 21 was less than two months away, bank panic was already in the air, and a slightly thinner James was buggered if he wouldn't be cashing in on it. Of course, it was possible that the panic was entirely unfounded, but the threat of financial chaos was still palpable, and was therefore still lucrative. And with a Porsche Boxster, whose acceleration was matched only by its depreciation, as well as a fake Tudor mansionette, which drained money from his bank account like a broken water main, James couldn't afford to remain unemployed indefinitely. Praying that news of his irregular programming methods hadn't spread too far, he once again set himself up as a contractor and went looking for very gainful employment. By the end of the week, which cost him, he calculated, £490 in mortgage payments and £180 in car devaluation, he had been offered a rolling one-month contract at the only other decently paying computer workplace in Birmingham – Intron. The money wasn't too bad, and, rather fatally, had an in-built incentive scheme. The more computers he fixed, the more money he made. At first, James valiantly battled the temptation to warp machines back to 1972. For three weeks, he loaded and unloaded software, checked program integrity, inspected systems, read guidelines, followed procedures and nearly died of underpay. He was, he reckoned, only on course for a frankly unsatisfactory £45,000 per annum.

This was no good. He had become accustomed to a certain standard of living. To step back from this would be like getting out of a warm bath and into a cold one filled with something unpleasant. James figured that if he simply turned one machine a day back to the heydays of tie-dyed flares and dangerous footwear, he could just about scrape by. Two machines a day, however, and he could live a little. Three and maybe he could trade the Boxster in for something Italian and even less sensible. By the end of the next week, therefore, James was corrupting four machines a day, dreaming of second-hand Ferraris and living, once more, like a king.

But before James had been allowed to work unsupervised, he had first been forced to serve a week's probation, with every move scrutinized by an assigned co-worker. This was Intron's scheme for ensuring their contractors knew what they were doing. Intron, after all, was an important company, with responsibility for the programs which ran components of the stock market. They couldn't afford to employ any old idiot, although clearly they had managed to employ a few. James's co-worker was called Archie. Whilst no idiot, James found him intensely annoying, and dull even by the rigid standards of tedium usual for computer programmers.

Archie had a bee in his bonnet about something. What that something was, James never discovered, but he was willing to bet it wasn't anything of any major interest. Archie made his first week a distressing affair, with only the thought of imminent pay-dirt to keep him from manslaughter. Added to the tedium of his company, Archie had some fairly distressing personal habits. He appeared to be collecting something, and something unpleasant at that. James had tried to pin it down, but progressed no further than a series of envelopes with uninviting descriptions. It was some time before he had managed to discover just what he was doing. Archie, he eventually concluded, was collecting himself. There was no other explanation for it. Many people collect things, Archie just seemed to have taken the idea a bit further. Besides, as James saw it, collecting yourself had several advantages over amassing beer mats, stamps or fag packets. For a start, and close to James's heart, the raw material was free, and easy to come by. Also, you weren't going to get bogged down in the company of similar people who wanted to trade a missing month of ear wax for an excess of navel fluff. There was a strong sense of self-sufficiency as well. Everything you accumulated had been made by yourself, one way or another. And, finally, there was always the chance that, given a lifetime's dedication, you could actually end up with a collection of ex-bits of you that outweighed the living bits of you. Technically, you would be more dead than alive, which was difficult to achieve with many other hobbies, except maybe bus-spotting.

The probationary period soon passed, and then Archie took a fortnight off, leaving James free to pursue his own agenda away from Mr Nylon's one-man mission to collect himself. Something, however, continued to undermine James. An idea expressed by a former colleague. Spartech's Darren White had told him that networks would be the real losers in his get-rich-quick scheme. Individual computers would be fine. It was just when a series of them were hooked up and got to talking with each other that problems would arise. Should one of them steadfastly believe it to be the start of 2001, and not the beginning of another flowery year in the early Seventies, all hell would break loose. A dissenter in the midst would spark an uprising of the sort that could only be crushed by vigorous unplugging. He either had to ensure all computers were similarly doctored, or none. The latter, for extravagant lifestyle reasons, was not an option. The former was impossible. There had to be a compromise. In the meantime, James proceeded to cash in regardless. And then, in the midst of a mild panic over the disorder which lay ahead, he had an idea. Why not set the *programs* back to 1972 as well. Although slightly more tedious, it would enable his *Back to the Future* machines to communicate harmoniously with each other, with the added advantage that a few of them might actually survive into February. If the programs themselves believed it to be 1972, then who were the machines to argue? So James, who was not accustomed to writing code, wrote some code, and loaded it on all the computers he warped back in time. As he proceeded to reverse the inevitable progress of the company, he did so with new-found enthusiasm. After all, a giant step backwards for mankind was a giant step towards a new Ferrari for James Birch.

A Man Could Lose Himself in London

I couldn't stay in Manchester for ever. It also didn't make any sense to stay with Darren and his rhyming girlfriend for much longer. The weekend was over, the place was a mess and I was, I noticed, beginning to annoy them. Dangerously early on Monday morning, before Darren got up for work and Karen went out shopping with my money, I picked through their video collection and came up with *Billy Liar*. A character who lived a parallel existence free from the inconveniences of reality. 'A man could lose himself in London. Lose himself. Lose himself in London,' Billy recited. After the film, I quietly gathered up my possessions, which now fitted inside a single suitcase with plenty of room to spare. In fact, my case was growing so thin that charities were thinking about launching an appeal. Save the Luggage 2000. All proceeds go to fattening up Ian Gillick's baggage and giving it a decent life by the sea. I picked the case up and headed for the door, and soon flagged a taxi down. We trundled towards Piccadilly, and I bade another city farewell.

It wasn't that I wanted to lose myself in London, however. Rather, I wanted to find something. And I also needed time out from being pursued by Brummie gangsters, so that I might actually be able to think of a new strategy to save my ever threatened lifestyle. Three and a half hours later, I was in another faceless hotel room, near Euston station. After a small amount of unpacking and pacing about, I flopped onto the bed, lifted the receiver out of its cradle and wedged it between shoulder and ear, all the time watching myself in the wardrobe mirror. The dial tone gnawed away impatiently at the seconds of my prevarication. In films, the thing to do would be to dial the number and then remain stubbornly mute as the call was answered. I should draw erratically on a cigarette and sigh a terse smoky breath as the voice said Hello? Is there anyone there? If you don't answer I'm hanging up . . . I should shake my head and replace the receiver, the pain of hearing the other voice choking my words. I continued to watch my face, trying to picture myself in a film or soap opera, on the perpetual verge of making that one important call to that one important person. Pushing my finger onto the small rectangular button which served to cut the connection, I saw that my face was flushed. I fingered the piece of paper I had carried with me since the day I left England. In real life you don't get multiple chances and endless coincidences. In real life, you get one go, if you're lucky, and that's your lot. You cannot blow it again and again. Which was, effectively, what I had managed to do over the last few years.

I replaced the receiver, walked over to the wardrobe and opened it slightly. Sitting back on the bed, no longer observing my reflected spinelessness, I tried to gather some composure. Suitably calm, I finally dialled the number and let it ring. And ring. And ring. Eventually a male voice answered.

'I'm listening.'

I was intrigued and had a go at a suitable answer. 'I'm talking,' I said.

'I'm listening,' the voice repeated impatiently.

'Who is this?'

'Who do you want it to be?' the voice questioned.

If this was some sort of clever word game I could see that I was going to lose. 'Sue,' I answered.

'Just Sue?'

'Yes. Just Sue,' I repeated.

'Not on my list,' the man said, and put the phone down. I sat and stared blankly at the receiver for a second before having another go. This time I dialled each digit of the number carefully and in slow succession. The phone was answered more promptly.

'I'm listening.'

'Look,' I said, 'is Sue there?'

'I don't have a Sue. Sue is not on my list.'

'What list?'

'The list.'

'Can you help me out?'

'I'm listening.'

'I want to contact Sue.'

'I said I don't have a Sue.' Again, the line went quiet.

I sat and fingered the crumpled sheet of paper. Usually, I would have been annoyed by such a deficiency of telephone manners. Now, though, I was intrigued. A list of names? Curiosity helped me dial again and sparked some confidence. 'No Sue?' I asked with forced hopefulness.

'That's what I said.'

'Who do you have then?'

'Who do you want?'

'Anyone.'

'Look, the only ones here at the moment are Marge, Charlotte, Helen, Roxanne and Astrid.'

'Astrid?'

'Yeah. You want Astrid?'

'What's she like?'

'Pure as the driven. Where are you?'

'A hotel in Euston. Why? Do you deliver?'

'Yeah. Cost you, though.'

'How much?'

'Double.'

'When?'

'Give me your address.'

'Look, are you sure you don't know where I can find Sue?'

'No. Do you want Astrid or not?'

It was time to make Hotel Life a whole lot more interesting. Especially for the people in the room opposite. 'Yeah. It's the Euston Ibis, room . . .' I stretched the phone cable to the door and squinted through the spy hole. '124. Anyway, how much is it going to cost?'

'Depends how many minutes you want.'

'Dunno. Ninety?'

'You sure?'

'Yes.'

'Right. Be with you in an hour. Sort the money later.'

'Right. Bye.'

'Bye.'

I extracted a miniature can from the minibar and shuffled a chair over to the door, where I could monitor the corridor from the safety of my room. Sue was once again consigned to a guilty feeling that I washed down with beer.

I nosed around the room, turning lights on and off in order, until I had explored them all. Then I investigated the trouser press, which was, as far as I had ever been able to discern, a kind of vertical sandwich toaster for pants, which no-one ever used. Who wanted toasted trousers anyway, I wondered? Next, I extracted all of the minibar's contents and calculated a grand total for its consumption. A suicidal £214.70. Street value about £2.50. The bathroom had escaped my scrutiny, and I endeavoured to put this right. The contents amounted to one mini-frisbee bar of soap, purportedly French but manufactured under licence in Smethwick (London, Paris, Smethwick), one sachet of shampoo and one of conditioner, a hair net, should you wish to keep your hair dry whilst you showered, which seemed to defeat the object, and absolutely no toothpaste. Not that this was unusual. Sewing kits, pillow chocolates, envelopes and fucking hair nets, but never any toothpaste. Long-term hotel use was just asking for dental trouble. What hotels had against toothpaste was a mystery. Everybody who has teeth cleans them at some stage or other, but very few people sit in hotel rooms effecting emergency sewing repairs or toasting trousers. Toiletries aside, there were seven towels, stacked in ascending order of surface area, beginning with face cloths, stretching to two of modest size, a rougher-feeling bath mat, and ending with a pair of reasonable-sized pieces of fabric that you could just about dry your halitosis-ridden body with in an emergency. Eventually bored with the bathroom, I carefully replaced all of the minibar's valuable items, and decided I now knew enough about my room to be happy.

I looked at my watch. I had wasted enough time and so walked over to the chair and listened for interesting noises. Ten or so minutes later there was a knock outside. I stood up and peeped through the spy hole. A chubby, scruffy motorcycle courier glanced impatiently up and down the corridor. He certainly didn't look much like an Astrid, and I thanked my lucky stars that I hadn't arranged to spend ninety minutes of my time locked in a room with him. The door to 124 opened and the courier produced a small envelope from his shoulder bag, which was thrust through the aperture. It was difficult to see the occupant's reaction from my vantage point behind the shoulder of the courier, but it didn't appear particularly forthcoming. In fact, as the courier demanded 450 quid, cash, Room 124 became considerably less welcoming, and the courier considerably less patient. A small row began to surface and I listened intently.

'Look, here's the fucking Astrid, just give me the money.'

'Astrid? What do you mean Astrid? I tell you I have no idea . . .'

'Come on, don't mess me around. Tell you what I'll do. Four twenty-five, but that's it. You take the Astrid and I'll leave politely.'

I tried to fathom it out. Certainly, from the appearance of the package, if Astrid was a woman, she was a little on the thin, dwarfish side for my liking. And for a small lady, Astrid was also very expensive.

'Please, take whatever is in the package and leave me alone,' Room 124 tried again.

'You wanted Astrid, I've brought it to you. I won't tell you again. I want the money.'

'But what *is* Astrid?'

'Astrid. You know, acid. Or maybe you're not getting the lingo. Maybe you want Helen?'

'Helen?'

'Smack. Heroin. Or something harder? Some Roxanne? You know, rocks, man.'

The penny dropped on both sides of the corridor. Room 124 thrust the package back at the courier and slammed the door. I watched him shake his head and swear, before replacing the envelope in his bag and mooching back towards reception. I wondered what the others might have been. Marge. Marijuana? Charlotte. Charley, maybe. But Sue had seemed to register a reaction. Sue. I began to wonder what sort of drug Sue might be. In my not so recent experience, a rare, addictive and wonderful one which I could never seem to quite lay my hands on. I picked up the telephone again. She had to be out there somewhere.

Spy Hole

Reading is one thing, Archie shrugged, but doing is quite another. Having spent several nights learning and relearning the *Reader's Digest Book of Decorating*, he had felt reasonably confident of transferring words into wallpaper. However, he was forced to concede that the book must be wrong. Wallpapering was simply not possible. It was like flight, or filling out tax returns or some other such allegedly achievable goal. The physics of the situation just weren't right. And, Archie said to himself with some satisfaction, you cannae change the laws of physics. The first few days had been OK. He had drilled a perfectly satisfactory hole in the front door and installed a security feature, although there had been, in all fairness, a slight debate about the actual merit of said feature. But he had just been doing his job. Install it backwards, Jeremy had advised. Nobody will notice and spying in will be easier. This had turned out to be patently untrue, and Archie had been forced to fit it correctly. A couple of skirting boards had been painted without too much mutilation of the carpet, a door had been sanded without any obvious structural damage, aside from a deep gouge which he had disguised with an uneven lump of Polyfilla, and an area of plastering had been effected, which admittedly wasn't still plastered, due to the fact that most of the stuff had slipped down to the floor soon after its application. Jeremy and Brian were paying the actual decorators a healthy sum to allow Archie to do the job, so he wasn't too concerned about the lack of progress he was making. Until, that is, he had come to the wallpapering. As, for around the twentieth time, he held a sodden strip of paper to the surface of a wall which remained unwilling to get to know it intimately, Archie felt his patience wane. He screwed up the paper and threw it to the floor, where it suddenly seemed to get quite a liking for sticking to things, and refused to leave the company of the carpet for several minutes. Darren came into the room and, catching sight of Archie losing a wrestling match with a length of wallpaper, scratched his scalp irritably.

'Used the right key, then?' Darren asked him. Archie *had* used the right key to let himself in. Obviously. If he had used the wrong one, he would still be outside. As far as he was concerned, Darren had asked and answered his own question and there was therefore no need to reply. Had he been in a less awkward situation than actively spying on someone in their own home, he would have pointed this out. In the absence of an answer, Darren nosed around for a couple of minutes before calling up to Karen, who appeared in a long T-shirt and socks. Archie averted his eyes, unused to seeing females in so few items of clothing, particularly on Monday mornings. 'He's gone,' he said to his girlfriend.

'Where?'

'London. There's a note.'

'What does it say?'

'Gone to London. Be in touch. Ian.'

Archie pricked up his ears. At last, mention of Gillick. London. So he had been here in this very house, maybe over the weekend and he had missed him. He attempted to swear. 'Fudge.'

Karen glanced at Archie with an expression of both curiosity and menace, and then back at her boyfriend. 'You'll be late. It's nearly ten.'

'It is impossible to be late for academia.'

'I thought you told me that science waits for no man.'

'Well, it'll have to wait for me,' he said, carefully opening a kitchen cupboard which was clinging precariously to the wall. 'I haven't had my Shreddies yet. Anyway, what time does your shift start?'

'Not 'til twelve.'

'And you call *me* a slacker.'

'I'll call you a lot worse if you don't get a move on.'

Archie mumbled something and went outside while Darren fixed some breakfast. He took a mobile phone from his pocket and dialled Jeremy. 'Jeremy? It's Archie. White's house, Manchester. Look, Ian's been here and gone over the weekend. London, by the sounds of things. No, I didn't get the chance. What, now? But I've got to finish the decorating – I'm fitting a kitchen today and – I had to go back to Birmingham on Friday. It's not my fault. There's no need to swear. You didn't say I had to be here at the weekend. No, I don't do that to my mother. Or to farmyard animals for that matter.' Archie held the phone away from his ear and found the button to switch it off. For a man with such a genteel name, Jeremy certainly had a foul mouth.

If My Life was a Film

Sue was standing almost within touching distance and hadn't seen me yet. Her eyes darted around the gloom, and a couple of men stared back at her. She took a self-conscious step towards the bar and ran her hand along its lacquered surface. A barman raised his head in her direction and asked her what she wanted. I mouthed the words 'Pernod and black' as Sue said, 'Gin and tonic.' Taking her glass, she turned round, a little unsure. She appeared very uncomfortable. I decided to put her out of her misery, and waved. There was a moment of hesitation which made me suspect that I had changed in her eyes, before she walked over to my table.

'Not drinking the cough medicine any more then?'

'I'm not doing a lot of things any more.' She sat down and crossed her legs, which I took as a bad sign. 'In particular,' she said, 'not drinking in places like this.'

'Why? What's wrong with it?'

Sue swirled the ice and lemon of her drink. 'Well, for a start, it's a singles bar.'

'You're joking!'

'Do I look like I am?'

In fairness, she didn't. In fact, she didn't look happy at all. 'No. So what else aren't you doing any more?'

Sue sighed. 'I just mean I'm different now. I was

thinking about this on the tube. Talking to you on the phone yesterday was like talking to my past.'

'Cheers.'

'No, I mean I felt like I was a new person, and that you hadn't changed at all.'

'Suppose not,' I said for the sake of no argument. Even if you do change, the chances are that no-one will notice unless it's to their advantage to do so. 'But anyway, I wanted to see you to get a few things cleared up.'

'I don't really see what else there is to say.'

'Well, sorry, for a start.'

She took a swig from her glass, tipping her head back and maintaining eye contact, giving the deliberate impression that she was looking down her nose at me. 'Sorry?'

'Yes . . .'

'Sorry for the fact that I waited round for a year for you to call me from France? Sorry that when you did at last invite me over, you never even showed at the airport and I had to spend a miserable two days in Nice alone with my luggage, before flying back on my own? Sorry because you then waited six weeks before ringing me from America to let me know what had happened? Which, incidentally, I still don't believe. Or sorry because after failing to get in touch for almost a year you are now once again bothering me?'

This wasn't going quite as well as I'd hoped. 'Yes,' I mumbled. 'All of them.'

'Really, if you hadn't sounded so desperate on the phone, I wouldn't be here. And I'm not really happy about you ringing my parents to get my new number.' They hadn't been particularly happy either. She took another down-the-nose sip. 'So what have you got to tell me that's so important?'

It had all been crystal clear at the time, but now didn't seem quite so sorted. I had had the semblance of a speech lined up, with a humble beginning, an enticing middle and an overwhelming end. I was going to convince her that, finally, we should be together. 'That we should . . .' My patter was suffering stage fright in the glare of Sue's eyes. 'I mean things have been a bit fucked up, you know . . .'

'No. I don't know.'

'And I just thought that now I was back for good, maybe we could, as you're not seeing anyone, get together occasionally.'

'Why?'

'To have some fun.'

'With you?' she snorted. 'Now that is funny.' I hadn't expected this to be easy, but I also hadn't anticipated being savaged. Things didn't appear to be improving and so I kept quiet for a minute, which allowed her to start again. 'So you want us to get together, and you arrange to meet me in a singles bar?'

'I didn't realize. Honest. It just looked like a decent place for a drink. I don't really know London.'

We sat in silence again for a while, not quite looking at each other. Sue lit a cigarette and asked, 'So where are you living?'

In a hotel, I told her. To avoid washing up? she asked. Mainly, I said. And do they serve your special breakfast every morning and the same evening meal every night? I replied that I wished they did. And do you wake up at the same time and get home at the same time each day? Sort of, I nodded. Wear black socks on Monday, blue on Tuesdays . . . Sometimes, I said. During our time together, I had developed a clockwork existence of well-oiled routines, which gave me the advantage of being able to live with my eyes almost closed. Sue hadn't been quite as enthusiastic about my system. In fact, my pre-planned behaviours had encouraged her to spontaneously leave me one day. Shopping on Saturday, the same items every week? she continued. There seemed little point in fighting. I just lay down and endured the beating I figured she owed me. She was slowly shaking her head. 'What was it you used to say, Ian? Routines make life go faster. That was it. But that was the great irony – you were so stuck in your ways you could hardly move.'

'And you're not stuck in your ways?' I retaliated, having taken sufficient stick. 'Working nine to five, panicking five to eleven, sleeping eleven to seven? An extra two hours in bed at the weekend, hanging out with your dizzy friends, endlessly shopping and taking things back? Come on, your life is hardly a riot of impromptu activity.'

'Isn't it?' she asked.

I ventured that no, it probably wasn't.

Sue finished her drink and glanced around the bar, as restless as the remaining ice.

'Another?' I asked, almost desperately.

'Better not,' she said, stubbing her fag out. 'Look, Ian, I think I'd better be off. I'll ring you sometime.' She had a miserable attempt at a smile, stood up and left. We both knew full well that she didn't have my phone number.

Luckily, all was not lost. Everything was still going to be OK. I had a back-up plan for just such an emergency. Five pints and a club would get things sorted.

Around beer four, my mood declined further, however. There was a TV screen in the corner of the bar showing what appeared to be a romantic film, something like *Truly Badly Weepy*. I tried to ignore it but the film sucked me in. As I watched, I began to grow bitter that things could have been so different if only my life was a film. I would bump into her repeatedly, having botched chance after botched chance to make something happen. Instead, I knew I wouldn't see her. If my life was a film, I would have started out despising the girl, and ended up loving her. Instead, I rather liked her from the outset. If my life was a film, every feeling I had would be echoed by an ever-present orchestra. Instead, the jukebox was playing something shite. If my life was a film, we would be toasting our champagne future together as credits flowed over us. Instead, I finished my fourth beer and let the numbness flow though my veins. If my life was a film, it would be over by now. Instead, I found myself wishing it was.

And then the director smiled on me and offered me a co-star.

Spank

The only route out was annihilation. I needed to waste a large sum of money listening to music I didn't like and drinking beer I couldn't taste. I needed to experience that curious sense of freedom which comes from dancing in front of strangers when you are too pissed to feel self-conscious. I needed noise and lights and people. In short, it was nightclub time. The venue was underground, not in an exciting clandestine way, but in a subterraneanly sweaty manner. The singles bar had been littered with gaudy flyers for clubs with suggestive names, and I had picked the gaudiest and most suggestive from the pack. And here I was at Club Spank, leaning unsteadily against the bar, getting in the way of fellow drinkers, clinging to the very structure that was undermining any remaining co-ordination, and completely failing to get spanked at all. The music was crap – it seemed on reflection to be some sort of student night – but this was good. I wasn't here to enjoy myself. At the very least, I was hoping for a protracted bout of sickness. The trouble was, upset though Sue's rejection had made me, I realized I wasn't as emotional about it as I might have liked. I wanted to feel worse. At least after several rounds of vomiting and with a bugger of a hangover, I would be a bit more distressed.

I ordered another pint of mock Tetleys and noticed that without sustained concentration, my vision was deteriorating. Another good sign for reasonably imminent pain. I glanced slowly up from the depths of my drink to be greeted by an inquisitive smile. Tetley Vision allowed me only to focus on a small part of her face at a time, as if the whole picture was too much to take in at one go. Eyes were shining, mouth was grinning, teeth were glistening, and nose was nosing. I was no expert, but I think she was interested in me. I straightened slightly and felt an unwelcome surge of sobriety.

She stepped forward and stood close to me at the bar. I consumed greedy lungfuls of her perfume. This was a golden opportunity which would take some blowing, even with my track record. Given a lifetime's practice, though, I considered myself more than up to the challenge. I thought about a lucky mouthful of beer but decided against it. Any more Dutch courage and I would be sticking my finger in dykes. Not that the idea didn't appeal, but this didn't seem like that sort of club. I half glanced at her, keen to appear neither single nor lecherous nor both. Desperation, bitter experience had proved, could be detected by females at distances of up to several miles. She was inches rather than feet away. Maybe my desperation was too close for detection, like flying below radar levels.

All I had to do was say something. It was that easy. A life spent opening my mouth for voluminous guff to utter forth, and I was having difficulty saying the single word I wanted to say.

'Hello.'

She had beaten me to it. 'Hi,' I said, as soberly as six pints would allow. More a sort of Hiaaaaaii. I turned to face her and smiled. Now all I needed were a few hours of conversation.

She smiled back. 'Hi.'

Come on. Anything. Any old rubbish just to get the ball rolling. I took the plunge with a chat-up line which would have made adolescent attempts seem debonair. 'Is it me or is it loud in here?'

'It's you.'

'You don't think it's loud?'

'Not especially.'

'Oh.' Maybe something a little less rubbish. 'Ian, by the way,' I told her, offering my hand. She smiled and her face lit up. More accurately, she smiled and a disco light caught her features full on. Either way, she was shimmering. As I took in her cropped auburn hair and warm grey eyes, I decided I might be in with a chance.

'Helen,' she said, refusing my sweaty palm and grinning in the stroboscopic lights.

I liked Helen. There was something remote about her. I soon discovered what. It was her boyfriend. He travelled a lot and was abroad at least half of the time. Helen, it appeared, required someone altogether more local to fill in whilst he was away. I put myself forward for the job. After Spank we returned to her flat where I spent half the night urinating. It must have impressed her, because she wanted to see me again, particularly as her boyfriend wasn't around much for a while. During most of December we had a very cosy arrangement which saved me considerably on hotel bills and took my mind away from the imminent loss of my livelihood. As we continued our on/off relationship of mutual convenience, however, I became less and less interested in Helen, and increasingly obsessed with the man in whose bed I was sleeping.

High Infidelity

While I nose around the flat checking out your knick-knacks, books, records and gadgets, I once again find myself thinking about you. Helen is talking to you on the phone and I am under strict orders to be deadly quiet. When she puts the phone down and you start your journey back to her, I will be by her side. While you check schedules and calculate the hours until you are in her arms, I will be in her arms, working out whether we should make love again. But don't get the wrong idea. We are both looking forward to your return. I will be able to go to a hotel and spend a day or two on my own. Your girlfriend will be able to resume her cosy existence with her live-in lover. Things will return to normal, or thereabouts. Until you go away again. She knows I only want her when you are not here, and I know that she only wants me when she cannot have you. We are both happy with this arrangement. And it *is* an arrangement, as cold as reality, a date written discreetly in her diary, something cryptic like 'All day conference', a commitment to fulfil, an obligation to meet. So, as you ring from the station or airport and your voice limps out of the speakerphone, saying just six more hours, six more hours, and I will be yours, remember that I am sitting quietly next to her stroking her hair, listening to the tannoy in the background, the people rushing past you, the general sounds of imminent departure, thinking about the near desperation in your voice, seeing the cool middle distance in your girlfriend's eyes as she tells you that she too will be counting the hours, knowing that she will instead be counting the hours that she can spend with me.

Sometimes we lie in your bed and discuss the chance that you will come home unexpectedly early. We make a game of it, trying to decide what she would say, where I would hide, how she would get you out of the way while I escape. She tells me that you will never come home early, never do the unexpected, and that is what she likes about you. All the same, when you're not here, we like to imagine that you are the impulsive, spontaneous sort and that there is a distinct possibility you will catch us. Lovers need things like this to talk about. That's why dining out was invented. Meals come served with their own conversation. Do you want to try some of mine? The service is good here, don't you think? The crockery, a bit on the twee side for my taste. White or red? If a couple can't think of a decent stretch of conversation while they enjoy a meal, there really isn't much hope for them. If a meal fails, the final bastion is the cinema. Truly, this can paper over a couple of hours of otherwise silent frustration. But meals and films pale into insignificance compared with the conversational possibilities garnered by the unexpected return of a jealous lover. What makes this even more exciting is that the closer we get to your return, the more sex we have. It is last throes stuff, admittedly, and wonderful at that. You only have to return say an hour early one day, and we are in with some fairly interesting scenarios. I don't know, maybe you've wondered why our girlfriend never leads you straight upstairs when you return, eager to renew her acquaintance with the body which has deserted her for a week. The reason is that the bed is still warm. Probably, she says that she wants to be sure of you first, to get to know you again, just to hold you for a while. This may be true, but there are truths and then there are truths.

There is a much more fundamental reason that I'm interested in you, though. Once again I seem to have crawled inside someone else's skin. First Marcelo, then Archie, followed by Darren and now you. I have found a new host organism, and this time without really trying. It is almost becoming natural for me to burrow my way under the surface of someone else. I feel as if I'm eating you from the inside, breathing your air, invading your living space, even, at times, penetrating your girlfriend. I am occupying your life, abusing everything you try to keep precious, and all for my own selfish needs.

And one day I woke up in your bed and realized that I had had enough of being a parasite. Ultimately, if you steal enough identities, you lose your own. I bade farewell to your girlfriend. It was time to move on, time to make amends, time to encourage the real Ian Gillick to step forward into the spotlight.

Crap Expectations

The house was fine. I admired the décor. In fact, it was more than fine. It was positively opulent compared to its former glory. They might as well have pasted £10 notes to the walls for all the money it had cost me. Despite this, I had bought them a couple of peace-making presents. For Darren, a posh suitcase to replace his stolen one, and for Karen a series of executive stress toys to take her mind off the general public. Both seemed relatively appeased, and generally happy and together in their newly refurbished home.

New Year's Eve 2000 was an important night. Tonight I was rich, and tomorrow I would be poor. I was early and nervous, in a large party full of strangers. More people arrived in dribs and drabs, a fair cross-section ranging from the almost nerdy to the firmly nerdy, with the occasional nutter thrown in for good luck. One of the latter sub-type told me that his name was Sam. He didn't really introduce himself so much as come over and tell me he liked my jumper. Jumble sale? he asked as an opening gambit, pointing at the top I was wearing. Diesel, I told him. Same thing, he said. Darren joined us, and began to quiz Sam about his love life. I watched the two friends, occasionally glancing around the room, wishing that I had a love life worth discussing.

'So I'm thinking of settling down,' Sam said.

'Why?' Darren asked, looking a little taken aback.

'Well, you know, I'm getting on a bit. Mind, I've had a fair innings. Started with Amy, an A, worked my way all through the alphabet to Z, and now here I am back at Alison. Seems to make sense to stop there.'

Darren still appeared sceptical. 'Hang on. Who was the Z?'

'Zoe.'

'Oh yeah, I remember. Short girl with thick glasses. What about the Q?'

'There wasn't one.'

'The I?'

'I didn't say *every* letter of the alphabet.'

A reasonably attractive female entered the room and quickly left again. Darren continued to quiz Sam, whose resolution was seriously wavering.

'OK. What about U?' he asked.

'Look, there was no U. Just—'

'O?'

'OK, maybe not so many of the vowels.'

'So you stuck mainly to the consonants?'

'I guess.'

'What about X?'

'No,' Sam was forced to concede. The battle over his virility was beginning to swing Darren's way. I began to take more interest in the proceedings.

'V?'

'Come on, how many female names start with V?'

'Vera. Veronica. Vicky. To name but three.'

'OK, OK. But you're deliberately sticking to the obscure consonants.'

'Right, we'll go through the regular ones. B?'

'Easy. Amy Brown.'

'What? You're counting surnames now?' Darren demanded, obviously sensing victory.

'I didn't say I wasn't.'

'You implied it.'

'Look, all I said was that I'd been from A to Z.'

'And with how many in between, exactly?'

Sam appeared to be counting. I finished my drink. 'A few,' he said eventually.

'Somewhat less than twenty-four, I'm guessing,' Darren countered.

'Maybe. But what about you then, stud-features?'

'Well, neglecting vowels, surnames and rare consonants, I'd say eight or nine.'

'So which one? Eight or nine?'

'Seven. And you? Honestly?'

Sam shrugged. 'About the same.'

'Hardly a whole language then,' Darren said after a couple of seconds. 'More a small spoonful of alphabetti spaghetti.'

Sam smiled, and I allowed myself another scan of the near-empty room. 'How's Karen?' he asked.

'Oh, fine. Still fed up with her job, though.'

'She should get herself sacked. Made a career out of it myself. Keeps me happy.' Darren went off to grab me a refill. Sam filled me in on the details. He had, he told me, been gifted with a spectacular inability to hold on to gainful employment, coupled with an equally impressive lack of ambition, and every single day that he slouched out of bed at eleven a.m., he thanked his lucky stars. Whilst others jumped up at 6:30 to perform laps, reps, and squat-thrusts, to consume bran flakes, OJ and coffee, to digest stock prices, mergers and takeovers, Sam would stir contentedly beneath his duvet. Sometimes he would set his alarm clock to normal people's breakfast time, just to enjoy the fact that he wouldn't be joining them. If he was feeling particularly adventurous, he would even get dressed and peer outside his window at the gloominess beyond, before slipping back into bed and gloating some more. Truly, Sam enthused, there are few greater or more thorough pleasures than lethargy in the midst of surrounding endeavour. I glanced at my watch. 11:53. Seven more minutes until financial collapse. Seven more minutes and I would be joining him in unemployed gloating.

Not How It Happened

And that was that. The same as any other. One enormously anticipated let-down, just like every previous New Year's Eve, though this year the countdown was like the disappearance of my income. Ten grand a month, nine grand, eight, seven . . . all the way to zero. But I cheered with everybody else. It's hard not to get carried along in the enthusiasm for the festivities, no matter how bad you know next year is going to be, or even how duff all your previous 31 Decembers have been. For of all the nights of the year, regardless of whether it spells the end of a very cosy lifestyle, New Year's Eve is destined to let you down. Never was this more true than for 31 December 1999, which was as bad as all the other ones, only more expensive. You know full well that the greater the expectation of an event, the greater the event has to be to meet those expectations. You effectively price yourself out of the market as far as having a good time goes. It can't just be an enjoyable night, it has to be fantastic. This is in stark contrast to the best nights out you actually have, which often start with the fatal words 'A quiet pint or two' and culminate with you sitting unconscious on the toilet in a curry house minus a couple of kidneys.

31 December 2000 was different, then. Whereas a change of the date often heralds an alcohol-fuelled bout of unrealistic optimism about the virgin twelve

months ahead, I knew that my year was already spoiled. I would have to find a job somewhere. Routines would have to be re-established. The endless cycle of going to work and resting from work would resume. I shivered. It wasn't just money or work, though. I felt as though I had lost. The previous three years had been a victory, an escape from the mundane, a holiday from normality. I swilled some flat champagne around my thin, white plastic cup and swallowed it. The bubbles had long since departed, leaving behind a bitter reminder of their good times.

I stumbled over to Darren and held the cup out for a refill. 'None left,' he said. 'Beer OK?' I nodded in silent defeat, the music drowning the need for further conversation, and swapped the cup for a bottle. It was once again time to move on. I wondered whether I might be able to slim things down to a single carry-on bag now. Such was the rate at which I was losing possessions, a suitcase seemed an extravagance. Someone passed me a spliff and I took a couple of drags. It was strong and I was out of practice. I sat down on the floor of the front room, with my back against a radiator, feeling the fuzziness of the drug mingle with the warmth of the heater. Next to me was a girl who was looking sorry for herself. I watched her out of the corner of one bloodshot eye. She was picking squares off a glitter ball which someone had stolen from a nightclub. I passed her the spliff and we began a heavy, stoned, dislocated conversation about our lives. As she continued to extract mirrored fragments from the surface of the globe, we disassembled our lives into short splintered paragraphs.

She told me her life was like Bremsstrahlung, the X-rays which passed through her body when she shielded herself inappropriately from radiation at work. Too much shielding, or the wrong type, and you do more damage than just standing in front of radioactivity and letting it do its worst, she said. In short,

Bremsstrahlung is making things worse for yourself by trying to make them better. It is suffering brought on by attempting to protect yourself from the world.

I told her that I am the ambitious man who is petrified of failure. I am the lover who is afraid of not receiving love. I am the party animal who can't bear to be alone. I am the generous man who holds grudges. I am the confident man slowly drowning in a murky sea of inferiority. I am all that I try not to be. I am everything that you don't see. I am an expert liar, an actor. I take what eats me from the inside and force it out of my sweaty pores as if I have conquered it. I joke about my weaknesses before others get the chance to notice them first. I live my inadequacies, possess them, own them, wear them. But I never beat them. I can only hope to appease them.

She told me that she had soaked up a little of each of her lovers on the way, so that she had become a melange of different people, never in her own company long enough to hear her own voice. And this worried her at times. She had wondered what it would be like to be alone and how perfect it would be to be independent, in the way that others wondered what it would be like to be held by someone. Now she was alone, and all she could think about was being surrounded by somebody.

I said that believing in things is like whistling a tune you've just heard and trying to keep the memory whilst all around you people play a multitude of different songs on different instruments. You desperately try to cling to that one tune in your head amongst the cacophony, and all the other songs seem much more catchy and inviting.

She said that the single worst thing about being human can be summarized by the phrase Familiarity Breeds Contempt. Familiarity Breeds Contempt means that in the rare instances you happen to stumble across a genuine pleasure in life – a person, an experience or an object – the chances are you'll be fed up with it before you've even had a chance to enjoy it. Everything gets taken for granted. The new becomes stale and then becomes old. The old is discarded in favour of a different new, which doesn't necessarily have to be any better, it just has to be different. But what if every time you did something you could live the same fear, the same trepidation, the same excitement that you felt the first time you did it? Now that would be living.

I told her that sometimes I feel as if I'm in a coma, and all the voices and music I hear are from anxious friends and relatives trying to wake me, trying to bring me back to my senses. I said that noises and voices drift into my semi-consciousness where they almost seem to mean something, all desperate to pull me out of my torpor.

She said a man hears what he wants to hear and disregards the rest.

I said you've stolen that from a song.

She said that she was just singing.

I said don't give up the day job. And then asked her what she did.

Scientist, she told me, a colleague of Darren's.

And what's your name? I asked finally.

Sarah, she said.

Ian, I told her when it was my turn.

Well, Happy New Year, Ian, she said.

Happy New Year, Sarah, I replied.

I kissed her on the cheek.

Obviously none of our conversation came out like this at all. It was, more than likely, a series of rambling paragraphs punctuated by a string of umming and ahhing that would have embarrassed a hippy, laden with gaps of silence which held for years, interrupted by frequent fits of giggling, occasional trips to the toilet and sporadically being fallen over by frivolous scientists who had got a bit carried away. However, I would like to remember the former version. And given the well documented ability of cannabis to erode short-term memory, I decided to recall it this way until I forgot all about it anyway.

In the morning, just as in the evening, I found it impossible not to get carried away with the prevailing spirit of the remaining people at the party. I grew sick of hearing the annual pronouncement of a New Dawn on 1 January, but still not sick enough to disagree. Things had changed, very real things, and, in turn, adjustments would have to be made. It was time to confront my past.

Parasites Lost

It wasn't as if I knew their address, more that I knew where I stood a chance of bumping into them. Indeed, one particular pub sprang to mind as a potentially suicidal venue for drinking: the Jug of Ale, where I first encountered the two nameless parasites who had been pursuing me all this time. I had no doubt they would still drink there. They weren't the sort of characters who got high on selecting a new wine bar to peruse each week. I had already spent a couple of days at my old house, frantically hoovering, turning lights on and off and generally trying to attract as much attention as possible to the fact that I was back in Birmingham. But they failed to take even the remotest interest. They had obviously given up monitoring my house for signs of life. I had to take a more active role. Originally, the idea had been to meet them on my own ground, like an easy home leg with psychological advantage, rather than a difficult away match in front of a hostile crowd. Whilst I didn't anticipate much in the way of violence, I would have more control in my own house. My nerve wouldn't hold for ever, though. If I was going to confront them I had to do it soon. For nostalgia's sake, I took the Number 11 Outer Circle bus.

The pub, much to my shock, had undergone refurbishment. Suddenly I was worried that they might have moved on, given this was no longer the type of establishment local hard men were particularly fond of. Evidently the Jug of Ale had been purchased lock, stock and beer barrel by the Wonking corporation, which specialized in transforming pubs with authentic character into pubs with mock authentic character, via the investment of huge sums of cash. The Wonking brewery also specialized in a succession of increasingly weak puns based around the vague similarity of its name to a swear word. Inside, you would be assaulted by Wonking bar staff, Wonking toilets, Wonking beer, Wonking peanuts and, given the brewery's propensity for attracting the kind of punter who found such things consistently funny, Wonking wonkers. Nowhere, however, were there any Wonking parasites. Students, yes. Psychopaths, no. Student psychopaths, maybe. I sat at an unoccupied table with a book and pint of Wonking ale, which really did taste as if someone had Wonked into it, and prepared myself for a long, hard day of drinking and reading.

By late afternoon, I noticed an odd shift in the balance of things. I was now pissing and sweating considerably more than I was drinking, which didn't seem right. Despite a consistent intake of fluid, I was draining away. The only way out of this insane logic would of course be to stop consuming large volumes of liquid, which didn't make a lot of sense. All in all, I had drunk myself into a dehydrated quandary, and it was surely only a matter of time before I came to resemble some wrinkly old bastard who had just finished a long soak in a bath of vinegar.

The pub emptied for tea and I was getting too pissed to read. The one remaining barmaid kept her eye on me. I didn't know what she was expecting me to do, apart from suddenly get up and desiccate in front of her eyes, so I kept on drinking. After a while, I stumbled for another piss, which brought my tally for the day up to eleven. Six pints, eleven pisses, two nervous dumps, two packets of crisps, a sandwich, three chapters, one premature hangover and absolutely no Wonking.

Back at the bar, I ordered an emergency pint of water. And then I saw them. They hadn't seen me, and they idled over to prop the bar up. I wondered whether this had been such a good idea. Even from a relative distance I could see the advantage of staying well away from them. But things had to be sorted, and I had to get on with this new chapter of my life. I took an unsteady lurch in their direction. Concentrate on appearing sober, I told myself, slurring the words. Both of them glanced towards me as I approached, and quickly returned their eyes to the direction of their pints. I leant against the bar, inches away. I was breathing their smoke, hearing their words. They continued to chat. A substantial period of time spent searching for me hadn't greatly honed their powers of observation.

'He's a soft shite. Couldn't even hang fucking wall-paper. One more complaint about that specky cunt from the boss of the decorators and I was going to have to lamp him.'

'Yeah.'

'*But, Jeremy, I read up on it in a book,*' the smaller of the duo said, in an imitation effeminate voice.

'Book,' the bigger one snorted.

'I mean, what's the fucking point? Two weeks pissing about, surrounded by Manc bastards, endless calls to my mobile like *Jeremy, what does "grouting" mean?* And *Jeremy, how do I get paint out of a carpet?* And *Jeremy, do you think Brian could give me a hand with some tiling?*'

'Tiling,' the larger of the two grumbled. 'Like I'd help that cunt do any fucking tiling.' I surmised, pissed though I was, that I had finally stumbled across my assailants' names.

'And then, just when I thought I'd heard the last of him, he calls to say Gillick has been and gone, and he missed the cunt.' I stiffened at the sound of my name. Up until now, it had been a cosy tale of ineffectual decorating. Now I was in the story. 'Blind bastard.'

I decided to point out the irony of slating someone else's myopia. 'And which cunt might that be?' I asked, stepping up to the pair and smiling.

And then everything goes slow motion, as if occurring in Beer Time.

They glance up and something registers. They exchange looks. 'Fuck me,' Jeremy announces. Brian steps forward and towers over me. He appears about to lunge. I am suddenly scared. An unconvincing version of sobriety kicks in. I brace myself. 'Bri,' Jeremy barks, and Brian takes a pace back. 'So, Ian fucking Gillick. What the fuck are you doing here?'

No punches have yet been thrown. I feel a little confidence return. 'I've come to straighten a couple of things out.'

'Yeah?'

'Look, there's no point in still trying to find me. There's no more money. We've both just been shafted by some changes going on in banking. All the code has been updated, when a new operating system was installed.'

'Meaning?'

'Just that certain things have happened. Ask Archie. Things there's no way of fixing. Christ knows I've been trying – that's why I'm back.'

'And why the fuck should we believe you?'

'Would I be here?'

'What about the rest of it?'

'Spent.'

'All of it?'

'All of it.' There is a sudden gleam of anger in Jeremy's eyes. He is in my face, and wants to hit me. It is time to play my trump card. I reach into my inside pocket and take out an envelope. 'All of it except this.

Here.' I pass it to him and he snatches the envelope, ripping it open.

'How much?'

'Twelve and a half. That's all there is. It's yours. And here,' I unfold a couple of cashpoint receipts just to prove there's no other money, 'my two bank accounts – just enough to get me to the end of the month.'

'And that's the fucking lot? That's what we've been running around for all this time? Twelve fucking grand?'

'Look, you kept your initial stake, the two hundred and fifty thousand, I didn't rip you off for that. It's not like you've actually *lost* money.'

Jeremy scans the receipts and jeers. 'We've wasted a fuckload of our hard-earned chasing you about. Flights to Nice, bribing decorators, you fucking name it. A lot of people were expecting to make a lot of money, and you cunted them. And not nice people like me and Bri. People who would be happier if you were dead. People who wouldn't take this piss-poor amount of money, which barely covers our fucking expenses, and just walk away.' He slots the money into an inside pocket. 'We're going to be watching you, Gillick. If you're fucking us about again, then maybe we'll call some of those people.' He drains his drink. 'You have been very, very fortunate.' He turns to leave. 'And if I was you I'd stay the fuck out of this boozer.' Brian swears at me, and they leave their cigarettes still smouldering and walk out. My plan has worked. The short-term gain has momentarily helped them forget their long-term grievance. I order a beer to celebrate.

User

I am a user. Everybody is a user. Everybody, one way or another, uses everybody else. We are all symbiotic to some degree. The same is true of animals, though in the animal world there are categories of use: mutualism, where both parties benefit; parasitism, where one party benefits and the other suffers; and commensalism, where both parties benefit and suffer at the same time. For humans, the lines are more blurred, though most human relationships owe a debt to the last, and many contain an element of all three. All in all, in the human world, I have known a fair number of mutualists, some decent commensalists, and an unhealthy number of parasites.

Into the commensalist category, I reluctantly placed Darren. I had been using him and he had been using me, and we both seemed to be doing equally badly. Now, though, I had no more use for him. I had climbed inside his skin and used him as a disguise. I was ready to relinquish our symbiotic relationship, and hoped that he was about to stop using me as well. There were, after all, no more of my wages to find their way into his bank account. Even Spartech would have cut the money supply by now.

As well as my symbiont, I had entertained a couple of parasites. Jeremy and Brian wanted to use me and then harm me, and I can't say that I blamed them particularly. But whereas the only feeling I had towards Darren was a mild irritation at his reckless spending of money I hadn't earned, my parasites inspired a plethora of symptoms, including a damp forehead, an erratic heart, suspicious eyes, ever-attentive ears and unreliable bowels. These two relationships served to illustrate the crucial difference between symbiosis and parasitism – parasites are only really happy when they know you are suffering. Symbionts, on the other hand, are only happy when they know you are both suffering. However, I had now got rid of my parasites as well. I was free from the constraints of dependency and exploitation. I was no longer a user and I no longer felt used.

I once had a dream about using. The room is NHS white – not bright and gleaming, but tired and shop-worn. A doctor sits opposite me, behind a messy desk. She is intelligent and proficient, and has seen my type before. 'So how long have you been a user, Mr Gillick?' she asks.

'As long as I can remember,' I tell her. 'Probably longer.'

'Can you recall a time when you weren't a user?'

'I think the times I can't recall are the times I was using the most.'

'And when would this have been?'

'Childhood.'

'Really?'

'Yes. Every child is a user.'

'Why do you think that is?'

'Nature. A child can't do much. A child needs to use.'

'Who would you use?'

'Parents, mainly. Other children sometimes.'

'When did your using start to get out of hand?'

'It is not out of hand.'

'But you fully accept that you're a user?'

'I am a controlled user.'

'Does that not strike you as a contradiction in terms?'

'No. I use and then I stop. It isn't a problem.'

'And yet you have come here.'

'Of my own free will. I can control my use but that doesn't mean I'm happy about it.'

'So what do you want me to do about it?'

'I want you to tell me that it is OK to use.'

'And if I can't?'

'Then I will walk away from here and continue using.'

'What form will this use take?'

'The usual. At work, at home and in play.'

'What will you hope to accomplish?'

'Simply dulling the pain of life.'

'How?'

'By using others to make life more easy for me.'

'And you think this is what everybody does?'

'Yes.'

'Then we are all being used to make everybody else happy, which makes us unhappy, and so we all use others to make ourselves happy. Is this not an endless, self-defeating circle?'

'Yes.'

'And you want me to tell you this is OK?'

'Now you're catching on.'

'But in doing so you will be using me.'

'Of course. I'm a user. That's what I do.'

'I would feel used.'

'That's the point. I would feel I had used you and would be happy that you condoned it.'

'That wouldn't cheer me up, though.'

'Maybe you should become a user, then.'

'I already am.'

'How?'

'I'm thinking of using you as an interesting case to present to colleagues.'

'You haven't asked my permission.'

'You wouldn't have found out.'

'People would be laughing at me.'

'Maybe. You wouldn't be aware of it, though.'
'So that makes it OK?'
'Yes. If I'm a user.'
'Well, I don't want to be used like this.'
'Users never do. They hate being used. That's why they're users in the first place.'
'So you think I'm a user because I hate being used?'
'No. I think you're a user because you're selfish.'
The dream faded and I woke up thirsty. Sue stirred. We were living together then. What's wrong? she asked. Thirsty, I said. Do you want some water? she yawned. Yes, I told her, if you don't mind. I listened to her stumble out of bed and down the stairs, and tried to get back to sleep. I had something to tell the doctor in my dream. Some people, it appears, are happy to be used, if only to shut you up.
Now, having lost both my parasites and my symbiont, I felt strangely uninvolved in the proceedings of life. I finished my pint and headed for the gents. To live is to be used. Unused and alone, my life blood might just as well drain away.

Pity

Blood drains away onto the floor. Chest is raw. Lungs crushed. One arm grazed and weak, the other throbbing at the wrist. Jeans open at the knee. Iron filing taste. Something small and hard. Spit it out into my palm. Part of a tooth. Try to stand, hand outstretched against the tiles. Rub my index finger in the gap between my teeth. Things not right. Finger catches on jagged ridges. Straighten and look in the mirror. My mouth is red. Teeth like I've been sucking disclosure tablets and catching bullets. Grimace. Top two incisors are chipped. Have lost a quarter of one, half of the other.

Someone comes in to piss. I stare into the tiles. Porcelain and enamel. Long, slow blinks. The man leaves. I watch him. My temple is pounding. Rub it with the weak arm. Some lubrication. Red fluid on my sleeve. Porcelain and enamel. Lean over the sink, coughing. Try to stop but my lungs are intent on continuing. Itchiness in my throat. Cough harder and retch, once, dry, twice, wet. Thin, ditchwater fluid pours out. I am not vomiting. Someone else is throwing up through my mouth. Beer sluices through my nose, my eyes crying in pain. Vomit until I'm dry, and then some more. Dry retches through a bloody mouth and a scraped nose.

I head for the door, still heaving. Bartop phone. Hands almost too numb to dial the taxi number, like trying to tie your laces on a freezing day. There is a song on the jukebox. I hear the intro and rack my brains. It is on the tip of my tongue. Any second now I will recognize it. Where to? the voice asks. Selly Oak Casualty, I say. The chorus is approaching. And then I get it. The song I used to hear in France. The silly love song that used to pick me apart. Now I am truly falling to bits. Ten minutes, the taxi woman says. I am singing silently along. I put the phone down. Another song comes on. Time passes, shuffling and staggering by.

A man enters the pub and approaches me as I cling unsteadily to the bar. Taxi, he says. I nod and follow him out to the car park. I walk close to him, afraid they might still be here, lurking in the dark, ready to administer a final beating. The knackered Nissan Bluebird starts up and the driver turns to me as I slump in the back. Watch the upholstery, he barks. I don't mind you bleeding, but you don't do it on my seats, OK? I nod, mute with pain. From now on I try to stem any leaking drips from my body.

We clatter out of the car park. The bastards, I slur. Stole my watch, ripped it off my wrist. Even took my wallet. Forced me to give them my PIN numbers, took my bank cards to clear out my other accounts. And then they held me down and did the unspeakable to me. I clench my right fist and mouth the single word 'Cunt', tears welling. Nearer the hospital, I put bits of blurred information together. Must have hung around outside, watching. Then when I went to the toilets . . . Archie. Double cunt. I could see it through his glasses. Pity. Standing over me as they kicked and punched. Staring down at me. Go on, Magoo, they said, get stuck in. Kicked me with his Clarks brogues. Of course I didn't hold it against him. It wasn't as if it made any difference. The pity, though, that was what really hurt. Sympathy from an anorak. They must have phoned him to come and join in the fun.

My diaphragm twitches and I retch, eyes bleeding.

The driver swings round. The upholstery! he shouts. Watch my bloody upholstery! There is no need for worry. My stomach is empty and is simply squeezing itself dry from time to time, trying to purge the acid from my body. I attempt to pass out.

Snakeskin

Having suffered a major beating, I found myself depressed. I stayed at home and lay on the sofa, the TV muted, my wounds healing with a worrying lack of urgency. They had been here, and turned the place over. Presumably while I was getting stitched back together in Casualty and seeing the emergency dentist, they were ransacking drawers and upending furniture. Even my sacred Birthday Morning Album had been attacked. All the Polaroids had been tipped out and mixed up so that I was confronted by an ageless set of images of myself scattered over the floor. Nothing was missing, though. They were obviously after more important things than televisions and hi-fi, like any bank cards or money I might have neglected to mention.

At first when I returned from Casualty, there was only blackness. My front teeth had been capped, and felt like intruders in my mouth. I ached as if my body was one large, seeping dead-leg. No position was comfortable – any contact with any part of me hurt. I swallowed anti-inflammatories through my swollen throat and poured beer over my ceramic caps. The enamel had been broken, to be replaced with porcelain. Blackness gave way to mood swings. Again, I had time to think, which was bad. I found I could only despise myself, though, and granted Jeremy, Brian and Archie just cursory moments of ill-will for the attack.

Gradually, fleeting moments of near-contentment levered their way through the haze of self-loathing. When I did squeeze some happiness into the long hours of recuperation, however, it disappeared as quickly as it had come. For every positive thought I tried to muster, a negative one crept up promptly behind and strangled it.

Before my beating, I had always felt that life never seems to mean enough at the time you are living it. Everything is too easy, nothing matters, the highs escape like bubbles, floating out of reach, empty of substance, always moving away from you. And if you do happen to catch one and try to squeeze the joy from it, suddenly your hands are empty and clammy, the thing you were chasing having somehow eluded you, even though you were clearly holding it in your grasp only seconds before. Lows would remain, however, and it was all you could do to get their stain off your hands. Now, as I stared into my painful fingers, there was a new stain. It was blue and uneven, the result of a struggle. I had picked at the scabs but the blemish ran too deep. I examined their handiwork. The unspeakable act, the unspeakable word. C-U-N-T tattooed across the fingers of my right hand, letters in the places where rings should dwell. I made a fist and inspected the sickening image of the word. It was, I decided, time to invest in some jewellery.

It took just over four weeks before I felt well again. And when I did, I felt better than ever. While I hung around getting reacquainted with my house, things began to change inside me. As my bandages and plasters were all finally removed like a discarded membrane, a very new me struggled out to emerge in the sunlight. Or rather a very old one. Day after day, innate behaviours had been stitching themselves back together to form a mesh of actions. My brain had shut down and happily conceded defeat. Arms and legs had taken control. The mechanics of living became all that mattered. My routines were once again established. I had come full cycle and was reborn. It wasn't quite a metamorphosis, more a snake slithering out of a dry, discarded skin, shiny and new. The sun was beating down on my patterned back, and I felt strong. I took deep, cool breaths which seemed to inflate my whole body. When I closed my eyes, all I could see was a serene darkness. There was no longer any baggage. I was streamlined and sleek, and ready for anything which came my way. I was in control because I had order amongst all the chaos. I awoke at the same time every day, ate the same breakfast, the same lunch, the same evening meal in order throughout the week. I visited the same shops and bought the same products. I watched the same programmes at the same times. I flossed my teeth from top left to top right, bottom right to bottom left. I bought the same paper and read the same sections in the same order. I showered every day and washed my hair and shaved on alternate mornings. The house was tidied on a strict rota, and the washing up done once a week whether it needed it or not. I filled the washing machine on Sundays, rinsed whatever was inside on the standard bachelor 40°C cycle, and unloaded it on Mondays before it had time to rot. I even visited the toilet at measured intervals. Nothing could defeat me now that my routine existence had been resurrected. In just four short weeks, I had built a small haven of predictability in a sea of disarray. In fact, the more I thought about it, the more I wondered how I had ever let it all slip in the first place.

Can Buy Me Love

It had started insidiously enough, as insidious things do, by definition. They don't have it in them to start up with a great big fanfare of announcement. Instead, insidious things prefer to sneak up on you in a dark alley, to jump on you when you are least expecting it and knee you in the bollocks. So it began innocently. I was unable to find any sliced bread in Nice. Not the world's greatest dilemma, admittedly. But without bread, toast was out. And without toast, breakfast was in danger. And without breakfast, well, I was in trouble. I did the only thing anyone in my predicament could do – I experimented. I went to the boulangerie and bought a croissant, and, when I got home, attempted to slice it in cross-section for toasting purposes. With a great deal of difficulty I had also managed to get my hands on some marmalade. Not that the jar looked to have been desperately close to any oranges, or other fruit for that matter, but it certainly could have been marmalade, particularly when examined from a good distance in poor lighting. The croissant was having none of it, though. Croissants are built to flake rather than slice, I found to my cost. So toasted croissant was out. Milk had been fine. No problems. Cornflakes were easy too but muesli appeared to be a non-starter. The French didn't seem to be big on Swiss breakfasts. In the face of such ignorance, I resolved that neat cornflakes would have to do from now on. And so, with a broken croissant, a vacant grill, an unopened jar of alleged marmalade, a bowl of pure cornflakes and an empty stomach for company, I sat miserably in my kitchen, with a feeling that all wasn't right with the world, as the true horror of life without a proper breakfast chipped insidiously away at me.

Bit by bit, I tried to patch together a new breakfast. Normality, I began to appreciate, is an infinitely variable thing, dependent on time, place and circumstance. I resolved therefore to build myself a new normality, starting from breakfast and working chronologically onwards. Breakfast now comprised one croissant, two pains au chocolat, a three-quarter glass of orange juice and a cup of English tea, of a type seldom drunk in England. I figured that if I could just get my first meal sorted, everything else would fall into place. But it wasn't that simple. The new breakfast left me unsettled, off-balance even, and the repercussions spread like ripples through the rest of my daily actions. I quickly found I was shedding routines. And losing these slowed me down, because the real function of routines is to make life go faster. With all this time suddenly on my hands, I had the opportunity to think. And the more time I had to think, the less happy I became. I started to explore myself, to work my way in. I sat and thought of nothing else for hours on end. I worked through decisions I had made, motives I had developed, feelings I had suppressed. I took the whole woolly jumper of my existence and began to pick it apart stitch by stitch. The more I unravelled, the less reason I happened upon, and it soon became clear that there was very little underlying sense to the majority of actions I had filled my adult life with. There was simply a need to protect myself from the unknown and the unexpected. Almost all my actions could be judged in this way. An opportunity, a choice, an opening. The decision – what will I have to alter? How much effort will it be? How can I keep my life the same?

I tried to understand what scared me about the unknown but got no further than everything. I began to change with surprising rapidity, and this was unsettling. I could almost watch it, it was so quick. I was living the change, and a very different me was emerging. If I had a new breakfast, I reasoned, I could have other new things. Suddenly free from its cage of pre-planned actions, my brain ran amok and I did what any self-respecting partial hedonist would do. I set about trying to take the pleasure out of life. I used my money purely for destructive means. I systematically tried to undermine any genuine feeling I had ever had in my life. I destroyed hunger, yearning, hope, beauty, love, understanding, patience, kindness and fear by buying each one of them in turn. I started with the love. I bought myself a girlfriend. Not literally, but it was a close call. Nadia, Marcelo's ex-girlfriend, was excited by my ability to spend money. She didn't like me particularly, and the feeling was mutual, but she did a damned good impression when the need arose. I thought about a letter to the Beatles, pointing out the error of their words, but decided they'd probably blame it all on John, who was dead anyway.

One night I gave all I had left from an evening's gambling – about ninety quid – to a beggar, just to see whether I could buy ingratitude. I followed him round, and when he seemed in danger of squandering it, asked him to lend me a little of my money back. Did he fuck. Point proved. I had bought ingratitude. I bought despair, by wasting more cash in a week on clothes which made me look like a wanker than I had given to charity in my whole life. Shallow, frivolous vanity has always been a quick road to despair.

But as I progressed with my scheme, I came to appreciate that many feelings came naturally with the territory and didn't really need much encouragement. Avarice, greed and envy didn't cost me any money at all. As soon as I had money, I got envy. I wanted more money and envied those who were wealthier than me. And the more money I had, the more acute this feeling. There were also some which were annulled by the wealth: daydreaming, understanding and patience all disappeared as I continued to spend my riches. The only feeling which remained immune from persecution was hope. Hope snapped me out of my lunatic scheme. Hope in the shape of an African girl in rags.

Now, with an almost fatal absence of cash, I was back to being nice but dull. I had cast off a skin of superficial being, and innate behaviours had struggled back to the surface. Cured of the desire for change, I was ready to slide along and get lost in the daily hubbub of existence. As far as I was concerned, a boring life would suit me fine. It had certainly done so before.

Caring Too Much

Today is a big day, I mouthed to myself in the bathroom mirror, opening the cabinet and pulling out a box of assorted plasters. I pocketed a small handful of the narrow rectangular variety, shut the door and checked my tie. Job bait, I said. Then I ruffled my hair, and examined it from a couple of reflected angles. Girl bait, I announced. I inspected my face. I was fully recovered. Bruises had turned from black to yellow, leaching silently away to leave only pink. Cuts had closed up, risen on scabbed backs and then peeled off. Capped front teeth mingled inconspicuously amongst natural ones. It was difficult to tell now. Only one injury remained. I left the bathroom and headed for the front door. This morning, breakfast had been taken fifteen minutes early. I had failed to watch any TV, and flossing would have to wait until later. I had a job interview. On the bus, I reread the letter. 9:15, Human Resource Department, Intron UK. This was the one place I had been avoiding. Intron was my former workplace, the only other employer in the Birmingham area which dealt with financial programming. Spartech was a non-starter, since I had walked out one afternoon and never come back. Although Intron wasn't without its problems, one of those had recently been removed. Archie, to be precise. Whilst phoning around former colleagues, I came across the welcome news that he had resigned in the previous month. No-one was exactly sure why, though there was talk of a personal hygiene issue. Quite what this meant was not expanded upon.

During the four weeks I spent convalescing, a new need presented itself to me. Changing countries, girlfriends, jobs and possessions suggested an antidote: permanency. I needed something permanent. I took four plasters out of my pocket. One by one, I peeled off their backings and wrapped the sticky portion around successive right-hand fingers, obscuring the T of my index finger, the N of the middle, the U of my ring and the C of my little finger. Then I had one final glance through the contents of the letter before filing it in my suit pocket. With any luck, I was about to become a Permie. The bus approached the leafy industrial estate which hid Intron from the view of people who had sensibilities to offend. Before it ground to a noisy halt, I tried to get my story straight. What, this? Nothing really. Fell off my bike, scraped my fingers against a wall. Inside the building, a few people said hello – workers I recognized from my previous stint at the company. One of the interview panel was Ruth, my former boss. Told you you'd be back, she said. I smiled.

After the formality of the panel's questions, Ruth took me to one side and told me that the job was mine. Although I'd stumbled badly with one of my answers, she said that the members of the board had generally been impressed with the way I handled myself? Was this an obscure way of calling me a wanker? I wondered quietly. Ruth continued to walk me through the building towards the exit. So come on, Ian, what *are* your biggest faults? she teased. As I had done in the interview, I once again remained silent. Lying, stealing, cheating and ripping your company off would have been the obvious answers, but didn't seem like job-winning responses. You know, Ruth, I said, as she opened the door, I think it's caring too much. About yourself, she said, smiling and shaking my hand. Maybe, I replied, grinning back and heading in the direction of the bus stop. Just maybe.

Ceiling Stars

In the afternoon, I hung around the litter of New Street station, browsing books, listening to announcements and thumbing magazines, until Sarah arrived on the Manchester train. She looked different, maybe because I was sober. Not worse-different, just different-different.

'You look different,' she told me as I kissed her on the cheek.

'It's the suit,' I said. 'And the lack of a party hat.'

'What about me?' she asked. 'Now you can see me in daylight.'

'Exactly the same. But slightly less stoned.'

'Incredibly tidy though,' she commented.

We were standing in the sitting room of my house. I took her coat and hung it up. Evidence of all the atrocities inflicted upon the interior either by myself or by the thugs had been removed. 'Haven't had much else to do recently,' I said, following her eyes around the room. The red, gaping, paint-spattered hole in the carpet had been covered with a rug. Dust had been not merely displaced to a new venue, but actually hoovered away. Magazines, books, CDs and letters had all been sorted. Upstairs, the perma-clothes of my bedroom floor had been washed, dried and hung up, though not ironed, for obvious reasons. And, through the back window, even the garden had been tidied to appease my unobservant neighbour.

Sarah continued to nose around. 'Not bad for a single bloke.'

'What, the house or the bloke?'

'The house.'

'And the bloke?'

She looked me in the eye. 'Still deciding. I mean I didn't know whether to be flattered or scared that you had tracked me down through Darren.'

'Scared,' I said, 'that I should count scientists among my friends.'

Later, I took Sarah out to celebrate the fact that I had a new job. The evening was not a resounding success. She had, I learned, lost her father to cancer a year earlier, and was still not out of the woods yet. In lieu of grieving, Sarah had thrown herself into her work, which hadn't come naturally. When not slaving over a hot test tube, she had tried to party as much as possible and had, as she readily admitted, become a walking work-hard-play-hard cliché.

'It's the photos which really get me,' she said, lighting a cigarette as we sat down in the lounge of a high street pub.

'Why?'

'We're all there, grinning and showing our teeth, and Dad is just staring into the camera. Every picture's the same.'

'He didn't just object to having his photo taken?'

'No.' She sighed a smoky breath. 'It was like he could only tell the camera about his misery. Of course what's also amazing is the fact that I could have spent day after day with him and failed to notice his unhappiness, and yet in photographs, frozen instants, it can be so obvious to me.'

'Photos don't always tell the truth, though.'

'True. But the real bugger is that all I have now to remind myself of him are those bloody photos, where he always looks as miserable as sin.' A tear poured over the lip of her lower eyelid and toppled down her cheek. She swept it away with the back of her hand as if this was a familiar event. I didn't know what to say and so kept quiet. Sarah stubbed her cigarette out and composed herself.

'Another drink?' I asked, standing up.

'Yes. Get me a tequila.'

'You sure?'

'Reminds me of good times.'

'Right.'

I returned after a couple of minutes and we talked some more. After a while, our glasses were once again empty and an uncomfortable edge settled into the proceedings. 'Do you want to make a move?' I asked, eventually. We were discussing cold, uninvolving subjects to try to move away from her father's death.

'Might as well,' she said.

We walked home in silence. I held her while she cried on my bed. Later, she slept and I lay next to her in the half-light, staring up at my ceiling. The previous owners of the house had stuck luminous stars to it, mapping out intricate constellations against the dark blue surface. Every night when I turned the lights off the stars continued to sparkle for long minute after long minute, until one by one their fluorescence died and they disappeared into the gloom. Really, I ought to have painted over them, but so far I had been unable to bring myself to do it.

This is Your Life

The irony didn't elude me. I was a Permie, the very person I had despised all along. And I shared a prison cell office with a Tractor, the exact being that hated Permies. I had come full circle. As much as I had tried to escape the dull inevitability of my former existence, it had ruthlessly tracked me down and taken me captive. I was a slave to the mundane once again.

The Tractor's loathing was palpable. It was there in his eyes as he looked at me, summing me up, literally at times. He was thinking fifteen quid an hour for the Permie, and forty for me. I wondered whether I had been quite so transparent when I had been a Tractor and the situation had been reversed. Maybe that was why Archie had tried to stitch me up. I winced as I thought about him half-heartedly kicking me. The twat. Couldn't even damage me properly when I was sprawling on the ground. I hated him for his weakness, and even more for his pity.

What made the current Permie–Tractor relationship particularly strained was the fact that I knew my cellmate. It was James, man of the reckless spending and even more reckless programming. He too had washed up at Intron after leaving Spartech. In the real world, it might have been of advantage to know my co-worker already. Here, however, the rules were different. James could hardly bear to look at me, except when he felt like gloating. At the forefront of cash-frittering technology as he undoubtedly still was, James found my acceptance of the Permie life not merely in bad taste, but on a par with paying the correct amount of tax. If anything, it bothered him more than my apparent change of name. Here was someone actively choosing not to earn more than a fair day's wage for less than a fair day's work. He was sickened to the core of his wallet. But there was more than rudimentary contempt about his attitude. There was fear. James looked at me and saw himself. The walls of his bubble were becoming dangerously thin. The millennium bug had come and gone, Symbiosis was essentially installed, the first of the first of the first was a fading memory and there was an alarming lack of anything to panic about. And with no panic, there would be no new contracts. James was, he worried, during his darkest moments of Ferrari servicing and house refurbishment bills, about to become me. He was about to become a Permie. He saw the car I drove, the absence of silk in my ties, the Burton's label on my suit and was gripped by dread. In fact, the only item he respected about me was my Rolex. I didn't have the heart to tell him it was fake. That really would have depressed him.

The single thing that could possibly have given James any hope was the fact that Symbiosis was far from firing on all cylinders. Like other similar organizations, Intron was busy transferring its banking and investment architectures over to the new language. But things weren't working well at all. Instead of harmony, there was disharmony. Programs which should have talked to each other refused to do so, and went off in strops. Workstations routinely crashed, and applications shut themselves down of their own accord. The network had become one enormous battlefield. And everybody sat around scratching their heads and shrugging and wondering what the hell they could do about it, without ever coming up with anything constructive. One February afternoon as we filled our hours with the barren clatter of keyboard activity, I decided to ask James something which had been gnawing away at me since I had started working for Intron.

'James,' I said, peering over the top of my monitor, 'one thing still puzzles me.'

He made a show of finishing what he was doing before answering. 'Yes?'

'You had a system at Spartech.'

'Yeah.' James chewed his biro and screwed up his eyes.

'And it went a bit pear-shaped.'

'Mmm.'

'Then you joined Intron.'

'Hang on,' he said, wondering where my line of questioning was leading. 'Aspel's not about to jump out with a big red book, introduce loads of hangers-on I thought I'd managed to ditch and say "This is Your Life", is he?'

'Not exactly. But when you first came here, what did you do?'

'What do you mean? I did the same as everyone else – a load of Sym stuff.'

'And?'

'And what?'

'Look out in the car park. See that heap of shit there – that's my car. One careful owner, a dozen fucking psychopaths and more scratches than a bag of cats. Now, head right a couple of rows.'

'Yeah?'

'That's yours. Two previous owners, both of whom were probably loaded, and one current psychopath.'

'So?'

'So your car's worth almost as much as my house. Something's got to be wrong. Even an overvalued Tractor like yourself couldn't run a car that foolhardy on your money.'

James smiled. 'What you're implying, Mr Gillick, is some sort of scam.'

'Exactly.'

He tilted his executive-type office chair back at an unhealthily smug angle. 'Well, you never know. Anything's possible.' Then James stood up and walked out of the office, leaving the suggestion that he was once again doing something questionable hanging in the air. For two days I continued to pester him whenever I could, in between being shown the ropes by a couple of programmers from the next office, who were vainly battling to get Symbiosis to fulfil its function. From time to time during my induction I was left to my own devices, with the recommendation that I 'get to know the network'. This was when I would try to wear James down with my interrogation. Eventually, bored into submission, and having strung things out long enough, he cracked.

'So come on, James, put me out of my misery. What's your plan?' I asked for the hundredth time.

'Jesus, this is worse than Spartech. And there aren't even any lunches going.'

'I'll buy you a sandwich.'

'Fucking hell. Don't get carried away.'

'And a drink. And crisps of your choice.'

'Some chocolate?'

'Name it.'

'A Snickers. Kingsize.'

'Right. Anything else?'

'Yeah. Bring them to my desk.'

'Then you'll let me in on your secret?'

'And an apple.'

'OK. An apple. Then you'll tell me?'

'Maybe.'

In the canteen, I picked through my total coinage. £3.89. Just enough for James's generous lunch package. My meal would have to wait. This had better be worth it. 'So come on, let's have the gory details,' I said, unloading the collected booty on James's desk. With a little cajoling he began to spill the beans.

'It's fiendish, Gillick. Devilishly fiendish.' James opened a sandwich and grinned. 'And it's all thanks to you.'

'How do you mean?'

'Well, as you gaze sick with envy every morning at my prancing horse . . .'

'Mincing pony . . .'

'You really should know that without your unwitting help, I'd've been driving something as lower class as your thing.'

Eager to punch him, but even more eager to hear him out, I encouraged James to continue. 'I don't follow you. What has this got to do with me?'

'I can trust you?'

'I didn't tell anyone about your Spartech thing.'

'Right. Here we go then. You remember saying that it was OK to alter computers, but programs would fall apart if any single machine had the wrong date?'

'Yes.' And I also recalled finishing his pint while he damned near shat himself.

'Well, I had a bash at programming. I put some code onto the network which told it to ignore any machine with a clock date in the Seventies. Look, here's the batch file – have a butcher's.' I got up and walked round to his side. 'Even now, there are dozens and dozens of networked PCs which do bugger all but reroute to other servers.'

'So everything's been fucking up because half of the machines which run Symbiosis simply shunt their business to ones which haven't been tampered with yet by you?'

'That's about the size of it.'

'And you get your contract extended trying to get Sym to run on every workstation, and continue to rake the money in, while everyone assumes we've just got massive glitches in the programming which need to be sorted?'

'Aha.'

'So loads of Tractors in the company are wasting days and nights trying to fix something that you're spending your days installing?'

'Nice, eh?'

'Not bad,' I was forced to agree. James was eating the company from the inside out. There was a kind of beauty to it. The whole organization was devoting its hours to fixing a problem that one of its staff was creating. James continued to claim healthy amounts of overtime, which was spent inventing new ways to keep the system from functioning properly. I was quiet awhile, thinking. 'Not bad at all. But fairly minor league, on the grand scale of things.'

'What do you mean?' he demanded. To have any part of his financial arrangements described as anything other than excessive was a deep insult.

'I mean it's a nice little scam . . .'

'Little?'

'But people have done better.'

'Like who?'

Hungry and let down as I felt after the amount of effort I had put into getting the truth out of him, James's second major confession had nudged me somewhere. As I sat and listened to the pride he took in such a small-scale bending of the rules, I was moved to enlighten him about the true dimensions of a proper scam. My swindle had been big, very big. 'Like me.'

'You? What are you up to?'

'Nothing. I'm happy how I am. But I did do something once.'

'Yeah? Come on!'

'No, really. Something major.'

'Where? In the States?'

'No. Here.'

'Here? Intron?'

'Yep. I wasn't the only one in on it. But it was big, and I made a lot of money.'

James pricked up his ears. I had tickled his G-spot. 'Big?'

Getting the Job Done

I spared few details, and as I talked about the ins and outs of the Original Swindle I watched James's pupils widen with excitement. And when I'd finally finished telling him what a real scam should be like, it became obvious that he was going to treat me with a new-found respect. I had made a lot of money by doing something vaguely illegal, which encompassed his two great passions in life. OK, I had now frittered that money away, having set up home in three countries only to leave everything behind each time, the apartments in Nice and LA draining the dregs of my foreign bank accounts as rent continued to be collected by direct debit, but, through James's eyes, a swindle was a swindle, and you couldn't do much better than that. He no longer glared at me with Tractor derision. I had been initiated into his club.

For the next couple of days, James remained so pleasant that I began to seriously regret opening my heart to him. At least when he looked down on me, we didn't talk much. The more we chatted, the more he let me into his world, and the uglier it appeared. The man was without soul. His humanity lived entirely within the bounds of his bank balance. He entered the building in the morning, cheerily greeted all the fellow Tractors, gladly discussed the problems of Symbiosis with managers, tutted at the lack of progress that was being made, and scratched his head in meetings when people tried to come up with solutions to the problem. He was admirably good at playing the innocent. When we weren't conversing, James worked with alacrity. He devoted increasing amounts of time to maintaining his scam. There was a battle going on, and he needed to stay one step ahead of colleagues who were trying to rectify the problems that he was causing.

From time to time, he talked openly about it, like a minor league criminal boasting about a conquest. I listened to his meanderings with rapidly evaporating patience. To him, we were partners in crime. At last, he said, there was someone who understood what it was all about. He followed me around like a bad smell and bought me endless coffees, though he always kept the receipts, muttering about legitimate business expenditure. He even offered to let me sit in his car, as long as I didn't touch anything. I declined. James similarly rejected the opportunity to sit in mine, on the grounds that people might see him. But it was no good. Things had to return to normal, and soon. I couldn't bear the prospect of being treated like a beloved crony any longer. Also, the air of suffering within the workplace was growing daily more acute. Tractors were getting fired as progress failed to be made. Some of them were James's friends, and I watched him make a big show of commiserating with them when they received their notice. And then one day, a seemingly unconnected event got me thinking. All wasn't necessarily well for James Birch. A senior manager had grabbed me and asked me a question. James's life was, I suspected, about to take a downturn.

One morning, when James was still treating me with respect, he launched into a lengthy explanation of a new twist to the swindle which would fox the opposition for a bit longer. 'They'll never see through that one. Fucking magic. So I reckon I'll easily get another three or four months out of it, and then, I dunno, the next thing I suppose,' he said.

'Sounds good.'

It was time to put James out of his misery and share my news with him. I wanted it to be gentle, though, so I introduced the information slowly over a number of minutes, giving it a chance to sink in fully.

'You bet.'

'But don't you ever worry that your scams could get too good?'

'What do you mean "too good"?'

'I mean let's say Symbiosis continues to fail.'

'Right.'

'But to fail so badly that Intron decide the Tractors aren't getting the job done, and outside help is needed?'

'They won't.'

'It happens.'

'So they get new people in. Big deal. No-one's going to suspect that there's rogue code knocking about. New systems always have teething problems.'

'Not this bad, though.'

'I dunno. Look at the DSS, or that passport fiasco, or any other time when entirely new software has been installed.'

'That's different. They were public sector – who was going to notice an increased level of incompetence in the DSS?'

'Still the same principle, though. Software is tricky stuff and doesn't always work. In fact, if you think about it, that's largely how we make our money – by milking programming conflicts. Only this time, the milking's a bit more clever.'

'But suppose they did get outside assistance in, and the new people were smart. What if they knew more about the system than you did?'

'I'd like to meet them. I've been doing Symbiosis for, what, eighteen months now. Come on, there can't be many punters with a better idea of the language.'

'Except the guys who performed the initial testing on it.'

The penny was beginning to drop. 'What do you know?' he demanded.

'Not much. Just that a friend of mine is on his way over. One of the fund managers trapped me a few days ago. Put me on the spot and asked who I used to do Symbiosis testing with in the States. Said they wanted outside help straight away.'

'The States?'

'Be here by the end of the week, apparently.'

'Yeah?'

'Looks like it. He worked for one of the first companies to evaluate Sym in America. Bit more than coincidence, I'd have thought.'

'Mmm.' James frowned and pretended to continue with his work. I stared out at his car and smiled.

Arrivals

Greg's flight was early and I almost missed him. He had strolled out of Arrivals, confidence ebbing as faces thinned and name signs died out, until the realization dawned that no-one in the lounge had come to meet him. Someone in the car park had, but he wasn't to know that. I, meanwhile, was sitting fifty yards away, reading a paper and occasionally glancing at the clock on my dashboard. Just be landing, I said to myself as he sat down on his expensive suitcase outside the main terminal and peered forlornly at freezing Limeys shuddering about their business. And later, I estimated that he would just be taxiing in as he stood up and headed for the cab rank. When I did finally venture over to meet him, he was asking a driver how much it might be to the centre of Birming-*ham*. The cabbie was telling him that it might be thirty-five quid. I told him it *might* be thirty-five quid if you happened to be American, but to the rest of us it was generally fifteen. We headed out of Birmingham International in a considerably cheaper form of transport. As we negotiated the A45 towards town, Greg did a good impression of not being overawed by the West Midlands. However different the perma-frost of Birmingham must have appeared from the perma-sun of Los Angeles, there were, as I pointed out, obvious similarities between our two cities. Both had seemingly been designed as experimental areas where increasingly complex road systems were tried out on unsuspecting motorists, and both were a long way from being architectural masterpieces. Admittedly, that was about it, but my attempts to persuade him that Birmingham was every bit as bad as Los Angeles, and in certain aspects even worse, appeared to cheer him a little. After a while he pointed generally through the window and asked, 'What *is* that?'

'*That*,' I replied, 'is what we call winter.' The grass was silver and the trees were naked. Even with the heater on our breath puffed out like cigarette smoke. 'And it's what you get if you visit England in February.'

'Mo'fo',' was his only reply, through a vapour-laden breath. Presently, he asked, 'And what the fuck is this?'

'This,' I said, 'is a car.'

'No. This is a heap of shit.'

I reminded him of the heap of shit I had bought from him in Los Angeles, which kept him quiet for a while. Twenty minutes later, I dropped him at the hotel I had previously called home, before fighting my way through the ten a.m. school-run-housewife-dangerous-pensioner traffic to get to work. James raised his eyebrows as I entered the office. 'He's here then?' he asked, with all the optimism of an English football fan during a penalty shoot-out. I nodded solemnly, to add to the sense of impending disaster, and sat down. 'Motherfucker,' was his only reply. Greg arrived in the afternoon, having showered and changed, and I was glad to be able to introduce them.

'Greg – James. James – Greg.'

'All right,' James said.

'Hey,' Greg replied. They didn't shake hands. I showed my old acquaintance the high spots of Intron UK, of which there were precious few, and again Greg managed not to get too carried away by his enthusiasm. He left early to get some sleep, and James and I sat quietly at our respective desks and pondered.

One-handed Reading

'No way. You're making it up.' Karen was not convinced.

'I'm not. I swear.'

'I don't believe you.'

'Why not? What's so unbelievable about it?' Darren asked.

'Well, what's the point, for a start?'

'I would have thought that was obvious.'

'But why don't lesbians just find a man?'

Darren stifled a laugh. 'Slightly defeats the object.'

'So they strap these things on and have sex with each other?'

'That's the way I'd imagine it happening.'

'I wouldn't have thought women wanted to do that.'

'You don't seem to mind being penetrated.'

'I'm not a lesbian though.'

'Just because they're lesbians doesn't mean they don't enjoy it as well.'

'But still, they could save themselves the trouble of buying these . . .'

'Strap-ons.'

'If they just found a man.'

'Again, I refer you to my earlier point.'

'I'm still not sure whether you're pulling my leg.'

'Ask anyone.'

'Anyone?'

'Well, not your parents. But anyone else. They exist. You see them advertised at the back of magazines.'

'What kind of magazines?'

'You know – gentlemen's magazines – one-handed reading material.'

'And do you have any such material?'

'I'd be too embarrassed to buy it.'

'But I thought most men had some sordid magazines stashed away somewhere.'

'Well, not this one. You can check through my stuff while I'm away in Colorado.'

'When's the taxi due?'

'A couple of minutes.'

'You know, I might go and get myself one of those strap-on things while you're away.'

'Yeah? What good's that going to do you?'

'I don't know.' Karen was silent a moment, images flitting through her mind. 'Maybe I could wear it inside out!'

The doorbell rang and Darren picked up his case. 'Taxi,' he said.

Karen hugged him. 'Have a successful trip.'

'You bet.' Darren opened the door and left. Good times here I come, he whispered to himself as he handed his case to the taxi driver. 'The airport, please,' Darren said, opening the rear door and strapping himself in. He had the feeling that this was going to be a successful conference.

Stick Shift

Before his arrival, I had imagined that Greg and I would quickly renew our mutual enthusiasm for junk food and beer. There were a number of drinking venues I had earmarked for us to try, with the aim of persuading him that pub culture was not, as he suggested, a contradiction in terms. I even thought he might stay with me at my house when Hotel Life wore thin. After all, we had been reasonable friends in Los Angeles. He even owed me money from my stay there, and not a trivial sum either. In the interest of attempting to resume our friendship, I let it pass. As I sat at my desk, several days after his arrival, I realized for the first time that things were going to be different now.

Greg was in the corner of the office, with his back to me, beavering away. From his first full hour in the building he had attacked the task at hand. He was on a mission, working through Intron's files with feverish alacrity, reinstalling software, fixing glitches and getting on people's nerves. I wanted to talk to him, not just about the people I had known in America, or the places we had visited, but about the very nature of what he was doing at Intron. He wasn't to know it but the harder he strove, the more he was wasting his time. There was nothing essentially wrong with the operating system that he was ploughing through. All of its many problems could be directly traced to a fellow worker who sat within feet of his desk looking worried. I didn't want to tell him straight away that the Symbiosis mess was James's doing, but felt a couple of minor hints might help him out and might also cheer me up a little.

Greg remained stubbornly caught up in his work, however, and hardly said a word. Increasingly, though, as the first week wore on, an unexpected liaison began to develop. When he wasn't hammering away at some unfortunate keyboard with all the gusto of a concert pianist undergoing electrocution, he was thick in conversation with James. Indeed, despite all the odds, the two seemed to hit it off, excessive sense meeting excessive non-sense in a no man's land of partial sobriety. But it quickly became apparent that theirs was not a friendship based around good times. Although neither of them was by any means comedic, or given to smiling even, there was a dour solidarity about their relationship which served to keep me at bay. James also became elusive. I was slightly hurt. Greg had been my companion before, and he appeared to be ditching me for the Big Spender.

Over the following ten days or so, Greg and James continued to pass more and more time together. They were almost always in the office before I arrived in the morning, and at night, as I watched colleagues leach out of the building like the colour from a stain before rushing to join them, Greg and James would remain quietly behind. They even ate lunch together. On the rare occasion when I managed to talk to Greg alone, he was uninterested, preoccupied and evasive. I felt as if I had introduced someone to my circle of friends, only for them to become much more popular than me, and for the circle to barely remember who I was. Although my pride was mildly bruised, I would get over it.

After work on Tuesday, I met Sarah at New Street station and we sampled the delights of Birmingham's China Town on Hirst Street. In fairness, it was more a village than a town, encompassing three or four restaurants which jostled for space amongst a cacophony of pubs, clubs and takeaways. Sarah was happier, and I was glad she had come to see me. Any distraction from Intron was a bonus at the moment. We forgot our troubles, eating, drinking and laughing them away, before catching a taxi back to the relative peace of Kings Heath. Later, I turned out the lights and we watched the stars in my bedroom die one by one. While Sarah monopolized the bathroom in the morning, I peeled a star from my ceiling and placed it in her overnight bag, imagining it glowing secretly all day, following her around as she headed back to Manchester.

When I arrived at work, having dropped Sarah at the train station, something unsettling happened. James's car screeched past me and parked in a space I had had my eye on. Only Greg was driving it. James had lent him his fucking Ferrari. James, the Midland Bank and his Ferrari were virtually inseparable. He wouldn't even permit people to look at the thing, let alone allow someone patently used to driving on the wrong side of the road to race it around the car parks of Birmingham. As he folded himself out of the Italian supercar, I began to appreciate that there was something different happening to Greg – he appeared to be becoming less sensible. He might even have been sleeping. He nodded at me and waited for me to park. We ambled towards the building in silence, while he crunched on some sort of savoury snack. When we entered the main security door I glanced back towards the car park. 'Some machine,' I said.

'You bet,' Greg replied, holding the door open for me. 'Stick shift's a pain in the butt, though.'

'Maybe you're using it wrongly.'

He stared at me for a second and then faked a laugh. 'Good one.'

'Look, Greg,' I said, blocking the open doorway, 'is

everything OK? I know you don't owe me anything, but I hoped we might go out for a couple of pints sometime.'

Greg continued to munch his snack food. On closer inspection, he seemed to be experimenting with a bag of pork scratchings, chewing them thoughtfully, no doubt weighing them up against pretzels and jerky. From his expression, it looked as if they had passed the Greg test of vitamin and nutrient deficiency. When he had finished the contents and tapped the upended bag to get every last morsel of goodness into his open mouth he said, 'Yeah, I'd like that.'

'Great. One night this week?'

'Can't. I'm busy with James.'

'What, every night?'

He screwed the bag up and put it in his pocket. 'Uh-huh.'

'Well, what are you two getting up to?'

'What d'you mean?'

'Just that you spend a lot of time with each other. Surely you must be doing something?'

'And you're implying what, exactly?'

'Nothing. Just . . .'

'No, really. Come out and say it.'

'I don't have anything to say.'

'Sounds to me like you do.'

'I was only—'

'My advice to you would be to stay the hell clear of us. Nomsayin'?' He glared down at me, angry all of a sudden. 'You nomsayin'?'

'Yeah,' I replied. 'I know what you're saying.'

'You bet you do.' Greg pushed past me, bumping my shoulder and muttering 'Mo'fo'' under his breath.

I sulked in the direction of my office, impotent, mute, perplexed, cursing the day I first encountered Greg. It was a symptom of the way you meet people in life. You weigh them up, reject them or accept them, whittle them down to a small group of humans you like and who like you, over the process of many months and years. But sometimes the rules are different. Sometimes you are forced to make rapid decisions. Sometimes there is no time to consider and ponder. Sometimes you end up in a foreign country alone, needing people, and you have to take a gamble. Greg was one of the first people I had met in LA. It had hardly been love at first sight, but he had helped me, which to some degree bypassed the normal rigmarole of assessment. There was no luxury of being able to decide whether or not to like him. I bought a car from him and he found me a job. We were friends of convenience.

I sat down on my chair and glanced over at James and Greg. France had been different. There was more time and I was closer to home. I could afford to be more selective. But now I was lumbered. A chance meeting 6,000 miles away had determined that something weird was going on in the close confines of my office. I felt an urge to escape and went to the Human Resource Department. With a little bit of pleading, I managed to book the next two days off, to create a decent-sized weekend. A few days away would do me some good. Besides, there were a couple of people I needed to see.

Rusting Gently

The gate to my parents' house was the first thing that I remembered – always open, rusting gently and strangled by weeds trying to squeeze its life away. Everything attacking it, and yet remaining resolutely open, oblivious. A man even tried to steal it one night, I recalled, as I approached the last roundabout before the drive. I had watched him grapple drunkenly with the structure from the lookout of my bedroom window. Comical though it was to watch the inebriate fight a losing battle with a gate, there was a principle here, and I felt a young-man's rush of anger. I got dressed and strode out of the house towards him. It was someone I recognized, slightly older, slightly bigger, very much stronger and certainly more violent. He stood and watched my approach with interest, leaving the gate to loll on its remaining hinge. I imagined he was increasingly excited about the chance of a fight. We squared up. He swore at me. I was in trouble. Suddenly there was another voice. My dad. Ian, get the hell back in here, he shouted. The drunk swore at me a final time and slouched off. I wrestled vainly with the gate for a couple of minutes until my dad spoke again. This time he was closer. Leave the bloody thing alone, he told me. My throat tightened and we walked back into the house, and I was trembling slightly after the threat of danger had subsided. It's only a gate, he said, shutting the front door.

But as I at last rounded the final corner and saw the house, I noticed that the gate had changed. It was clean, weed-free and, for the first time, closed.

An awkward guilt, of the sort which had been absent in my parents' company since teenage years, hampered my words. We sat around the old kitchen table and I tried to think of suitable phrases. My dad hummed a seemingly random tune for a while and then stopped. I wanted to tell them that I loved them, had missed them, had craved them at times, but found myself unable to do so. Mostly, though, I wanted to stand up and leave. I wanted to say the right thing and go back to my house. It was a shallow expediency and I cursed myself for it. Looking around the kitchen and recognizing the familiar spaces my parents had occupied, the objects they had used, the furniture they had sat on, I was aware of the burden that my exile had imposed. I found I was trembling again. This time, though, it wasn't the danger of confronting a local drunk. Rather, it was the blind acceptance of my parents. They were embracing my faltering words, welcoming my excuses. It didn't matter, they assured me. As long as you're back now, safe and sound, that's the main thing. I began to wonder whether this was just the initial reaction to seeing me for the first time in three years, and that the hard stuff was yet to come – the recriminations, the anger, the hurt. But no, there was just understanding, and relief almost. I had been prepared for rage, had even rehearsed lines and prepared to go on the offensive. I was quite unprepared for forgiveness. I was also quite unprepared for my next utterance.

Ours was not the sort of family where you told anyone you loved them. Indeed, I had never heard this happen since childhood. Somewhere during adolescence it had been lost, never to be found again on the other side. As an adult, I listened to friends who would end parental telephone conversations with epitaphs like I love you mum or I miss you dad. But I could never do it myself. None of us ever did. We would just say goodbye. That there was love, and a lot of it, was understood. It was just never said. So when I glanced up sheepishly, realizing that I had suddenly blurted out that I loved my parents, there was almost an insincerity about the silence which followed. I had uttered the unutterable and nobody knew how to react. I replayed the words in my head and they felt fake. I knew them to be true, it was just that the moment had come and gone and the words had slipped out as weightlessly as any others I had ever said. I imagined such an announcement should carry a great fanfare of poignancy along with it for the ride, but there was nothing but stillness. I blushed self-consciously.

My dad got up and filled the kettle. Tea? he asked quietly. Please, I said. Anything just to move on. No sugar though, he informed me. That's OK, I told him, I don't anyway. My dad had forgotten how I took my tea. He fished in various drawers for cups, saucers and spoons. Mum remained silent. I couldn't look at her. There was an acute sense of rejection. I had rejected them, and here they were rejecting me in return. Dad lined three cups and their accompanying saucers up on the work surface. He seemed to be making just enough noise to fill the emptiness that had taken my words. He clanked a spoon into each saucer, which was overdoing things a little. I met my mother's eye. She was crying, silently. The kettle switched itself off. She stretched a hand across the table, and said we love you too. Dad glanced over and smiled briefly. And then he started humming again.

Inevitably, after the forgiveness came the whys. Why did you move abroad so suddenly? Why would you never tell us what you were doing? Why didn't you come home to visit? Why did you lose contact with your friends? For each why I had prepared a because, most of which were half-truths, at best. Because I lost my job and got a large redundancy cheque, and wanted to go somewhere different. Because I was never doing anything remotely interesting. Because I lost my passport for a while, and then got a job in France which never gave me much holiday, and the same for America. Because it wasn't easy keeping in touch with them when I was abroad. For each answer, my mother gave me a reassuring smile and squeezed my hand, reluctant to let go of it, as if I would walk out of her life again if she did. Dad remained silent throughout. I had the uncomfortable impression that he didn't believe me, which was particularly uncomfortable because he was right.

Later, things returned to normal. By normal, I mean that I regressed to being a semblance of the person I was when I first left home. I found myself, rather awkwardly, becoming eighteen again. This usually happened to me. Somewhere, a clock had stopped when I left home, and whenever I returned the time was still the same. I would find myself happy to flop on the sofa and have tea and sandwiches brought to me, would get upset if I couldn't watch the TV I wanted to watch, would boycott any washing-up responsibilities, and try, on a good day, to get my clothes cleaned. My mother, for her part, was more than happy to fulfil her end of the bargain. On the rare, selfless occasions I had offered to cook or wash up, she had seemed reluctant, unhappy even, at the reminder that I had grown up and left her, and could now fend for myself. I'm not sure my father felt quite the same way. As long as his tea was cooked and the washing up accomplished without a lot of input from his side, he was reasonably content. I often wondered, stretched out on the sofa that had witnessed many wasted days in my youth, whether the clock moves on again when you return to the parental nest with children of your own. I didn't know. That still seemed a remote and rather unlikely scenario, and I found myself suddenly thinking of Sarah.

After tea, Dad insisted on dragging me to the pub. I didn't really want to go, having become emotionally attached to the sofa, but he wouldn't take no for an answer. Mum stayed at home and did mother things. Dad drove, and was particularly unfatherly.

'Come on, son, no bullshit,' he said, when we sat down with our drinks. 'I want to know what you've really been up to.'

'Like I said, just working abroad.'

'No-one just works abroad, leaves their friends and family and doesn't come home for such a long stretch. And that fancy watch, those clothes – I want to know what's been going on.'

'I've told you . . .'

'Your mother, she's happy to believe what you say. That's mothers. But me, you'll have to do better than that.'

We were sitting next to each other, both facing a fruit machine which was flashing away as if its life depended on it. I had chosen my seat first. Dad had obviously decided he didn't want to look at me. I sensed his anger and his hurt, without having to see his eyes. 'I want to tell you, Dad. Really, I do. There's loads of things . . .' I stared into the promise of the lights. 'But there's a lot more that I don't want to tell you.'

'Like what?' I raised my eyebrows. 'OK, daft question,' he said.

We left it there and watched the fruit machine in near silence. On the drive home, I began to think.

Screwdriver

Greg and James had to be up to something. They didn't seem to be natural friends. There was very little warmth between them, and even fewer laughs. Before I went to see my parents, Greg had been evasive to the point of active antipathy. Back at work, James's attitude changed. He began to treat me with contempt again, which was a relief. In fact, he now regarded me with even greater derision than when I had first rejoined Intron, which took some doing. Even the office cleaner, whose wages must surely have made James feel queasy, received a warmer reception than I did every morning. Over the coming week I barely did anything useful. I was too distracted, and spent many hours instead perfecting a system to make me look productive. By carefully adding poor spelling and inconsistent grammar to all work communications, I would, I hoped, appear too busy to have time for accurate typing. Of course, if I had been rushed I wouldn't have bothered writing any messages, practised imperfections or otherwise, but no-one had seen through this scheme yet.

As I added unnecessary commas and misspelled people's names, I had the opportunity to think. I pondered as I sat at my desk, in the canteen as I ate my meals and in the bath as I scrubbed the day's grime from my body. They were cooking something up. They had sniffed an opportunity. Greg had complete access to the network – all passwords, everything. James already had a small scam going on, and maybe with Greg's help this was going to become a big scam. This may have been pure speculation, of course, but I didn't see any reason why I shouldn't be in touch with my paranoia every now and then. It had proved to be right on an alarmingly high number of occasions during my life, though that may just have reflected a near-dearth of otherwise rational thought. With no evidence either way, I endeavoured to keep my head down and type as many second-rate e-mails as I could.

In the evenings, I bored Sarah rigid on the phone, asking and reasking her opinion on what was going on between my workmates. She suggested that maybe James and Greg had become lovers, and that their dourness was simply a long-running tiff. Whilst not an entirely convincing theory, it at least cheered me up a bit every time they sat close to each other whispering. I pointed out to Sarah that while computer programming was undeniably dull, it was not so mind-numbing that heterosexual male Tractors from different countries were perpetually jumping into bed with each other. Pity, she said. And then, as I walked down the corridor on my way home one night, thankful to be out of the office, a horrible thought came to me. James's scam was small potatoes, and would have been of no interest to sensible Greg. But something bigger and maybe he would have been tempted in. Something bigger like resurrecting my swindle. I stopped, the tune I was whistling ceasing mid-note as my slow exhalation became a quick intake of air. That was it. The bastards were stealing my idea.

The more I watched James during the week, and particularly Greg, the more convinced I became that my hunch had been correct. Phrases I heard them utter, manuals I saw them reading, the excitement I tasted in the air. They were also increasingly on edge and protective of their work. Collusion between them had given way to active hostility towards me. As time progressed, their apparent hatred intensified. I was the only person who could have any insight into what they were doing, and the more tangible their goal, the more threatened they felt. I might be wrong, of course, but the more I thought about it, the more sense recent events made. I had confided in James about the details of my Original Swindle. James was about to lose his livelihood when Greg discovered what he was up to. He could therefore kill two birds with one stone. Go for the big one and rope Greg in. And I had made it easy for him. Simply search for accounts set up just before I left Intron, see which of them didn't seem to be doing anything, just hanging there, and Bullshit Bingo! You had proactively outsourced considerable financial remuneration. With Greg on his side he would have access to the accounts. Then all that would be needed was a couple of fairly basic programs to divert the money into a bank account. Greg would get half of a large sum of money, plus the satisfaction of having fixed Intron's teething problems when James showed him exactly why Symbiosis wasn't delivering. James would sacrifice his scam for a far larger profit. Net result: two happy bastards, and one miserable Permie.

And then the first real evidence came to light. Suddenly Symbiosis began to click at Intron. System crashes petered out, and delay times plummeted. Tractors stopped losing their jobs and everybody cheered up. The network came dangerously close to doing everything it was supposed to do, and the reason was obvious, to me at least. James was removing his illicit code. This was not good news, however, and was an event I had been dreading. For James to make this sacrifice, they must have been able to smell success. And if Greg had done his job, then he wouldn't be around much longer. They must, I concluded, be on the very verge of taking my money. Helplessness abounded. I became increasingly desperate. I ate alone in the canteen and fretted. I parked my car outside my house and just sat there, worrying. I had cups of tea by myself and got jittery. Maybe it was the caffeine. Either way, in a few short days it would all be over. The money was passing to new owners, just as I had taken it from its old ones.

I had to confront them. I couldn't just sit by and watch the miserable duo bleed me dry. The feeling of betrayal grew stronger, and with it came anger. By Monday evening, I was ready to face them. It had been a long day and I had taken enough Permie shit. I was on edge, excited even, but still in control. Adrenalin was surging through muscles, making them hard. I paced around, thinking of tactics. Greg and James were nowhere, however. They had been out of the office for over an hour, and no-one had seen them. Something caught my eye as I fidgeted. A long, pointed screw-driver, used for reaching the backs of awkwardly positioned workstations. I picked it up. It had a fine Phillips head, which almost looked sharpened. I pushed the implement up inside the sleeve of my suit and then let it fall out again, catching the handle as it did so. I continued to play with the screwdriver as I waited. I was Robert De Niro in *Taxi Driver*, sliding the weapon out of my sleeve and asking the computer whether it was talking to me. Maybe the sight of a sharpened screwdriver would shift the balance. Maybe now they would see that I was serious. I flicked the weapon out and threatened the computer again. And then I caught sight of myself reflected in the window miming lines from a film with a household tool in my hand, and quickly ducked down behind a monitor. I crawled along the floor to the window sill and drew the blind, before returning the screwdriver to its rightful spot on James's desk, hoping that no-one had seen me from the outside.

Acutely embarrassed, I decided to give up on my

quest for confrontation. Finally, flushed, the anticipation of violence ebbing, I slunk out of the building. The early spring light was almost stretching to home time now, leaving behind a frigid dusk to negotiate through steamed-up windows. I pulled the car keys out of my coat pocket and approached my car. Twenty yards ahead, a figure slid out from under the rusty Peugeot. There was a surreality about the movement of the shape in the enveloping gloom. Nothing registered for a couple of seconds. I stopped, keys in my hand. The body stood up and stepped smartly towards me. It was Greg. He dusted himself off and glanced edgily around the car park.

'Greg, what the fuck are you doing?' I asked. Greg sauntered forward. We were dribbling distance apart. I looked up into his big round face with its thick brown eyes and spread-out nose. Greg was three or four inches taller and was standing as upright as possible to emphasize the fact. I imagined he was trying to use something approaching menace to get his point across. There was no doubt that he was bigger, heavier and stronger than me, but also slower, and if it came to a fight I envisaged him folding under a rain of quick sharp blows, preferably with something metallic. That's what I had imagined anyway, and on increasingly frequent occasions over the past few days. But the reality was that, even drowning in adrenalin, I was no fighter, and screwdriver or no screwdriver I lacked the stomach for combat. I was a runner, and a shabby one at that. Someone who had spent half their adult life in narcissistic gyms doing weights in front of mirrors was not someone to fuck with, particularly if you had spent half your adult life in pubs doing pints. I eased my posture as a sign of submission. Greg glared down at me. I repeated the question. 'What were you doing under my car?'

'I wasn't under your vehicle,' he said stiffly.

'What? I just saw you climb out.'

'No you didn't.'

'Look, Greg, for fuck's sake, what's going on?'

He kept eye contact. There was anger in his face. 'You messin' with me, mo'fo'?'

'It's the other way round, if anything,' I said. I was eager to know the truth but even more eager not to get beaten up. 'Come on, Greg, tell me what you're up to.'

'I ain't up to nothing.' His voice rose. He was almost screaming. The whites of his eyes and teeth shone out against the darkness of his skin, which was rapidly being swallowed by the gloom. 'Now stay the hell out of my face, buddy.' A reflex somewhere told me I was about to be punched. 'One more fucking . . .'

There was a scraping noise behind Greg and to his right. James. He had been crouching behind my car. Perhaps sensing bloodshed he stepped out of the twilight. 'Come on, Greg,' he said, 'it's not worth it.' He turned and walked towards the exit of the car park. Greg continued to bore into my eyes. He was having difficulty not punching me. 'Greg!' James shouted.

'My advice to you,' Greg said, talking quietly, 'would be to keep well away from us.' And with that, he turned and walked away.

Shaken but unscathed, I got in my car, locked the doors and started the engine. My legs were trembling and the car lurched forward under my shaky clutch control. As I left the space, the rear wheels went over something solid. Greg and James were no longer visible. I opened the door and had a look under the wheels. I had run over a pair of pliers and a hammer. At this rate it wouldn't be long until I had a full set of tools to my name.

Cavalier

'What the fuck's that?' Jeremy asked, pointing at the two large rucksacks Archie was struggling to pack.

'Just some stuff.'

'What sort of stuff?'

Archie pulled the drawstring of one of the packs, taking care not to damage any of the folders inside. 'Very personal things,' he said, 'items I don't want to be separated from.' Brian took the rucksacks, one under each arm, and threw them in the boot of the car. Archie winced. Just because they held bits of him that were no longer still attached didn't mean they were without feeling. Jeremy closed the curtains of Archie's front room, and told him it was time to go. 'I'm not sure this is a good idea,' Archie said, in a final, almost futile, attempt to extricate himself from the proceedings.

'Tough,' Jeremy replied. 'One for all . . . You remember.'

'But—'

'And anyway, it was you who started this.' He encouraged Archie towards the front door, steering him at the elbow.

'What's wrong?' Brian shouted from outside.

'Archie's going a bit queer on us. Start the car.'

Brian laughed, and the sound of his booming diaphragm failed to bring any reassurance to Archie.

Jeremy snatched Archie's keys and locked the front door, before pocketing them. 'Right. In the front.'

Archie opened the car door and slid himself onto the seat, while Jeremy climbed in the back.

'Which way?' Brian asked.

'M6. Aston Expressway.'

'Yes, boss,' Brian said, pulling away from the kerb and into the inevitable traffic.

Archie ran his eyes over the interior of the car as they headed down the Alcester Road. Mostly, it was tidy and in good order. Noting his interest, Jeremy piped up, 'Nice motor, eh, Magoo?'

'Yes,' he replied. Cars didn't hold much fascination for Archie, except for those with onboard computers, and even then it was more the computer than the car which held his interest. 'What sort of car is this?' he asked with little desire for an answer.

'Dunno. Cavalier, maybe. Brian?'

'Difficult to tell. Sierra, I reckon.'

'You mean you don't know?'

'Give me a chance. I only nicked it this morning.'

'It's stolen?'

'No, Archie. All those wires are hanging about the place for decoration.' Archie peered down towards Brian's right leg, which was pushed up against the dash, trapping a hardware shop's worth of cables.

'You honestly stole this vehicle?'

'Oh for fuck's sake. What do you think – we'd take our own transport for a job like this?'

'What if the police—'

'They won't.'

'But they might. I've seen a lot of *CrimeWatch*, you know, and they always get car thieves in the end.'

'Look,' Jeremy said, patience waning, 'the important thing is this. We go up to Manchester today, whatever vehicle we take—'

'Mondeo!' Brian shouted triumphantly. 'It's a Mondeo. There – on the dashboard.'

'Thank you, Brian.' Jeremy rubbed his hand down over his face. 'Look, Archie, you're with the big boys now, all right? We're going to Manchester so we can get back what's rightfully ours. Me and Brian have had a think about it, and this is the best thing all round. It might seem a bit drastic to you, but that's hard cheese. So sit still, shut up and let's sort this fucking thing out once and for all.'

'I just thought, given the circumstances—'

'Archie!' Jeremy shouted. 'Enough, OK? It'll only take a couple of hours and then it'll all be over. Now kindly do me the favour of shutting the fuck up. Right?'

Archie closed his eyes and nodded. Nerves began to form. He really wasn't at ease with this at all, and the further up the M6 they progressed, and the more signs he spotted for Manchester, the heavier the weight of dread which settled in his stomach.

Biological Control

I lay on my bed and stared up at the ceiling as I had done when Sarah visited. This time there were no tears, just bitterness. I recalled how I had even once saved Greg's skin, only for him now to be scaring me out of mine. I felt weak and impotent. For the first time in my adult life it was blindingly obvious that any notion I had about ever fighting my way out of trouble was a film-induced fantasy. I was no more likely to punch my way to victory than I was to receive an honorary doctorate in advanced shagging from the University of Amsterdam. But something had to be done. I ran through my options, trying to make patterns in the ceiling stars. First, I could shop them both to the Intron management. This was not a great idea – I would simply be implicating myself, and I didn't really have any evidence of wrongdoing. Second, I could do nothing and accept my lot. Fine, except the situation at work was becoming intolerable. I had now been threatened, and, whatever they had been up to, Greg and James hadn't been trying to make my car any safer. I decided to catch the bus into work in future. Third, I could get in touch with some old friends. This was, I quickly came to realize, a fantastic idea. After all, a problem shared was a problem halved. I flashed the light on and off to celebrate, and watched until all of the stars had faded.

In the morning, I went to work with new-found

enthusiasm. James and Greg continued to be as thick as people trying to embezzle already stolen money, and I kept largely out of their way. On the dot of 4:58 and 33 seconds, I left Intron and headed home on the bus. After a quick change, I drove to the pub. Some twenty minutes later, I entered and ordered a Wonking beer. I sat down and began to wait. I was excited. I drank quickly and breathed short, charged breaths. In other circumstances, I would have been terrified. Memories of a thorough kicking, my still-tainted right hand, porcelain and enamel, all would have had me on edge. But the rules had changed. I was dizzy with anticipation. I would be on their side now. Parasites were about to turn symbionts. No danger of any subsequent violence, and perhaps a share of the money if I played things well.

Another beer and a sandwich. Even the ham and tomato dullness couldn't blunt my light-headed expectancy. It was 6:30. I monitored the doors. Old jaded drinkers staggered home for tea and were replaced by fresh ones eager to take their places. The noise of the jukebox was eventually drowned by the voices of people trying to talk over it, and so the manager turned the music up louder. For Christ's sake stop them hearing each other seemed to be the message. 7:20. I went to the bar and ordered a bitter top, which was a shandy by any other name, except with slightly less ridicule attached. No-one, as far as I knew, had ever been called a bitter top-drinking nonce. 7:45 and my shandy was going flat. 8:11 and it was time to switch to soft drinks. I examined the change in my pocket. As a responsible driver of a motor vehicle, I had to weigh up the pros and cons – the bankrupting cost of a couple of cordials against a heavy fine for drink-driving. Bit of a close one, I'd have thought, which made me wonder why, if brewers were constantly banging on about the amount of time and effort they spent producing a perfect pint of beer, was it still cheaper than lemonade? On the basis of Stella Artois adverts, lemonade should be the ultimate connoisseur's drink, alarmingly expensive as it was. In fact, adding a dash of Coke or orange to a vintage wine could only increase its value. I swallowed my pride, and nearly a day's salary, and invested in half a Coke.

8:38 and still nothing. A packet of crisps, a visit to the gents, the jukebox was turned up a notch. Still no sign. I rang my answer machine. Sarah had left a message. I wasted another day's wages and called her, shouting down the line on the bartop phone, which greedily swallowed fifty-pence pieces like I was calling abroad. Which was no way to talk about my would-be girlfriend. Sarah shouted back, 'I can hardly hear you either. Where are you?' The Jug of Ale, I told her. 'Who are you with?' No-one, I said. But I'm hoping to bump into the men who beat me up. 'Whatever for?' she asked. I have a plan, I replied. 9:26 and still they weren't here. I began to suspect that they weren't coming.

My plan was this. I was, I realized, the middleman in an important equation. On one side of me stood a pair of parasites who were trying to hack into my old ghost account and empty it. On the other side was the pair of parasites who had encouraged me to set up the account in the first place. James and Greg were effectively doing their utmost to steal money which by rights should have been Jeremy and Brian's. It was my duty therefore to cut out the middle man, and introduce the two parties to each other – a case of using my old parasites to clear my new ones. A fine example of biological control, if ever there was one. However, for one undesirable species to wipe another out, they first had to turn up at the pub. 10:23 and this was looking unlikely. I drained my Coke and crunched the ice cubes. I would have to come again tomorrow.

Toys of Communication

Darren examined his bank balance with some dismay. In his heart of hearts he knew that no large sums of cash were going to be deposited into his account any more, but it didn't stop him checking. The one thing missing in his life, he had decided, was a minidisc player. Sure, he had a CD player, a Sports Walkman, a miniature electronic camcorder, a DVD player, a mobile phone, a laptop, a games system, a pager, a palmtop organizer, a fax machine, a scanner and a watch which automatically aligned itself with Greenwich Mean Time, but his existence was still lacking something. He could video himself receiving a fax which he had scanned into his laptop while listening to the disappointing sounds of Less is More and electronically diarizing events of the day ahead, but he couldn't record his CDs onto small pieces of plastic. He examined the insignificant piece of paper that the cashpoint had spewed out, which detailed his insignificant finances in tiny faded numbers. Darren sighed. How he would trade half of his gadgets for minidisc ownership.

He headed towards Dixons and ran through the items he could now happily live without. At the top of the list were his toys of communication – the mobile phone, the pager and the fax machine. He had bought them largely in the mistaken belief that being more accessible meant he would be more popular. This had proved to be a big error of judgement. He looked guiltily down at the phone bulging in his pocket. There had been times, Darren freely admitted, when he had phoned his own pager, paged an e-mail to his laptop, autoscanned it into his fax machine, and digitally faxed the message back to his phone. It was a beautiful loop of communication, the twenty-first-century version of talking to yourself. He had even managed to extend the loop into infinity, by setting everything to auto-dial. For a good half-hour, his various machines chattered away pointlessly, and Darren stood back from the circle and watched in fascination. The machines had become almost human. They gossiped endlessly to each other without ever saying a single thing of interest or stopping to think about the information they were regurgitating. In the end, he shut them down one by one, and left them off.

With no potential for communication, he felt a lot happier. But that was the very point of modern information transfer, as far as Darren could see. Being accessible, even to yourself, had become a bad thing. It is the inaccessibility of communication which will prove to be the greatest breakthrough – gadgets which keep people at bay and stop you being tracked down at any hour of the day will form the next generation of technological evolution. After all, status is directly related to access. The more difficult you are to contact, the more sought-after you become; the less frequently you can be reached, the more often people want to try to reach you. Darren realized therefore that by making himself more available, he had also made himself less popular, and resolved to be more elusive from now on.

Standing outside Dixons in the pouring rain, staring at the array of minidisc players, Darren decided to give it up as a bad job, and turned round and trudged homewards. Karen would have started tea, and the house would be warm and comforting. He examined his watch. 17:48 GMT. She would be wondering where he was. He still wasn't particularly happy about leaving her alone in the house half the day, especially since the visit of the thugs two months ago. He shivered, as rain dribbled down his neck. With luck they would never see them again. Besides, Karen and Darren had been getting along well recently. There was even the chance that they might make love later. Darren picked up his pace. Who needed gadgets when you had a girlfriend, he asked himself, taking his pager out and sending Karen a message telling her to unlock the front door because he was on his way home.

On the Verge

The next morning, James smiled at me, a knowing, telling, threatening grin which said we've almost got your money, and there's nothing you can do about it. I returned the smile, a grin which said you might have two legs now, but just wait until my friends get hold of you. Greg just nodded his head irritably, which suggested that he couldn't even be bothered to gloat any more. I nodded back, thinking of a nice headbutt which might be in the post for him. Maybe it was obvious to them that I knew what they were doing, but nothing was ever said. No words passed between us all day.

My plan had sparked some confidence though. I no longer felt as vulnerable. The big boys were about to join my side. Greg and James continued in their furtive collusion and I continued in my Permie confusion. At night I went to the pub and endured shoddy puns and shouted conversation. My friends neglected to turn up, however. This set the scene for the rest of the week. It started to dawn that something wasn't right. Night after night, Jeremy and Brian failed to take advantage of what I supposed to be their local. When drinkers like that consistently fail to make it to the pub, breweries get nervous. I wondered whether they had changed venues, and tried three other locals, to no avail. Certainly, any one of them would have been rough enough to satisfy Jeremy and Brian's delicate sensibilities. In these venues I was happy to take the plasters and rings off my fingers and wave my artwork about as a badge of honour. Days and nights became surreal journeys between intimidation at work and intimidation in pubs.

By Friday, I was becoming desperate. I had hardly been home all week, except to change my clothes and sleep. I spent more and more time in public houses, which in other circumstances would have been a blessing, but now was a sad reminder that Jeremy and Brian had disappeared. In increasing desperation, I asked around for them. Bar staff, punters, anyone I could find. Have you seen a couple of friends of mine? One's a giant of a man, wild as hell, and the other a mean-faced rodent likely to start fights . . . Perhaps unsurprisingly, no-one said anything. These were not the sorts of places which welcomed people turning up and asking questions, particularly about local psychopaths. I grew frantic enough to even think about trying to get hold of their phone numbers. Directory Enquiries, however, doesn't deal much in Christian names. The only other approach I could come up with was handing out my own number to suitably hard-looking characters, and asking them to pass it on to Jeremy or Brian, in exchange for cash. However, this plan also had its flaws. Giving my telephone number to dodgy punters to solicit men into phoning me for cash became something of a personal safety issue. I went back to what I knew best – sitting in the Jug of Ale and waiting. And then, on Tuesday evening, just as things were appearing almost futile, someone came into the pub and sauntered over to my table.

'Mind if I sit with you?' he asked.

I shrugged. 'Not especially.'

'So this is where you've been hiding out.'

'How did you know where to find me?'

'To tell the truth, I followed you from your house.'

'Why didn't you just knock on my door?'
'I wanted to know where you were heading.'
'So what do you want?'
'A word.'
'Yeah? And what might that be?'
'Get me a beer and I'll tell you.'
'Why on earth should I buy you of all people a beer?' I asked.
'I'll let you know when you've got me it.'
Reluctantly, I stood up and went over to the bar. 'The usual?' the barmaid asked. This was the real pisser about hanging around in such a substandard boozer – I was getting to be known as a regular. People would greet me as I came in these days, which was unnerving. I felt like Norm in a particularly poor episode of *Cheers*.
'No. A bottle of Bud, please. And two packets of pork scratchings.' I returned to the small round table and handed Greg the assembled health food.

Squawking

'So come on, let's have it.' I was in no mood to exchange pleasantries. Small talk always seems so pointless, like the squawking of a parrot, regurgitating the same remembered sounds over and over, just for the sake of filling the empty air. Faced with the threatening presence of Greg, I wanted to hear what he had to say and then get the fuck home, the minimum of messing about involved.

'Listen, buddy, I'm heading back tomorrow. Got my flight booked and everything taken care of.'

'Tomorrow?' I asked in defeat. I was shafted. My money had gone.

'Fifteen thirty,' he confirmed.

'So what are you doing here?'

'I've come to square a few things up.'

I scanned the bar in the vain hope of salvation. Jeremy and Brian could still walk in and save the day. Break a couple of Greg's bones, retrieve the money, maybe even give me a slice of it. This was, I conceded, an increasingly unlikely scenario, but that didn't stop me hoping. I decided to try to string things out a little, just in case. If I could keep him in the bar an hour or two, you never knew. Small talk might be a constructive use of time after all. 'And you're packed and everything?' I asked.

'Yep. All packed and ready to go.'

'Last night in the hotel then?'

'Uh-huh.'

'Be good to get home, I bet.'

'Yeah. Look, Ian—'

'Another drink?'

'No. I think—'

'Come on, I'll buy.' Greg scratched his head irritably. I picked up my empty glass, thought momentarily about smashing it into his face, shuddered at the needless violence Brian and Jeremy had introduced into my life, then headed for the bar before he could say anything else. Small talk wasn't going well. Short yes or no questions were hardly going to detain him indefinitely. I glanced at the time. 8:30, give or take. No-one new came into the pub while I was being served. Despite this, the landlord appeared to be considering whether to turn the jukebox up a notch. I needed to think strategically. What would Mary say? Supermarkets. Caravans. Gardening. Gossip. That was more like it. Think like the enemy. Baffle Greg with utter nonsense. I returned to the table, and gave it my best shot before he had a chance to speak. 'Don't know if you've ever considered buying a caravan, Greg. Very popular over here. Even started selling them through supermarkets. Large Tescos, I'm led to believe, are going to have them in their gardening sections. Which reminds me. I was reading a gardening magazine the other day – *What Garden* I think – and they had this section on celebrity allotments. You might have seen it in the papers as well. Apparently the England goalkeeper – that's soccer of course – has been having an affair with two—'

'Ian!' Greg had his hand up, palm facing my mouth, as if there was traffic coming out of it that he wanted to stop. 'Ian. For Christ's sake, man.'

'What?'

'You know what? You find me under your car with some tools. I threaten your ass. I say about two words to you in a month. I follow you to a goddamn bar. And you wanna talk about fucking goaltenders.'

'*Keepers*.'

'Whatever. I mean what are you hoping to achieve?'

'Nothing,' I said, guiltily.

'I'm leaving tomorrow, you never have to see me again. Don't we have something a little more important to discuss?'

'Like what?'

'Like what the hell has been going on?'

I rubbed my face. 'I've got a fairly good idea,' I said.

'Care to fill me in?' he asked. He smiled slightly as he did so. James's enjoyment at watching me struggle was wearing off on Greg. The Germans had a word for this malicious joy at someone else's unhappiness: football.

'If I must.'

'You must.'

Another glance around the bar. No sign of Jeremy and Brian. I wondered suddenly whether I had been wasting my time. 'I confide in James, James gets an idea, ropes you in, you both rip me off, you exit to the States, James buys a bigger house.'

Greg raised his eyebrows. 'Not bad.' He took a swig of Bud. 'But not good either. And tell me, what was I doing under your car?'

I had no idea where this was heading, but Greg no longer felt quite as threatening. He was leaning back in his chair, his hands playing with the bottle, occasionally eating some of his snacks. 'Certainly not improving it.'

'Fucking with the brakes,' he said, leaning forward.

'You wanker!'

'I told you, cool people say mo'fo'. But why do you think I was doing that?'

'So that I wouldn't be late for work any more?'

'Listen, this is no time for sarcasm.' Greg was in my face. 'The reason is that if I didn't do it, James would have done it. And if James had done it, you really would be late, if you catch my meaning.'

'So you're both a couple of cunts. What's your point?'

'My point is this, buddy. You haven't really been as smart as you think.'

'No?' I asked, anger welling.

'No. I kinda thought maybe you'da sussed things out by now.'

'What things?'

'I'll tell you. But first I need something.'

'A good kicking, by any chance?'

'Nope, little buddy. Just a favour. And believe me, it'll be worth it for you in the long run.'

When Greg had finished his drink and gone, I rang Sarah from the insatiable pub phone and told her we were making an important journey at short notice.

Departures

In Departures, I examined my two suitcases mournfully. They sagged in the middle like underfed bellies. Feelings of inadequacy once again surfaced. Checking luggage is like the final judgement. The saints on one side, the sinners on the other. Shuffle forward. Step up to the desk and present your worldly baggage. Put it on the scales. Weigh up your life. Excess baggage is God's way of telling you that you have failed the entrance test.

An hour and a half until the flight. The dead time of checking in and wandering about. Sarah continued to wrap her arms around me, stroke my hair, kiss me and generally not fuck off out of the way. The closer she held me the more I recoiled. I wanted her away from me. I ground my teeth and grimaced a nervous smile.

Fancy me? she asked. I looked away and mumbled of course. She had a genius for missing the signals I was sending her. My body was screaming Leave Me Alone. Now. Please Fuck Off. She squeezed me round the waist and pulled me close. Her tongue was in my mouth and I made a play at enjoying it. As I did, I fingered the key in my pocket. Locker 2167. I knew this without needing to examine the fob. 2167. The lockers were twenty or thirty metres away past Sarah's hair, which was clinging to my face, sticky like candyfloss from her hairspray. I could almost see the metal boxes. I took the opportunity to glance at my watch behind her head. The courier would be here in less than fifteen minutes. I needed to find a way of distracting Sarah. She let go of me and I dropped my head. Our suitcases sulked around our feet. Next to my anorexic luggage lounged Sarah's two obese cases, contents bulging over the waistline of their straps. She hunched over one of them, and began scribbling on a tag. Want me to do yours? she asked, gazing up at me. Hardly worth it, I said, half smiling back. The flight flashed up on the electronic scoreboard as being delayed. An extra half-hour, Sarah said glumly, straightening. Don't worry, I said, a couple of hours and we'll be out of here for good. We were not out of the woods yet, though. I watched the jaded arrive and the eager depart. Where was he? Where the fuck was he?

The airport clock said 13:17, and I felt a little nervous. I continued to monitor the entrance to Departures. Sarah pressed herself against me again and I tried not to push her away. She was in danger of ruining everything. And then came salvation. Just going to have a quick look round the shops, she said. Take your time, I replied. As soon as she had disappeared from view, swallowed up by people and their possessions, I grabbed a trolley and loaded the luggage onto it. Mobile, I careered towards the lockers like a *Supermarket Sweep* contestant on ice. 2167 took a while to find. Glancing around to make sure Sarah couldn't see me, I opened the metal box and peered inside. There, on its side, was a tatty case. I closed the door again and made my way to the exit, a tortuous few yards past the shops of Terminal 4 which were currently tempting Sarah with their many wares. I pushed quickly until I was outside. With the heat from the terminal on my back I stood near the door scanning the approach road. Coaches came and went, spilling their contents onto the tarmac at pre-assigned bays. Taxis clattered around like inefficient bees.

Pedestrians tramped over a zebra crossing whose white stripes were fighting a losing battle with black tyre marks. A TNT van approached and stopped suddenly and I pushed the trolley towards it. I grabbed the delivery man as he was about to walk past.

'I think you're here for me,' I said.

'You mister . . .' he scanned down his clipboard, 'Glick?'

'Close enough, yes. Here.' I handed him the locker key. 'The item is in this locker. You've got the address that it's got to be delivered to?'

'I've got the address all right, but it's not my job to go hunting around in lockers.'

I reached into my pocket and took out a £10 note. 'Will this help?'

'The locker's been paid for and everything?'

'Yes. But I'm late, so you'll have to get it yourself.'

He summed me up for a second before taking the note. 'Right you are,' he said.

'Cheers.' I swung the trolley round and made my way back to the last place I had seen Sarah. She was reading a magazine, occasionally gazing around the Departures lounge. I came up behind her and kissed her softly on the neck.

'Where have you been?' she asked.

'Just having a look around. Any sign of him?'

'No. You did tell him Terminal 4?'

'Yes. He'll be here,' I said, hugging her. Things were different now that I had sorted my business.

A few minutes later, Sarah called out, 'There he is.' I followed the nod of her head. She waved at him. 'We're over here. Greg, we're over here.'

Emotional Luggage

The flight to Los Angeles was, as promised, only half an hour late. When all the luggage had been checked in, Greg insisted on giving us some money.

'Come on, please, have some.'

'You've spent enough,' Sarah objected.

'Yeah. Fucking excess baggage. Seventy bucks. Bummer.'

'Well you are taking half of England's production of pork scratchings home with you.'

'I never realized they were so heavy.'

'We had a right struggle with them on the coach.'

'Must have about a whole pig in there altogether.'

Sarah still didn't appear convinced. 'But, Greg, you know where they come from? They're not made from whole pigs – just the yucky parts. They're horrible.'

'Look, in the USA we have beef jerky, pastrami, wieners, even fucking chilli dogs, and yet you Brits have managed to come up with an even more low-life food. It's a miracle! I love 'em! Can't get enough of 'em. And I reckon I'm gonna be able to sell these babies when I get back. Start importing them maybe.'

'I never thought I'd see the day that my cases were used for meat product transportation.'

'That reminds me – you gotta let me give you something for them.'

'Forget it. They're knackered.'

'Aw, come on. Here, Sarah, a couple hundred bucks

for yours, and Ian, you know what, here's five for yours.'

'Don't worry. Look, just do me a favour.'

'Name it.'

'When you get back to LA, sell that heap of shit car you sold me, and have a garage sale for my furniture. And sell our suitcases while you're at it. Keep what you want, give the rest to the LA Vagrancy Project. OK?'

'OK.'

'And could you give notice on my apartment? I'm still paying for the bloody thing. The deposit should cover the final month's rent.'

'No problem.'

'You'll miss it. Go on, get going.'

'Right. And don't forget to check your bank account on the first.'

'Don't worry.'

And with that, Greg turned round and walked smartly towards passport control. 'Come on, we've got a bus to catch,' I told Sarah. Free from the suitcases which Greg had borrowed, we ambled out into the cold air of the bus depot and boarded a National Distress coach bound for exotic Birmingham. Now that all business had been taken care of, I couldn't get enough of Sarah, and I held her close to me. There were many things I wanted to tell her, and an equal number that I didn't want her to know. Instead of telling her that I had stolen her colleague's suitcase and finally had it couriered back to him several months later, I told her that I loved her. Instead of telling her that Greg had resurrected my dodgy programming, giving me a very healthy pay rise, I told her that I would miss her when she returned to Manchester. Instead of filling her in on the other details – that Greg had duped James into removing his illicit code from the system, and in doing so had solved Intron's problems, I told her that I wanted to remove all of her clothes when we got back to Birmingham. Instead of informing her that James had done a runner and was facing an uncertain financial future, I told her I was going to buy her something nice. And instead of telling her all the other shady and dishonest aspects of my recent life, I told her that I would always be honest with her.

Around Oxford, Sarah said, 'You know, Greg seems like a nice bloke.'

'Don't be fooled by appearance, personality or a number of selfless deeds,' I replied.

'But you know what I mean. He helped you. He didn't have to do that, did he?'

'Didn't he?' I asked, smiling. 'Didn't he indeed?'

Rubbing Noses

I didn't need this. I was mid-shredded wheat. Two slices of toast, a quick visit to the bathroom, a mournful look in the mirror and it was time to leave for work. A relatively short trip across the LA tarmac and Phil Mannox would be eagerly anticipating another day of pushing me around and bullying me with his fascist workspeak. Greg was standing on my doorstep. He was almost pale. Not Caucasian pale, but certainly an Afro-Caribbean imitation.

'What's up?' I asked between mouthfuls of what had become my new staple breakfast diet.

'Trouble,' Greg said.

I stopped chewing. 'What sort of trouble?'

'Look, how much money you got?'

'In cash?'

'No. I mean how much can you lay your hands on right now?'

'What's the problem?'

'Please, Ian, I'm asking you to help me.'

'OK. But how much do you need?'

'I dunno. Ten thousand?'

'Dollars?'

'No, nickels. What d'you think?'

'I think something strange is going on here.'

'Come on,' he implored, 'get your wallet and let's go.'

I put my breakfast down, grabbed my wallet and

locked the apartment. Greg was already in his car. There was little time for misgivings. We headed up Gardner Street, with its apartment blocks bordered by perpetually watered shrubs, onto Fountain, and then dropped down onto La Cienega, lowering ourselves once more into the city's smog. The traffic was crawling, and the air-conditioning struggled to find any air worth conditioning. Cell phones were out all around us, mouths moving soundlessly. A girl applying layers of make-up in a Mercedes next to us, a mirror bolted onto the dashboard for just such a purpose. Bass bins booming in a Saturn behind. A guy leaning out of the window of his Explorer, trying to see what was causing the snarl. An unnatural blonde in a Cherokee elbowing in from a side street. Everybody edging closer together. Fenders almost rubbing noses. Pushing. Shoving. Barging. The whole city one machine, stationary, burning, anchored to the melting tarmac. Beads of sweat were forming on Greg's forehead.

'So come on, what's the problem?' I asked again.

'I'll tell you what the problem is. Fucking IRS.'

'Yeah?'

'Yeah. Bastards.'

'What do they want?'

'They want money. And now.'

'How come?'

'Long story.'

'You've not been paying enough tax?'

'Correct.'

'So not much of a story then.'

'Guess not.'

'But why the panic?'

'They're coming back with bailiffs in an hour. If I can't raise the cash, man, they're gonna take everything.'

We edged closer to my bank. It appeared that Greg had fallen foul of the tax authority by declaring his salary to be roughly half the amount his brother Carl actually paid him. Somehow this discrepancy had come to light. Zealously sensible Greg had ignored increasingly threatening letters from the tax office, and in doing so had managed to precipitate a crisis. Some seriously bad-ass dudes (Greg's words) were on their way right now to do his place over (mine).

The stop-start LA traffic lurched forward and we turned onto Beverley Boulevard and parked opposite the Rock Hard café. Outside, Japanese schoolgirls were taking each other's photos, excited to have journeyed halfway round the globe to stand outside a glorified McDonald's with a couple of drum stools in the window. Greg marched me out of the heat and into my local branch of the Bank of America, where normal air-conditioned service was resumed.

'You sure you have enough?' he asked.

'I'm sure.'

'And you're willing to help me out?'

'I'm willing. God knows why, but I'm willing. Now exactly how much?'

Greg looked shifty, unfolding a piece of paper he had been carrying in his jeans. 'Fifteen thousand four hundred.'

'Jesus.'

'And twenty-six bucks.'

'Any more?'

'Eighty-eight cents.'

'Right.'

'You know I'll get it back to you.'

'You'd better.'

The bank was alarmingly happy to give me such a large sum of cash over the counter. Greg was fairly pleased as well. It was a very satisfying wad of $100 bills. We headed back the way we had come. I trusted Greg implicitly – he was too dull to be dishonest – and hadn't been too perturbed about lending him the money. I was curious for more details, though, and asked him where he spent the money he should have been paying the government.

'You know. The usual,' he said.

'Like what?'

'The usual. Cars and chicks.'

'Which cars?'

'This one for a start.'

'And chicks? Which chicks?'

'Just chicks.'

'I've never seen you with a woman, Greg. I mean, no disrespect or anything . . .'

'Yes you have. Many times.'

We turned back onto Fountain. Traffic was barely moving in the opposite direction. Sprinklers embedded in the sidewalk showered fine mists of water over neatly trimmed strips of grass. I racked my brain. 'When exactly?'

'Think about it.'

'I am. When?'

'At work.'

'But there aren't any women at work. We're computer programmers – that's the law.'

'Wrong, dude. My brother does employ women.'

'Well, there's Toni. But she's Carl's . . .' Greg was smiling at me. We turned through a red light, an American manoeuvre which still made me nervous, and forked sharply into the underground parking bay of our apartments. 'You're joking.'

'Nope.'

'Seriously?'

'Seriously.'

'No!'

'Yes.'

'Fuck.'

'You said it.'

'But what about Carl? Doesn't he suspect anything?'

Greg put the engine out of its misery. 'Look at me, Ian,' he said, turning in my direction. 'Would you?'

I looked at him. He was as earnest and run of the mill as anyone I had ever met in the field of computing. 'I guess not,' I replied. 'And that's where your money's going?'

'What do you think? Chicks like Toni take a whole lot of investment.'

I wondered, apart from large sums of money, what Toni might be getting out of the deal. Greg was no George Clooney. George Bush was closer, although Greg dressed more conservatively and had a less dynamic outlook on life. 'Why didn't you say anything before?' I asked, hurt that I had missed out on this incredible gossip.

'I wanted to, believe me. But now I owe you, I figure I can trust you a bit better. Go opening your mouth and you'll lose a lot of money.'

Greg got out and walked briskly inside with the cash. I followed, digesting the news, wondering whether Greg had adopted an air of apparent sense purely to fool his brother. Certainly I would have stooped a lot lower if I'd thought I would get to sleep with the LA perfection of Toni. And as disguises went, it was a good one, although I had, at times, seen chinks of light in his armour.

Greg managed to appease the IRS bailiffs and began to repay my money. Three or four weeks later, however, I left the country in a hurry, expecting never to be fully reimbursed. Not unusually, I had been wrong. And I hadn't been so much reimbursed as reincarnated.

Manchester, So Much to Answer For

The doorbell rang, which was a rarity. Not because visitors were scarce now that the house had been fully renovated, but because the doorbell itself had been installed during a period of renovation overseen by a myopic handiman who had difficulty holding a screw-driver. Generally, people pushed the bell with growing pressure until their thumbs hurt, and then resorted to rapping their knuckles on the door itself. Today, however, the bell was working. Karen opened the door and was confronted by a large man.

'Got something for you, love,' he said. 'It's in the van. Don't suppose you could come and make sure it's yours before I lift it out?'

Karen had been down this road before and flatly refused to leave the safety of her doorstep. She stepped smartly back inside and closed the door, and put the safety chain on. The man sighed, and Karen watched through the spy hole as he walked to his van and returned carrying a heavy-looking package partially wrapped in tape. Only when the delivery man had passed his clipboard through the gap and Karen had signed for it did she open the door and lug the object into the living room. She examined it for clues. On closer inspection, it was a tired suitcase of some sort, which appeared vaguely familiar. Two leather straps with large buckles kept the thing together. Karen unfastened the clasps and unzipped the case. Inside were clothes which had seen better days. It was some time before she recognized them as Darren's. Intrigued, she began to root around, and came across a wallet which contained bank cards that her boyfriend had cancelled after his trip to the States. By now, Karen was enjoying herself. There was an element of lucky dip to the proceedings which beat the pants off watching dysfunctional families fighting on Springer-type TV shows. She pulled all the clothes out, and there, at the bottom, was a plastic bag. It was black with an unfamiliar logo. Her interest was piqued. Maybe Darren had bought her a present on his travels and had neglected to mention it. The bag was slippery. She ran her fingers over its shiny surface and felt a tingle of excitement. Finally, Karen opened it up, stared inside and smiled.

Recycling

First. Forty. Second. Seventy-five. Third. The ton. Fourth. One twenty. Fifth. Chicken out. Back off, ease down, eighty-five. Off the A road. Through estates at the very edge of Birmingham where shabby people live and fuck. Rough types who exist only for the now. Fags and booze. Tattoos and lovebites. Escorts and Metros. Stopping to stare at the Ferrari. Jaws dropping. Straining to catch a view of the driver. Impossibly rich. Who could afford such a car? How many of the rodents looked at the prancing horse and imagined it might belong to a computer programmer? James wondered, shifting down and revving the excitable engine. Through a mini-roundabout, a couple of schoolgirls staring, their male counterparts shouting Wanker! Fantastic. You couldn't bribe this level of jealousy.

So Intron had gone pear-shaped. Who gave a fuck? James Birch had the three Ss. He was single, sought after and seriously loaded. Give it a couple of months, find a new job, maybe in London where there was more opportunity, come up with a new scam. Simple. He would be back on the road to excess. He left the estate and headed back towards town on a grim concrete artery dissecting grim concrete housing. Approaching a garage, James glanced down at his fuel gauge. It was nearing dusk, and he was nudging empty, so he pulled up and refuelled. Fifty-seven quid for a full tank. James smiled. An hour's work. He sauntered into the garage shop. The young, spotty cashier pretended not to be impressed. James had noted this look many times, the double-take followed by a compensating expression of disapproval. Today just got better and better. He placed a gold card on the counter, which the youth reluctantly picked up and swiped through the till. After a second, the cashier frowned at him.

'That your motor, mate?' he asked.

James used his practised nonchalance to full effect. 'Yep. One of them.'

'Noice.'

'Thank you.'

'Can't accept this card though.'

'What?'

'Your card's coming up as, well . . .'

'Yes?'

'Stolen.'

'Stolen?'

'And I've got to keep it. Boss says so. Any nicked cards we've gotta keep.'

'*Nicked*?' James asked incredulously. As if James Birch needed to do something as crude as stealing credit cards. He composed himself and tried to rise above it. 'Right. Well, put it on this one,' he said, flourishing another card from his wallet and raising the stakes from gold to platinum.

James smiled out at his car. Garage strip lights were reflected in the paintwork, and appeared to be hugging the vehicle's many curves. The cashier swiped the plastic and cleared his throat. 'This one as well.'

'You *are* joking me?' James had never been so insulted. In fact, had he been accused of actually paying his taxes he would have felt more at ease with himself. He was sweating and uncomfortable. 'OK, I'm prepared to overlook your mistake. Now just put it on this one and I'll be out of this place.' To be on the safe side, he increased the stakes even further. Double platinum Amex, the royal flush of credit cards.

There was a slight delay before the cashier uttered the single word, 'Nope.' He was, James suspected, starting to enjoy himself.

There was only one thing to do. James would have to go for broke. He produced a card so magnificent that the garage employee would only be able to guess at the sort of funds needed to carry one. As he extracted it from his wallet, it seemed to glow, and the hologram hovered around the entire length of the card like a protecting halo. This was the four aces of debit cards, known by name only, seldom ever seen in the flesh. This was the Diamond Ruby Sapphire Treble Platinum Access All Areas Unlimited Funds Card. James himself had never used it, and carried it purely for the one occasion in his life when whopping it out might impress someone of a hopefully female nature. He glanced at the spotty male garage attendant and sighed. Turn this card down, he had been led to believe, and a gang of heavies would arrive and torch your establishment. The cashier swiped the plastic. James held his breath. There was a single impertinent beep from the till. The attendant smiled. James swore. 'Right. I want it back.'

'Can't. Very sorry, like.'

James was aware that the adolescent garage attendant didn't seem particularly upset. 'Look, give me ten minutes and I'll be back with the cash.'

'Right. But not with our petrol.'

'What?'

'You'll have to leave your motor. Company policy.'

'So how the hell am I supposed to get to the bank to use my one remaining card?'

'Bus? Taxi? Walk?'

'*Walk*?' This was taking the piss. James stormed out and onto the road. He would thumb a lift to the nearest bank, get the cash, and then get that fucking kid fired.

Smug Brummie bastard. He stuck out his thumb and scowled. Tasteless, mass-manufactured cars sailed by, oblivious. He tried to smile sweetly, and attempted to appear humble. After ten minutes, during which he swore silently under his breath at every vehicle that ignored his plight, a reasonably smart Volvo pulled up. James was secretly thankful – this wasn't the world's most embarrassing car by any means. The driver looked familiar. As he drew level, James recognized him. It was Interesting Dave from Spartech.

'James. Interesting seeing you here. Need a lift?'

'Dave. Am I glad to see you. Thanks.'

James squeezed into the car, which was already almost full. Inside, he was mildly put out to notice the presence of several other ex-colleagues.

'We're just heading to Sainsbury's, you know, the one with the twenty-four-hour garage and mother-baby parking on the other side of Solihull, past that office place but before the new cinema complex that my neighbour drew the plans up for, to get some paper plates for a party we're having at work to celebrate a successful quarter, and we're having sausages, cheese, lemonade . . .'

'Hello, Mary,' James replied wearily. 'You're not heading past a NatWest, are you?'

'As a matter of fact, we are,' Bob interjected. 'I think there's one up here on the left, or maybe the right, only two minutes away, give or take.'

'And your scheme, James,' Jan said, turning round from the front passenger seat, 'I can't remember if you ever told us what it was all about before you resigned?'

'No, I don't think I did.'

'. . . or we could always try the new Tesco's on the other side of the estate, where they've got this thing now that if you take in your old bus tickets . . .'

'Interesting.'

'. . . they'll recycle them for petrol vouchers . . .'

'Maybe it's not this road. They all look the same around here.'

'But it must have had something wrong with it as a scheme, otherwise you wouldn't have left. Surely you can tell us now?'

'. . . then the petrol vouchers can be used at any supermarket which has the scheme, provided you spend at least sixty pounds on barbecue equipment . . .'

'Hang on, it probably isn't this way to the bank – I think it's back the way we came. Five minutes, max.'

'Interesting.'

'Left at the top, Dave. Or straight on, maybe.'

'Because every scheme has a weakness, doesn't it?'

'. . . as long as the barbecue stuff hasn't been purchased in association with any other offer . . .'

'Stop! For fuck's sake, stop!'

'What?' Interesting Dave asked, slowing.

'I've seen a bank,' James said triumphantly. Dave drew to a halt and James got out, mightily relieved. 'Good to see you all. Hope to bump into you soon,' he lied. 'Bye.' The perplexed occupants in the Volvo pulled off and James swore in their general direction. He could well do without the company of fellow anoraks at a time like this. It was almost dark now, the sky more black than blue. He approached the single-storey bank, running across two fast-moving lanes of carriageway, and encouraging a couple of irate drivers to sound their horns. At the cash point, he inserted his remaining card and entered the four-digit code to his current account. The nightmare words This card has been retained. Please contact your bank for details appeared before his eyes. The fucker. It had swallowed his card. What was going on? First the garage made a mistake, and then this. Technology was getting its own back today. There was only one thing to do. He was going to have to hike back to the garage, take his car and grab some cash from home. He waited for a gap and then sprinted across the precipitously fast dual carriageway. And then, as he walked, cursing everything he could think of, an idea came into his head. A very unpleasant idea. The bank. His credit cards. Spartech. The end of his scam. Ian. That cunt Greg. This wasn't mere coincidence. Something was going on here. Someone was fucking with him. And then an even worse idea came to him. Maybe he had had his very considerable assets frozen. Maybe Spartech, who now knew of his scam, had contacted the police and had his bank account put out of use. James stopped dead. Of course. He had been shafted. Rumbled and shafted. He let out a scream, and stumbled into the road. A car zoomed by, perilously close. Fuckers, he screamed, as tears began to well in his eyes. They had taken his one true love from him. He lurched along the grass verge of the road, tears stinging his eyes. How could they be so callous? A lorry sounded its horn at him. What had he ever done to Greg and Ian that they should break his heart by denying him the single source of fulfilment in his life? Money was all that he had ever wished for. He had nurtured and protected it, kept it safe from the world, held it close to him, cherished it, obeyed it, worshipped it even, and they had stripped it away from his breast. The heartless bastards! He hadn't denied Greg junk food or deprived Ian of cheap cars. This was distinctly unfair. He wiped a tear on the back of a designer sleeve. Another car horn. He raised his fist and shook it at the speeding vehicle which whizzed off into the darkness. Wankers! he screamed. He began to jog on the uneven grass. A notion had come to him. He was going to get into his Ferrari and go and find Gillick. Let the bastard really have what was coming to him. It could only be a few more hundred yards to the garage. James increased his pace, and, as the momentum of a thousand superfluous lunches lurched within him, he stumbled and tripped. His right arm automatically flew out as he fell, and the tarmac of the road grazed his palm. James's head and torso landed partly in the road as well. There was a hush. A sudden stillness. A dog barking some way off. Tarmac scratching against his jacket. A hedge rustling. Long grass swishing. The material of his trousers rubbing. Tyre noise. Lights, getting brighter. The whistle of something moving quickly. Voices in a speeding car, inaudible to James.

'I told you Safeway's wasn't that way, but you wouldn't believe me.'

'Listen, my sense of direction is legendary.'

'Yeah, but for all the wrong reasons.'

'We're going to be late now. They close early round here.'

'OK, OK. I'll put my foot down a bit.'

'. . . but if you keep your vouchers, they're still valid up to and including . . .'

Thud!

'Jesus!'

'What was that, Dave? Heck of a bump there.'

'Yes, almost spilled my Ribena.'

'Dunno,' Dave reported, staring into his rear-view mirror at the gloomy stretch of road behind him. 'Nothing interesting. Probably just a traffic cone or something.'

Silence settled upon the occupants of the car. Each of them felt a small tingle somewhere at the back of their head, as if a significant event had occurred, but they couldn't for the life of them think what it was. The big, solid Volvo maintained its rapid progress towards the centre of Birmingham. Dave stared at the road ahead. Jan peered out of the window and into the gloom. Bob checked his watch, held it briefly to his ear, and checked it again. Mary drew breath. And then she continued where she had left off.

'Mind you, if we'd gone to Tesco's, as I said in the first place, we'd be back by now, and we could have filled up with petrol, bought all our party things, stocked up with sausage rolls and done some recycling . . .'

En Vacances

The rue de Plaza, Nice, 31 March 2001, 8:34 a.m. The streets were drying out and noisy mopeds were jostling for position. Archie carried his boulangerie booty up the hill and towards the apartment block.

'You're joking me, Archie,' Jeremy said as he entered the kitchen. 'Fucking croissants again?'

'D'you get any chocolate ones?' Brian asked.

'Couple.'

'Nice one.' Brian had secretly become very fond of them. If only they'd been fried and served with eggs, he would have been completely happy.

'As I have informed you before, Jeremy, it's all they eat for breakfast here.'

'Fuck me,' Jeremy said, holding the listless boomerang of bread in his hand. 'No wonder they never won any wars.'

'You mean apart from the Battle of Hastings,' Archie said, before quickly shutting up.

Jeremy glared at him. This used to happen a lot, but recently things had got a lot more friendly. If anything, Jeremy and Brian had relaxed since beating Ian up. They had dealt with a problem, tied a loose end, terminated the interdependency of their business relationship, as Jeremy had put it, after consulting a dictionary. And something else had changed, Archie noted. They now realized that Archie could be of more permanent use to them. Crime was changing, swindles were becoming digital. They needed him for their future success, and hence had brought him with them to France, to plan their next campaign. And what was even better was that they also respected him. All it had taken was giving Ian a good kicking when he was down, and a bit of amateur artwork with a needle and some ink whilst they held him still, and Jeremy and Brian no longer treated him with the contempt that had plagued his adult days. Really, Archie was forced to conclude, a little bit of violence and some amateur tattooing when he was younger and his life could have been so much better.

'You want a cuppa, Magoo?' Jeremy asked him.

'Please.'

'Brian?'

'Might as well.'

'Righto.'

At first, Archie had been firmly against the idea. For a start, he was terrified of the notion of air travel, and the manner of their journey to the airport in a stolen Mondeo had done nothing to placate him. But the flight from Manchester hadn't been too bad, and things were now settling down. Jeremy and Brian both had the semblance of tans where the redness had started to cool off. Archie had largely stayed out of the sun so far – it wasn't, after all, particularly warm – and had escaped the sunburn which the other two wore as a badge of British honour abroad. Indeed, they hadn't been at all contented until their skin looked distressingly raw. Then, and only then, had they settled down to the task of busily spending their money as quickly as they could, something they were remarkably adept at. Archie was well aware that he should also spend some of his before they came on the scrounge. But they were planning to stay a while. With just over £21,000 between them, following the clearance of Gillick's accounts and the sale of a rather expensive watch, as well as Archie's £3,000 redundancy settlement, they were aiming for a six-month jaunt. To help matters, the apartment was free, seemingly still paid for from one of Ian's French accounts. And, as a final bonus, there was a somewhat temperamental open-top Jeep available for their convenience. They could, as Jeremy pointed out, sell Gillick's possessions one by one until they ran out of cash. It was the ultimate free holiday. There was a kind of beauty to it, a back to nature sort of thing. They were recycling Ian's waste, living off the by-products of his life, scavenging his used resources, resources which had originally been taken from them. It was close to parasitism, but not quite. Really, they had all gained. Archie was going to say that it was almost symbiosis, but the word stopped his line of thought and changed its direction. Next February. The second of the second of the second. He had been busy writing a virus for Brian and Jeremy. Symbiosis was about to bite the dust.

THE END